M000074343

1

Yesterday's Hopes

A Slip in Time

Book Two

Jane O'Brien

Connect with Jane O'Brien:
www.authorjaneobrien.com
http://www.amazon.com/author/obrienjane
www.facebook.com/janeobrien.author/
https://www.instagram.com/author_jane_obrien/
Twitter: @authorjaneobrien

Contact: authorjaneobrien@gmail.com

Cover by: SelfPubBookCovers.com/ TerriGostolaPhotography

Books by Jane O'Brien

The White Pine Trilogy:
The Tangled Roots of Bent Pine Lodge #1
The Dunes & Don'ts Antiques Emporium #2
The Kindred Spirit Bed & Breakfast #3

The Lighthouse Trilogy:
The 13th Lighthouse #1
The Painted Duck #2
Owl Creek #3

The Unforgettables:
Ruby and Sal #1
Maisy and Max #2
Ivy and Fox #3
Georgy and Jack #4
Emmy and Clay #5

A Slip in Time:

Yesterday's Tears #1

Yesterday's Hopes #2

Christmas Novellas:

Pinecones and Promises

A Kindred Christmas

Dedication

This book is dedicated to my husband, who has been my best friend and love for over fifty years. Through the writing and editing of this book he has also been my nurse, after I had some major surgery. I wasn't sure he was up for the task, but he went above and beyond the call of duty. It was a long few months, but he stuck it out to the end, never complaining, but always there for me with a smile. We are soul mates and have known each other from the beginning of time and so the sentence of the following quote by Henry Van Dyke truly pertains to us: "For those who love, time is eternity."

Table of Contents

"Time is too slow for those who wait,

too swift for those who fear,

too long for those who grieve,

too short for those who rejoice;

but for those who love,

time is eternity."

– Henry Van Dyke. 1852-1933

Yesterday's Hopes

A Slip in Time

Book Two

Jane O'Brien

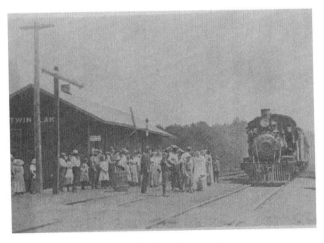

Twin Lake Depot,
Twin Lake, Michigan

Prologue

2019

Dora was still in her grandmother's favorite chair when dawn arrived. It was as if she were fixed into another world that she could not get out of. Half in and half out. Her mind would not budge. The trauma of the last few months was just too much for her. When nature called, she had no choice but to move, but she returned to the exact same spot, wondering what she was doing wrong. She was sure Franny had left from here. All the signs had pointed to it. Then it dawned on her that she needed to recreate the setup of the room. Still in a daze from lack of sleep and food, she placed the quilts on the back of the couch, and picked up the unfinished quilt including the individual quilt blocks. She lay the blocks around her feet and then placed the quilt top on her lap. She sat perfectly still for another hour, willing her transfer to happen, but when nothing did, she finally fell apart.

"It's not working. I was so sure it would," she cried. With sheer exhaustion, sobs wracked her body. She was missing her mother and father, and she needed her sister. "Why have they all left me?"

Tears from Dora's cheeks ran down her face. One single drop landed on the exact spot that Fran's had — the tearstained watermark. At that exact moment it fell, Dora opened her tightly closed eyes and watched the tear fall, as if in slow motion. She was aware of when it connected with the fabric, and that was the last thing she would remember. She felt like she was caught up in the middle of a tornado, spinning around and around. Her body violently tilted sideways and shifted back again. The very next thing she knew she was standing on a train platform, as a steam engine sped away from her, spewing a smoke trail in the sky. Still clutching her carpet bag, her eyes completely dilated, she swayed slightly and almost passed out. Nothing looked familiar; there was no one around. She was all alone on a wooden boardwalk in front of a train depot.

Dora looked around in fear, then weaving and barely able to stand, she simply said, "Franny?"

Chapter One

1875

As soon as Dora's head stopped spinning, she knew exactly where she was – well, not exactly. The wooden walk, a steam engine train chugging away from her, and a small train depot with a large water tower next to it. A big grin spread across her face. She had done it! She had actually traveled back in time. Then, immediately following her jubilation, concern set in. What if she was in another time, but not the right one? How could she be sure she was in the same place that Franny was? With all of the spunk she had been known for her whole life, she spun on her heels, intending to go into the depot and ask where she was exactly, but when she turned around, she found herself in the arms of a very handsome young man.

Ned London was covering the depot for a few minutes while his father delivered an urgent telegraph to one of his neighbors. He had intended to ask if the woman needed some help. It was what his father would have expected of him.

As Ned held Dora a moment to help her gain her balance, she had the opportunity to look into his green eyes. His sandy hair was almost completely covered with a cap, but she could see some stray pieces sticking out over his ears. He was just tall enough so that she had to tilt back her head to look closely at him. He looked surprised to find himself holding a woman, and at the same time, he seemed reluctant to let her go. She had no idea it was because she looked remarkably like someone else, the woman of his dreams.

Dora was enjoying being held by this strong man. Always a flirt, she decided to play the weak female expected of the times, but getting confused with how a southern belle would react to that of a pioneer northern woman, she fake-fainted into his chest. As she did so, she inhaled his manly smell, no deodorant or aftershave, just all male testosterone. She liked it a lot.

At the same time Ned was thoroughly enjoying the predicament he had found himself in – holding a woman who needed him. She smelled of lavender and lemons all at the same time. She was petite and must weigh no more than a wet hen, and when his arm found her small waist to wrap around, he gently guided her to the bench used for waiting travelers. A fainting woman was nothing new to him. Only a few short months ago, Mrs. Francine Clark had fainted on him in his wagon and again in her cottage, where she had rewarded him with a sweet kiss because she had thought he was someone else. He had fallen in love at first sight, but in the end she had broken his heart. The rejection was devastating for him. He had vowed never to put himself in that painful position again. But here he was, holding a

Francine lookalike in his arms, and not exactly sure how it had happened.

"Miss! Miss, can you hear me?"

Dora peeked out through her lashes, deciding she had given the young man enough of a scare. She feigned coming to, sat up, and said sweetly, "I'm so sorry. I don't know what came over me. It must be the heat of the day."

"Or perhaps you're tired from your journey," he said, with his face still close to hers.

Dora sat up, trying to act prim and proper in a way this century called for. She smoothed her clothing and fussed with her hair, which was pinned up in a tight bun underneath her bonnet. 'This is going to be fun,' she thought.

"I am ever so sorry. I guess I was surprised when my sister was not here to greet me, and it frightened me to be alone."

Ned was sitting up straight now, in order to give the proper amount of space between them; he moved over slightly but his arm lingered around her waist. "Who is your sister, if I may ask?"

"Francine Clark. Do you know her?"

'Well, that explains it,' thought Ned. "Sure I know her. Everyone here does. She's our new schoolmarm."

Dora grinned. "Of course she is. Can you let her know I'm here? I don't have a clue how to reach her."

"What's this?" asked a booming voice. Duane London, the station master, had returned to find his son with a strange woman practically wrapped up in his arms. It was very unprofessional. Duane was always professional and he expected those who worked for him to be, too. He took his job quite seriously.

Ned jumped up. "Pa, this is – I'm sorry. I didn't get your name."

"Dora Clark," she said, demurely.

"Yes, this is Dora Clark, Francine Clark's sister. And Miss Clark, this is the station master, Duane London."

"Why, I didn't know we were expecting anyone on this run. Welcome. So sorry I wasn't here to greet you."

"Nice to meet you, Mr. London. It's not your fault, sir. Francine wasn't expecting me. Well, she was, but I'm sure she didn't know I was coming today, and I see there are no buggies for rent. I thought perhaps I could hire a ride to her place."

"I'd be happy to take you there," said Ned.

"But, sir, I don't even know your name. Am I to get in a wagon in the middle of nowhere with a perfect stranger?"

"Oh, I can vouch for him," said Mr. London. "He works for me part time. This is my son, Ned – Ned London. He's also the blacksmith in town, and very well respected."

Ned tipped his hat and held his breath. He wanted nothing more than to escort Francine's sister to the Clark cabin.

Dora boldly looked him up and down, and then said, "I believe I can trust you, Mr. Ned London. Now, what will be the charge for this ride?"

"No charge, miss. It's a service we do for our passengers, when needed," said Ned, pleased to be allowed to escort her to the Clark cabin.

"You must keep terribly busy with your two jobs, then."

"Well, it's a small village and not much call for transporting passengers. And I'm only at the blacksmith shop three days a week."

"Well, if you think you have time and it wouldn't put you out too much, I would love to ride with you, Mr. London."

Duane London looked at his son. It was plain as day that he was already smitten with the new Miss Clark. 'Here we go again,' he thought.

∞

Just as her sister before her, Dora was a little awkward in getting up into the buggy, but she had seen enough TV shows and movies about the old west that she had an idea about how it was done. She lifted her long skirt with her left hand, placed her right hand in Ned's offered hand, then she placed her left foot on the foot plate, lifted herself as delicately as she was able, straightened her body up and swung her right leg in. She was very pleased with herself when she discovered that she was, in fact, sitting on the seat. Ned placed her heavy carpet bag in beside her, then ran around to the other side. In only a few seconds she was on her way to see her sister. Tears pricked at her eyes. She had missed Franny so much, and she had so much to tell her, so many painful things.

Chapter Two

1875

Fran and Luke were on their way into Twin Lake so she could deliver some eggs to Mercy Brody at the boardinghouse. It had been their weekly ritual; Miss Mercy required so many eggs to satisfy both her boarders and the customers at the restaurant she also owned, that she had made an arrangement with Francine to buy her extra eggs. It was one of Fran's favorite times of the week, because she could get out in the fresh air and see people to exchange gossip and discuss quilt patterns, depending on who was in town that day. But the best part was that she could ride beside her Luke, her hired hand, in public, and no one would ever be suspicious of the passionate nights they spent together. They held hands whenever Luke did not require his for the reins, and they allowed their thighs to touch in order to maintain contact, as all lovers like to do. Francine had never been so happy in her entire life, and by looking at Luke's smile, most of the residents of both Holton Township and Twin Lake said the same about him. Although they had no knowledge of what went on behind closed doors at the Clark cabin, some were beginning to suspect and others were talking that a marital union would be coming soon.

Fran was in the middle of telling Luke about her lesson plans and how she would deal with teaching children of all ages at once in the small one-room school. They would begin classes as soon as harvest was over, which was only a few weeks away. As she was chatting, Luke was listening to the sound of her voice and not necessarily to what she was saying. He could see some dust rise up ahead, and before long he noticed a buggy coming in their direction, just as he had suspected. A slight frown crossed his brow when he saw Ned. Although Ned had given up on his pursuit of Francine, Luke still felt a twinge of jealousy at Ned's handsome boyish charm. He was thankful Francine had chosen him, but he also knew that he still had demons from his past which could surface at any time, and he was afraid that during one of his dark moods, Francine would be driven to Ned's arms.

The couple were both surprised to see a young woman in the buggy with Ned. From afar she seemed to be someone neither of them recognized, but then her bonnet was covering some of her face from that distance.

When Ned realized who was in the approaching buggy, he waved. He seemed to be flagging them down, so Luke pulled to a stop, thinking perhaps there was some trouble. Luke saw Ned lean over to the woman and say something, and almost instantly the woman turned her face toward them and began waving. She tried to stand up in the buggy, but Ned pulled her down until they came to a stop.

"Franny! Franny, is it truly you?" Dora could hardly contain her joy, and if it had not been for Ned's quick thinking, she would have jumped off of the moving buggy.

Fran's head jerked at the sound of her sister's voice. "She's here; oh Luke, it's my sister. Dora, I can't believe you came." Francine put her hands to her face and sobbed.

"Hold on, Franny," he whispered, using the name she allowed him to call her in private. "Let me pull the wagon over."

Once the horse had pulled the wagon into a safe position, he helped Francine down and the two sisters met in the middle of the road. They sobbed and hung on to each other, sometimes hugging tightly and sometimes pulling back to look at each other's faces, checking to make sure it was reality.

"How? How did you manage?" asked Fran. But instantly she realized it was not the time or place for this particular discussion. She put her fingers on Dora's lips. "Let's talk when we get home." Then she hugged Dora

33

and whispered in her ear, "Be very careful what you say. Stay in character at all times." Then Fran turned to Luke and said, "Can we turn the wagon around, please?"

"Sure can, Mrs. Clark." Dora caught the little wink and smile Luke gave Fran.

Ned called, "Miss Clark, why don't you hop back in and I'll follow them to the cabin. You two can have your reunion there."

"Yes, of course, I'll be right there," answered Dora.

With one last hug, Fran whispered, "Choose your words wisely. Oh, and they think I'm a widow."

As Ned's buggy followed Luke's wagon, he watched out of the corner of his eye, not wanting to intrude on Miss Clark's emotions, but suddenly something occurred to him, and he had to say it out loud.

"I'm sorry to ask, but I'm confused about one thing."

"What is that, Mr. London?" ask Dora, as she dabbed at her eyes with her embroidered handkerchief.

"Well, Mrs. Clark came to us after her husband and daughter had died, and we offered her a teaching job. I guess you knew that. We all knew that she was married previously, so the name of Clark was her husband's surname. How is it that you are a Miss Clark, but still her sister? Wouldn't your last name be the same as Mrs. Clark's maiden name? Or are you a sister-in-law?"

"Oh," said Dora, knowing instantly that this was one of those times she was going to have to be very careful of, so as to not blow Fran's cover. His question explained why they called her sister Mrs. Clark. "Well, you see – has she already told you her maiden name?"

"No, we really know nothing about her, except that she is a relative of William and Sarah Clark's and she came from Canada. Did you come from Canada, too?"

"Why yes, I did, actually. That's why Franny – I mean Francine – did not know I was coming today. I caught an earlier train than expected. And as far as my last name, it is a very strange story." Dora was improvising something as she went along. "My last name *is* Clark but it's spelled differently. There are a lot of Clarks where we come from." At this point she realized that she didn't have a clue what he knew about where they came from. She proceeded with caution. "My last name is Clark with an e. C-l-a-r-k-e. So Franny, I mean Francine, went from being a Clark with an e to a Clark without an e. Completely different families."

"Very interesting. It was nice that she did not have to change her last name except to remember to spell it correctly." Ned chuckled, completely satisfied with her answer.

Dora breathed a sigh of relief. She decided that she was better off remaining quiet until she had the facts from Franny. "Now, if you don't mind, Mr. London, I'd rather ride in silence, so as to take in all of the beauty of this countryside."

Ned was a little put off at first until she complimented his township. He was born and raised right here in Holton Township and worked in Twin Lake in Dalton Township all of his life. He was very proud of the woods and many small lakes in the area. Besides it was great farmland. "Of course, Miss Clark, I understand completely. I shall not talk again until we arrive at the cabin which will be shortly. Enjoy your ride." He smiled at her pleasantly, not at all sure how to take this beautiful but strong young woman. She was nothing at all like Francine when she first arrived. But then, no one would ever be like his Francine, not even a lookalike sister.

While Luke and Fran rode back to the cabin, they quietly talked about Dora's unexpected arrival. Luke glanced at Fran several times. She seemed to have gotten her emotions in check, but he could tell there was something still on her mind.

"Are you okay, Franny? You seem to be troubled about something. Aren't you happy to see your sister?"

"I'm overjoyed, Luke. I can't tell you how many times I wished for her to join me. I'm just hoping she can adjust to this way of life." Instantly Fran realized her mistake. She had cautioned Dora to be careful, and now she had made a flub herself.

"Adjust? How do you mean? Is America so different than Canada?"

"Oh, no, I meant to farm life. Dora has been raised as a city girl. She's used to more people being around and being closer to certain activities."

"Well, we'll make sure to take her to town often, once she's settled in, but Franny, what does that do for us? You having a visitor?"

The look on his face was almost comical, but she knew exactly what he meant. They had had a perfect setup for romance. Luke, being a hired hand, could come and go at will, always with an excuse that she needed some work done. He often complained that there was too much for one man, and said that he had begun sleeping in the barn because he finished so late. But the truth was that the two lovers shared a bed several times a week and he often spent the night in it, and the many nights they had shared had not dimmed their passion for one another. Luke was worried that their arrangement was coming to an end very soon.

Fran looked into Luke's gorgeous grey eyes; his concern had brought out a darker color than normal. "We'll work it out, don't worry. I'll talk to Dora. She can be quite – quite modern in her thinking. She'll understand. But I am more worried that I don't have another bed. She'll have to sleep with me until I can work something out about the other bedroom."

"I can build a simple bed frame, that's no problem, but what about the bedding?" Luke would be sure to make the building of another bed top priority.

"I have extra quilts, but soon it will be colder and I'll need more. But what about a mattress?"

"We'll buy some bed ticking for the cover with your egg money, and I can get some straw from Pa. We always keep enough extra around in case we have company and Ma wants to freshen a bed."

"Thank you, Luke. You always look out for me." She gave his arm a squeeze. Then Fran leaned closer and said seductively, "I'd kiss you if they weren't so close behind." She was pleased to see his dark eyes lighten to a light steel blue. She ached to touch the little wrinkles around them.

"I'd love that more than anything. I can never get enough of you, Franny; you know that, don't you?"

"I do, Luke. I'll meet you in the barn as soon as I get Dora settled. It might be a while. We have a lot to catch up on."

"And I'll get started on that bed frame right away. I can't get it done soon enough. Good thing we have some wood left over from when we had to reframe the chicken coop after the storm. I can use logs for the rest." Francine's smile was all he needed to reassure him that things were not going to change between them. As soon as school started and Franny was assured of her teaching position, he planned to make their liaisons permanent.

Chapter Three

1875

The wagon and buggy turned into the drive to Fran's cabin. She glanced back to see if there was a reaction from Dora, but she couldn't tell if her sister recognized their grandparent's house. But then why would she? Fran had not.

This 1875 small log cabin looked nothing like the 2019 house their father had grown up in and the one they had played in, while learning valuable lessons in life from their wise grandparents. Even though Dora had not taken to the self-sustaining way of life their grandparents had lived, Fran's sister had still loved this place when she was a child. It was paradise for a kid. Their parents, Frank and Elaine Clark, had let them run wild, with only a warning about the creek. There was really nothing to fear here. There were very few bear here in 2019, and the only ones to worry about were mothers with cubs in the spring; otherwise they were fairly skittish and ran when they heard a noise, and the children were always noisy. Coyotes were the same, never attacking humans, and they were rarely seen during the day. The Massasauga rattlesnake is the only venomous snake in Michigan, and even then only harmful to small children. Even if it did strike, as long as an anti-venom was received quickly, there was no major threat. The snakes would normally hide as soon as they heard any human sound and were rarely even seen, the loss of their habitat making it more difficult for them to thrive. The children had been cautioned about such things, and learned about the threats in school, but no one ever truly worried about them.

As the two sisters were helped down from the wagons, Fran watched Dora's face for any kind of reaction, but all she saw was a big grin. Dora had suspected where Fran was living, but had not been sure. The front of the envelope that Fran had left for her in the trunk simply said 'Mr. and Mrs. William Clark, Holton, Michigan.' It was the only thing that gave Dora a clue that Fran was living in their grandparents' town, but since she had never heard of William Clark, she was not sure what to expect. She was pleased with the little cabin. It was everything she had ever read about pioneer life, and the beautiful summer flowers only added to the charm. But other than the Michigan woods and farmland, nothing looked familiar.

Fran glanced at Ned. He seemed lost, not knowing if he was needed any longer. Fran walked to him and took his hand, "Thank you so much for bringing my sister to me, Ned. Once again, you have been my savior."

Ned blushed. The touch of Francine's hand warmed his heart. Even if Luke had won her heart, he would always have a soft spot for her. "You're more than welcome, ma'am. I'm so glad you have family with you once again."

Dora stepped forward to add her thank you, also. "Mr. London, you have been most kind, and you have made my trip from the train depot quite enjoyable. Thank you for your kindness."

Dora leaned forward and kissed Ned on the cheek. He blushed a bright red, and mumbled, "It was nothing, miss. I was only helping out." He looked down at his feet and scuffed a shoe in the dirt. "I hope to see you again sometime, if you don't mind that is. I'd love to show you around, like I did for Francine."

Dora was enjoying his boyish charm, and she was pleased that she was still able to catch a man's eye, even in the 1800s. "I'd like that, Ned -- may I call you Ned?"

"Yes, ma'am, I mean, Miss Clarke. Call me Ned. Everyone does."

"Then you shall call me Dora. Everyone does," she teased.

"I'll do that, Dora. It's a very pretty name. I'll enjoy using it."

"I'll see you soon, then, Ned. Have a pleasant afternoon."

It was an obvious invitation for him to leave, but Ned's feet were not moving. Once again he had fallen in love, but this time with a different Clark sister. He knew immediately it was not a good idea, but he had no choice. 'The heart wants what it wants,' he thought. He sighed and turned to get in the buggy, but not before he took one last look at the most beautiful creature he had ever laid eyes on.

When Dora turned around, she saw a look of displeasure on Fran's face, but Luke was grinning from ear to ear. He recognized her type. Fran's little sister was a real pistol.

"Come along, Dora. I want to show you everything," called Francine, as she led her sister inside. Luke followed behind easily carrying the heavy carpet bag, as if it were a feather pillow.

As soon as Francine opened the door, a rather large creature jumped up to welcome her. Dora squealed, and then laughed with joy when she realized it was a dog.

"Down, Moose," commanded Francine. "Sorry, he's the size of his namesake, but he's still a puppy."

"Oh, he's just adorable!" Dora bent over to ruffle Moose's fur, and he melted against her leg, his tongue hanging loosely, and his mouth hanging open in a doggie grin.

"Look at him. He's in love, just like all the men you meet. How do you do that?" Fran shook her head in amazement.

Luke raised an eyebrow. He was glad he had chosen the first Clark woman he had met. Franny was happy, smart, sweet, and vulnerable at times. He liked that in a woman. This one was going to be trouble for whatever man she set her eyes on. Heaven help Ned!

Once Dora had pulled herself away from Moose, she had a chance to look around the cabin. Luke had not been there the first time Fran had entered this cabin; Ned had been the one to let her in, so he had no way of knowing that Dora's reaction was the same. First confusion and then complete awe.

Fran watched as Dora's eyes swept the small space, from the kitchen to the fireplace to the placement of the bedroom doors. Then Dora began to grin, as she nodded her head in recognition. She looked at her sister, while pointing her finger at her surroundings.

"Isn't this –

"Yes, it looks remarkably like the one at home, doesn't it?" Fran cut her off, afraid she would say something that Luke might pick up on. Fran had still not told Luke about her time traveling, not knowing how he would react to the fact that she was from the future.

"Oh, yes, it's just like our grandmother's place." Dora had caught on quickly, and covered before she said anything to compromise Fran's position here. "It must make you feel quite homey and comfortable."

"Yes, it has been a comfort."

Luke stood quietly by through their exchange. Even though the words sounded fine, he could detect an underlining conversation between the sisters that he was not privy to. He cleared his throat to remind them that he was still there.

"Mrs. Clark, ma'am, I think I will be going now. I'll let you ladies catch up. I'll tend to the animals and then be on my way."

"Oh, yes, Luke, thank you for taking me to town. It was a shame we had not made it to deliver those eggs."

"Oh, I'll take them in for you. It's not a problem."

"But it's such a drive."

Dora was watching the exchange. She was sure they were procrastinating their separation.

"Just doing my job, ma'am."

"All right, then. Thank you."

Luke tipped his hat and as he left he said, "It was nice meeting you, miss. I'm sure Francine is pleased to have family here."

"And nice meeting you, too, Mr. Grainger. I'm sure we'll see each other again soon."

"That you will."

When he walked out the door, Dora noticed Fran was standing perfectly still as she followed him with her eyes. Dora grinned.

Once the door was closed, she demanded, "Now, give me the scoop. Is my sister in love?"

"What made you say that?" she asked. "Is that the first thing you came up with after arriving from another century?"

"Oh, Franny. It's written all over your face. I love that you're happy." She kissed her sister, and then said, "Now, spill it."

Fran laughed out loud. She hugged her sister tightly, "I'm so happy to see you. First, let me show the house."

"I can see it. There's not much to it."

"But you do recognize it, right?"

"Yes, yes I do. We're in Gram and Gramps house, aren't we? There's the fireplace. How could I not remember that? Oh and the trap door to the cellar."

"It is, but it only goes down a few feet. It must have been dug out deeper, at some point."

"Yes, but the kitchen is where Gram's study is. Of course! That's what she used to say. They moved the kitchen when they added on the back for more bedrooms and an indoor bathroom. Oh no! You're not telling me there's no..."

"I am telling you that. You'll have to get used to going in the outhouse."

"Franny, I don't think I can!"

"Well, it's that or a thunder pot."

"A what?"

"Also known as a chamber pot, kept under the bed for night time."

"Oh please, no."

"Yes. Now come with me to the bedroom, my bedroom." Fran opened the door and Dora stood in the opening, tears filling her eyes. "This is it. The room where they spent so many nights together. Where we crawled in bed with them when we had a nightmare. I think it's even the same headboard and footboard, isn't it, with the turned spools?"

"I believe it is. The Jenny Lind style was quite popular, or is, I should say. I seem to recall that it was the type of bed the popular singer liked to sleep in. I remember reading that Jenny Lind toured America in the 1850s, so they all know who she is here."

"Yes, the Swedish Nightingale, right? So that means this bed in Gram's house is about 150 years old, but here it's only a few years old. Amazing." Dora stopped talking a moment and gasped. "Isn't that the trunk? I mean THE trunk?"

"It is," smiled Fran, "but here's the thing. Luke made it for me."

"He made it for *you*? But that's impossible. You've never been here before. You weren't born until 1991, and yet it's identical to the one Gram stored her quilts in."

"That's right. But I was here the day he brought it into the house, and I was told by my friends, one of whom is his mother, that he made it for me, the new schoolteacher."

"Oh, yes, Ned told me you were the 'schoolmarm,' he called it."

"But look inside." The two women bent over the trunk as Fran lifted the lid.

Inside there were a few quilts folded on the bottom and the quilt blocks that Fran had made.

"The signal blocks!" Dora exclaimed. "But they look new. How could they have been used for signals if they were already in the trunk?"

"No, they weren't here when I arrived. I made them to contact you. I remembered from teaching about the Civil War how the Underground Railroad used quilt blocks to send out messages."

"That's what I thought, but they look brand new, and when I saw them they looked – well, over a hundred years old."

"You mean they aged?"

"They must have. And this envelope, too. It was old and faded. All I could read was the address on the front, and the date stamp. It's what tipped me off to your whereabouts. Well, at first I wasn't sure about anything, but then I started to put the pieces together."

"I was hoping you would. But didn't you get the message on the back?" Fran turned it over to show Dora what she had written. 'I am here and I am well. Fran.'

"No, there was nothing on the back, at all. This would have helped me a lot. I was so worried. We all were." Tears filled her eyes as she thought about home and her parents. How could she tell Franny? But it would have to be done. She would wait until she was asked more questions.

"I can't wait to hear about it all," said Fran. "I'm so sorry to have scared you, but I had no control over it."

"Yes, I could see that, once it happened to me."

"Look, Dora, I really have to talk to Luke. Would you like to rest a bit on the bed until I get back? I remember how exhausted I felt when I first arrived."

"I think you're right. I am suddenly feeling very tired. It must take a toll on the body – passing through, I mean. I have a very strong need to close my eyes."

"Take off your shoes, and crawl under the covers if you like. I'll close the door and you can nap as long as you want. I want you well rested. We have a lot to talk about -- home, Mom and Dad, Kevin, and I have a lot to share with you, too." When tears filled Dora's eyes, Fran knew that Dora was hurting. Wondering if she had had a problem with Kevin, she hugged her sister tightly and kissed her on the cheek.

"Get plenty of rest. This is a hard life, Dora. You're going to need your strength."

Dora laid back on the bed and almost immediately passed out from exhaustion. Fran covered her with the quilt and tiptoed out. She almost tripped over Moose, who had been resting just outside the door as the sisters talked. He whined a little, seeming unsure of what was happening. Fran gave him a reassuring hug while softly speaking words of love. His tail thumped heavily on the wooden floor, and when he saw Fran move to the door, he jumped up to follow.

"Come on, boy, let's find Luke."

Chapter Four

1875

Fran found Luke in the barn, rubbing down Traveler. She stopped a moment to watch him work. His hands traveled over the horse's body with such gentleness, brushing with one hand and then stroking with the other. She heard his voice as he whispered calming words while he groomed. She remembered how those very same hands had recently stroked her body, and she got a thrill all over. He must have sensed her at that moment, because he turned his head and smiled.

"Did you miss me already?" he teased.

Fran stepped forward and said softly, "I did. I had other plans for this afternoon that did not include a newly arrived sister."

Luke loved how bold this woman could be. His heart began to beat faster; he had no choice but to leave the grooming for another time. He stepped quickly toward her and took her face in his hands, looking deeply into her eyes. They kissed with a common desire, one that would not be quenched until they had satisfied their needs. But when Luke remembered the visitor, he pulled back, placing his hands on her shoulders.

"What does this mean for us, Fran?"

"What do you mean?"

"You know." He blushed, and Fran chuckled at his discomfort. "We've been sort of playing house. We always knew it couldn't go on, but now we'll be forced to call it quits while Dora is here."

"I've already thought about that. Dora is quite modern thinking. I'll tell her about us and ..."

"No, you can't. Even a sister can't keep a secret like that. People will suspect even more than they do now.

And if they figure us out, you could lose the teaching job that you have not even started yet. You know what kind of scandal it would cause. I hate putting you in this position because of my, uh, needs."

"They're my needs, too, Luke. It takes two to do what we've been doing, and I am a willing participant."

He grinned, something he had been doing more and more lately. Fran loved seeing him happy, and it felt good knowing that she was a small part of his happiness.

"My question to you, my sweet Franny, is what does it all mean for us? Is she here for good, or just a visit? When can we return to how we were living?"

"I'm not sure, Luke. We haven't had a chance to talk about it, but once she gets settled, we'll have a long chat. She's napping now, so we'll talk when she wakes."

"She's napping? Why didn't you say so?" he growled. Luke pulled her into a clean stall filled with fresh hay. He wrapped his arms around her, and they tumbled down as they giggled like children.

∞

A half hour later, the two lovers adjusted their clothing, smoothed down their hair, and kissed goodbye. It was torture to separate, especially since they did not know when they could see each other again, but promises were made to try to meet in the barn in another day or two. Fran knew she would have to tell everything to Dora so that could be arranged, but she was worried that once she did, the magic between her and Luke would disappear. Maybe their passion was only strong because they were meeting secretly, and since their joining was taboo without the sanctity of marriage, it would die out soon. She feared losing him, so she would do everything in her power to prevent that from happening. She needed to hear his words of commitment often, because once he found out who she was and where she had come from, he would know how she had deceived him. And it was true. She had. He was a prideful man. He would be hurt, that much she knew for sure. Fran waved goodbye as the wagon pulled away, her heart and lips already aching for him to return.

As Fran walked back into the small cabin, she marveled at her life. Only a few short months ago, she was in the 21st century with all of the modern conveniences, and here she was, in 1875, and fitting in just fine. It had not been easy, and she knew if Dora were to stay she would have to make the same adjustments. And since she had not yet been able to talk to Dora about it, she wasn't even sure if it was possible for Dora to get back. Maybe the two sisters would be spending the rest of their lives together in this century. And if that happened, how would their parents handle that? Had it already been discussed? Had Kevin given Dora the go ahead to try to bring Fran back? There was no wedding ring on Dora's finger, so obviously they had postponed the wedding. Was it because of her being missing? Had she caused her sister to put aside the day she had been waiting for her entire life? These were questions she intended to clear up tonight. It was going to be a long one. Luckily, she had just filled her lantern with oil.

Luke had killed a deer yesterday, so she had made venison stew with her garden vegetables, and there was plenty to go around. Fran felt bad because she knew Luke was planning on sharing that meal with her, but there would be more days when she could cook for him. For now, it was all about the future, or her past. Whatever she called it, she needed answers, and she was excited to hear what Dora had to say.

∞

Dora slept for another hour, so Fran took Moose for a walk around the garden to see what new items were ready to harvest, and when she returned she began setting the table for supper. She tried to be as quiet as she could because the cabin was so small that every noise could be heard, but in a few minutes Dora woke anyway.

"Hi. You're awake!" Fran walked over to give her sister a hug.

"Yes, I really didn't want to get up, but I smelled something delicious. What are you making?"

"It's venison stew."

"Venison? You know I don't care for venison." Dora screwed up her face in displeasure.

Fran laughed. "You'll learn soon enough that you eat what's on the table or you go hungry. There's no fast food here, you know. And sometimes even meat is hard to come by. You're lucky. The first few weeks I was here I thought I would starve. If it hadn't been for Luke and Ned and their families and friends, I would have."

"Sorry, Franny, I know I should be appreciative. It's going to be hard to get used to things. I can see that now. I'll try not to complain. But where did you get the deer meat? Don't tell me you killed it yourself!"

"No, but I could have if I wanted to. Luke and I have been hunting together on more than one occasion. He got this one yesterday, and brought it by for me. He's been very thoughtful in that way." Fran's eyes went a little dreamy when she thought of all Luke had done for her, and all of the pleasure he had brought to her.

"I can see how thoughtful he is. And he's a real hunk! Now tell me about it." Dora pulled out a chair as Fran put the finishing touches on their meal.

"First of all, you can't use words like 'hunk.' I still catch myself using modern phrases, and I have to cover my tracks. Be very careful or you could give us away. I don't want to be tarred and feathered for being a witch."

"Do they still do that?" Dora was horrified.

"Oh, I have no idea. I'm just saying you have to stay in character all the time. Eventually, you get used to living here and their speech and their ways of doing things seem normal. On a few occasions I've had to blame my mistakes on being Canadian."

"Okay, so fill me in. What's that all about?"

Fran pulled out a chair and sat down, while she waited for the biscuits to finish baking. "Well, when I showed up unexpectedly at the depot – is that what happened to you?"

"Yes, it was! And then I fell into the arms of that handsome Ned London."

"Oh, dear, I did too!" The sisters had a giggle together before Fran continued. "Well, it seems that the town was expecting a woman named Frances Clark to come from Canada to be their school teacher. When they asked my name I instinctively knew I should use Francine Clark, so Mr. London thought I was her. I had no luggage and was quite dazed, so he assumed I had been robbed or perhaps lost it on the train. I was told that the other Frances Clark had recently lost her husband and child in a house fire, so they all began to call me Mrs. Clark. They've taken real good care of me. The town got together and had a box lunch auction to raise money for the school and collect items for the house. I'll tell you all about it later. But first I want to know about how you got here. How did you manage to do it? And can we get back?"

Dora went on to tell her how she had had all of her clothes made for the proper time period, how she was so careful to use only natural fibers and fabrics, how she had collected a few coins and bills which were in existence in 1875, but when she got to the part about trying to transport herself here, Fran called a temporary halt. She had to get the biscuits out of the oven and dish out the stew. Once their meal was on the table, Dora proceeded to give her the rest of the details.

"I tried over and over again, and nothing I did worked. One night, I dressed fully in the clothes I am in now, and I stood in the middle of the room without moving for what seemed like hours. And nothing happened. When my legs got tired I sat in Gram's chair, and that's when it hit me. I needed to recreate the room exactly as you had left it, so I spread all of the quilts around, placed the new blocks at my feet, and held the unfinished top on my lap. Still there was nothing. I was exhausted and depressed, and I missed you so much. When I started to cry I saw, almost in slow motion, a tear fall directly onto what looks like a watermark on the quilt top, and at the exact moment they connected, I began to spin and sway. Then I suddenly found myself at the train depot in Twin Lake standing all alone on the boardwalk."

Fran was silent a moment as she took it all in. Dora took the time to shovel the stew in her mouth. She ate like a starving person, exactly like Fran had done when she first arrived.

"Mmmm. This is really good. Do you have more?"

"Of course. But don't lose your train of thought. I think we're onto something." Fran got up to fill the bowl and she brought more biscuits and butter to the table. She was so thankful that her butter churn was working now, and Dora would not have to endure the hardship with food that she had had to. She placed the bowl in front of Dora, and her sister began to shovel more food in. It was almost comical considering she never ate like that, always worrying about her figure, and that she had never liked venison.

"Dora, now that you have told me your experience, it has brought back memories of my own time travel. I was pretty blank until you mentioned that teardrop. I do remember crying and watching a tear fall onto the quilt. I'm pretty sure that the woman who left it behind cried when she made it, because she didn't want to move. I think she intended to leave it here so she could finish it one day when she came back, but I doubt if they ever do, because the cabin stays in our family, which is theirs, too, I guess."

"Now, I'm confused," said Dora between bites. "This milk is fabulous, by the way."

"Fresh from the cow," smiled Fran.

"No pasteurization? Don't you get sick?"

"Not so far. But there's no choice, so you eat or die."

"Well, all I can say is, it's like my taste buds are working overtime."

"So, more about the quilt," said Fran, trying to get the conversation back on track. "I know we are connected to this family. I got a letter from the woman who lived here. Her name is Sarah Clark and her husband is William. She thought she was writing to her cousin, the school teacher."

"I never heard of them."

"But we never got into genealogy, so who knows. But they are related; they have to be. This is Grams' cabin, right here in Holton. Wait till you walk back to the creek with me. It brings back such memories, and yet we're almost 150 years before our time."

"Do you think that the tear stain contains DNA? I've been reading so much about it lately. They use it to find lost family members, in family tree research, and in court trials. It's even been used to set innocent men free from prison."

Fran's eyes opened wide. "I think you're on to something. DNA was left behind in the teardrops, and when our tears merged with the 1875 tears, since we are Clarks, it brought us back to the original cabin. That's it! You're a genius, Dora."

"Genius or not, what does that do for us?" asked Dora.

"Maybe we can do the same thing in reverse. If we cry on it, maybe we can go back. Hey, why did you come if you didn't know how you could get back? What's going on that you haven't told me? Why aren't you married yet?"

"Oh, Fran, I have so much to tell you." Dora's eyes filled with tears. She swiped them away, and then laughed. "Maybe I should capture these and bottle them up. We might need them again someday soon."

"Tell, me, Dora. What's happened?"

"Yes, I will, but first I need to use the – um -- outhouse."

Fran burst out laughing. "It's out back. I'll take you. I have to use it, too."

"Oh, Franny, I don't think I can go in one." Dora scrunched up her face in disgust.

"It's that or the woods."

Dora pouted, and said, "Okay, lead the way. But if I throw up when I come out, don't laugh."

Chapter Five

1875

After their trip to the half-moon, the sisters went to the barn where Fran introduced Dora to Traveler, her horse, and Laney, her cow.

"Laney and Traveler?" laughed Dora. "I can see that you were the one to name them. Mom would roll over in her grave if she knew she was named after a cow!"

Fran stopped in her tracks. "Dora, what an awful thing to say. Mom, will take it as a joke, I'm sure. She has a great sense of humor. Wait, you said 'roll over in her grave.' Dora! What haven't you told me? Is Mom okay?" Fran's face went white and when she saw the tears well up in Dora's eyes, she knew without being told. "Please, Dora, tell me it's not true. Dora?"

"It's true, Franny. I wanted to tell you, but the timing wasn't right. Let's go inside and sit down."

"No! I won't hear it! Besides I need to secure the barn and check on the chickens. You go ahead. I'll meet you inside." Fran turned and walked away.

Dora was confused. She hadn't expected this reaction. The old Fran was very sensitive and would have fallen apart, but Fran did seem different, now. She was stronger, both physically and mentally, and she had more confidence. Dora slowly walked into the cabin, leaving her grieving sister behind, knowing that she had not yet related all of the bad news. It was going to be very difficult to tell her everything.

About an hour later, as the sun was beginning to set and a beautiful deep red sky was covering the fields and lakes of Michigan, Fran walked in the door. She found Dora sitting on the floor stroking Moose, crooning words of adoration in his ear. He was eating up the extra affection. He now weighed close to 120 pounds, but he still acted like a baby.

Dora stood up and went to Fran to wrap her arms around her. "I'm sorry you had to find out like that. It wasn't my intention."

"I know, sweetie. Let's sit on the bed. It's softer than the floor. You can tell me all about it as we get ready for the night." After spending some time alone and trying to adjust to what she had recently learned, Fran felt like she was ready to hear whatever Dora had to say.

Dora took Fran's hands in hers. "Honey, this is going to be hard. Harder than you can imagine."

Fran stared at her for a second and then said, "Go ahead. Tell me."

Dora took a deep breath, then she forged ahead, trying to tell everything in order. "Well, you knew about Dad's heart problem."

"Yes, of course, but what does that have to do with Mom?"

"In a minute. Be patient. Franny, Dad had to have another stent put in, and he improved in leaps and bounds, but during a checkup, they discovered he had stage four pancreatic cancer. He died six weeks later. He's gone, honey."

"Dad? But I thought we were talking about Mom? What are you saying?"

"Yes, Dad died a few weeks after you left. Mom was so distraught with losing you and him both, so soon after losing Gram, that she couldn't eat. She got real weak and it wreaked havoc on her body. She lost so much weight, Fran. She didn't even look like herself anymore. When I was finally able to get her to eat, it was too late. The extreme weight loss took a toll on her body. She suffered a fatal heart attack. We lost them both, Franny," she cried. "We lost them both. I had to come find you. You were all I had left." Dora sobbed in her sister's arms.

Fran numbly stared into space. It was too much to comprehend. All this time she had been planning on returning to them, and now there was no one there. Gram, Dad, Mom – all gone.

"It's not possible. It can't be," she whispered, but when she looked at her sister's devastation, she knew it was true. They hung on to each other and sobbed until all of their tears had dried up.

When Fran felt like she could breathe again, she said, "Honey, I'm so glad you had Kevin. He must have been a rock to get you through this. Is that why you postponed the wedding? It wasn't just me; was it?"

Dora took in a deep breath and looked at her hands, wringing them until her knuckles turned white. "That's just it, Fran. There is no Kevin and me any longer. He was not there for me when you left, and I finally broke up with him. I soon discovered that he had been having an affair with a girl in his office. He got her pregnant and they got married right away. He didn't even have the decency to show up at either one of our parents' funerals."

"You had to go through all of this alone? You poor baby. What a jerk! You're better off without him."

"Dad never liked him, did he?"

"No, he didn't. I guess he knew something we weren't aware of."

"So, Franny, that's why I came. I had no one else. I had to find you, or I thought I might die, too. But now we can find a way to go back together. We have each other, right?"

"We'll always have each other, no matter what."

"No matter what? What does that mean, Fran?"

"It means, I've been struggling with whether or not I want to go back. And now that you're here and our parents are gone, I might want to stay. Will you stay with me, Dora? You're all the family I have here."

"But you're not really alone, right?" And finally a small smile escaped Dora's lips.

"No, I'm not. I might be in love. No, I know I am in love, but it scares me."

"Why?"

"What does it mean? Think about it. If I hadn't come here, Luke would have found someone else to marry, and he would have had children, and a family tree would have been formed. If we stay together, do I disrupt that whole line? Maybe the Clarks, our Clarks, were never meant to marry the Graingers. Maybe the cabin would not have been passed down to Gram and Gramp. Maybe you would not have had a sister. I wish I had done some family research before I came here, but of course, I didn't know that was going to happen." Fran sighed.

"Well, one thing is sure, we know you can't have children, so it's impossible to screw that line up too badly."

"Right," said Fran softly.

"I'm sorry to bring it up so coldly, but it's probably for the best in this situation, don't you think?"

"Still to have Luke's babies? Can you imagine how beautiful they would be?"

"You've got it bad, girl."

"I'm afraid I do. But enough talk. I'm exhausted. Crying always tires me out. Let's hit the sack. Oh, and be careful with phrases like 'you've got it bad'. We don't know how long any of them have been around, so I stay away from them as much as possible."

"What do you do if something slips?"

Fran laughed. "I blame it on Canada."

The girls crawled into bed together and held each other for a while, then Fran said, "Yikes! I forgot how cold your feet are. Move over, please." And they giggled until more tears came. When their wet DNA had dried up, they fell into an exhausted sleep.

Chapter Six

1875

Fran was in a deep sleep, her hand dangling over the edge of the bed, her mouth hanging open. A wet nose pushed itself at her over and over, followed by a few licks. Moose whined quietly, but knowing he was on the verge of a full out bark, she forced herself to sit up. Her sister looked very peaceful, apparently she had not heard a thing, so Fran tiptoed out to take care of Moose's needs.

Still in her camisole, she opened the door to the fresh morning air. The huge dog pushed his way past her and bounded down the steps. She gave him free run now, not so much worried about him being attacked by a coyote or bear. Most likely he would be the aggressor, and chase any unwanted critter away from the cabin. It gave a sense of comfort to know he was looking out for her. Moose was the best gift Luke could have given her. Luke; her eyes got misty whenever she thought of this new man in her life. She stretched and yawned, her breasts pressing against the thin fabric of her undergarment, revealing the dark circles beneath.

"Now that's a sight I enjoy seeing in the morning."

Fran jumped. "Ooh, you startled me! Where did you come from?"

"I was going to start building that smoke house, but I was afraid to wake you two with the pounding noise, so I stood at the side of the house to see if I could hear movement. Just then you came out. When I saw you standing there in the morning sun, looking like a picture any artist would be pleased to paint, I was frozen in time." Luke moved closer to her while at the same time she gravitated toward him, in a dreamlike manner.

"Luke, I missed you so much last night." As they came together Luke pushed her around the corner. He crushed his lips to hers and pinned her to the house with his strong arms holding her arms above her head.

"It has seemed like days since we were together," breathed Luke into her hair, his hands trying to cover every inch of her body at once.

"Silly, it's only been since yesterday afternoon. Mmm, do that again." Fran threw back her head and moaned.

Luke continued with his kisses down the crook of her neck, but when he moved even lower, Fran came to her senses. "Luke, we can't. Not here."

"Why not. Nothing has stopped us before. We've been all over the farm." His eyes twinkled with the memories of their passion.

"Because my sister is in the house. She'll be waking any moment, maybe she already has."

"What are we going to do about it? I need you, Franny."

"Well, for one thing, you work on that new bed, so she can have her own room, then maybe, I can sneak you in."

"That will help, but it still won't be enough privacy for my little she-cat. And not soon enough for me." He nibbled at her some more.

Fran sighed. She was both embarrassed and excited at the thought of her behavior when she was with Luke during their intimate times. She had never thought she could let go so completely with anyone. But when it came to Luke, there was no way she could hold back. She was putty in his hands.

Luke laughed out loud when he saw her blush.

"Shhh, quiet." Then they both broke out in giggles. "Now, get back to work. You're welcome to join us for breakfast, if you like."

"I might just do that. Thank you, ma'am." Suddenly formal, he winked at her, tipped his hat, and sauntered off.

She loved the view as he walked away. Fran exhaled loudly, but as soon as she turned the corner of the house, she was shocked to see Dora standing there.

"My, my, my. What has become of my big sister? And look at how you are dressed—or not dressed. What will the neighbors say?"

Dora squealed when Fran ran after her. It was just like when they were teenagers. Once inside the house, they laughed until their sides hurt.

"Okay, forget whatever you saw or heard. Promise?" begged Fran.

"Are you kidding? I'm going to hold this over you forever."

"All right, but then I'll have to remind you of the time I caught you and Jimmy Moore making out in the back of his Chevy and your top was off."

"Hey! We were in love."

"You were only fifteen. Jailbait."

"Yeah, you're right. I was lucky it never went any farther. I did have plenty of fun before I found Kevin, though. But once we were together, I never wanted

81

another man. I thought it was true love forever. How could I have been so blind?"

"Some men change after they get what they want. Not that I have any experience." Fran moved to the stove to start the coffee. "My only boyfriend in school was Joey. At first he was a convenient date and I did have a little crush, but after school, when he joined the Air Force, I really did fall in love, or so I thought. But let me tell you, it was nothing like what I feel for Luke."

"I can see that. Is there anything I can do to help?" she asked, gesturing at the sink.

"You can set the table – for three, please."

"Perfect. I can get to know this man of yours. Does he treat you right, Franny?"

When Fran turned around, her sweet smile said it all. She wiped her hands on her apron and started to say something, but changed her mind. A look of concern crossed her face.

"What is it?" asked Dora.

"I don't know what to do about telling him – you know about...."

"Well, we have time yet, to make a decision. I want to explore this new world."

"Decision?"

"About us going back together."

"That's just it, Dora. I'm not sure I want to. How can I leave him?"

"But how can you not go with me? We only have each other now."

"Are you determined to go back?"

"It's why I came. To take you back with me. I never once considered staying."

Fran's eyes filled with tears. She knew this would come up one day, but she had not wanted to face it. And now Dora was here, and her chance to return had come with her. They now knew that the DNA in the tears was the answer. She was sure they could make it work, but it would tear her apart to make this choice. Twisting her hands with anxiety, Fran knew it wasn't meant to be decided just yet; she had a lot to think about first.

Just as she was about to continue their discussion, Luke knocked. She was surprised that he had not just walked in as he normally did, but happy he had knocked instead, because he would have seen them both in despair. She wiped her tears away and opened the door.

"Come in. Breakfast isn't ready yet, but you can have some coffee while you wait."

"Thank you, ma'am."

"Oh, for Pete's Sake!" exclaimed Dora. "I know all about you two, so stop with the formalities."

Luke was shocked at her boldness at bringing the subject of their shared love out in the open, but he was relieved. He would no longer have to tiptoe around the issue when he was with the two of them.

"Now, sit down, and let me get to know this man of my sister's." She winked in a flirtatious way, making Luke suddenly shy and uncomfortable, but when he heard Dora's teasing giggle, he relaxed a bit.

'These Clark women sure are a strange bunch,' he thought.

Chapter Seven

1875

Dora sat at the table gently stroking Moose's large head and scratching behind his ears. He turned his head around and looked at her with adoration, his big brown eyes blinking slowly.

"Will you look at that?" laughed Fran. "You even have Moose wrapped around your little finger. How do you do that?"

"Do what?" Dora kissed the top of Moose's head, causing him to sigh with pleasure.

"Cause men to melt at your feet. You have always been able to get them to do whatever you want."

"Not always. I couldn't get Kevin to marry me."

"Well, Kevin's another story. I believe he loved you in his own way, but he wanted a harem on the side."

"Then that's not love; is it? And the truth is that any female can get any man to do her bidding. A little attention and a stroke of the ego is all that's required. They're such simple creatures."

"Really!" laughed Fran. "I beg to differ. Luke is anything but simple. He's quiet and sometimes moody, a deep thinker."

"Haven't you figured him out yet?"

"No," responded Fran, "and I'm not sure I want to. He'll tell me all about himself when he's ready. Besides, I made a promise to myself to tell him my true story on the day he tells me everything. Then there will be no secrets between us."

"Are you sure that's wise? Telling him about where we come from?"

Fran looked up from the sink where she was cutting vegetables from her garden. "I don't think I can keep living a lie. It's very difficult, Dora, loving someone and not knowing if they can accept the true you."

"Well, I would wait until he has no choice. Maybe after you get married?"

"Who said anything about marriage? How can I even consider that? It's what keeps me awake at night. Is it fair to allow his feelings for me to continue when he doesn't know what he's in for?"

"I don't see why not, but he'll need an explanation. You might want to go back, and it would break his heart to know you left him to return to another century. He would never have a way to contact you or to follow your life. He would never know if you married and had a family."

Fran rubbed at her eyes. "I can't think about it now. It's just too much to deal with." She threw down her dishcloth and took off her apron. "Let's see if we can get you unpacked. I might be able to squeeze out some space in my dresser for you. Luke fixed it so it's not as beat up as it used to be. He's making me a wardrobe soon, so we can hang up our dresses."

"He's quite handy, isn't he?"

"Most of the men here are. They have no choice but to learn, but Luke is an exceptional carpenter. He has a real talent."

"What about that Ned? What kind of talents does he have?" giggled Dora.

"What about him? Dora, please leave him alone. If you have any plans of going back, you cannot start something with Ned. I'm afraid I already broke his heart."

"You did? I wasn't aware of that. Was it because you went after Luke?"

"It wasn't like that. I didn't plan it, and besides I never truly thought you would come. I had given up all hope of figuring out how to get back. I needed someone. Luke makes me feel secure and safe."

"You see? You use men the same way I do. That's what they all want – to be your savior and protector. It's in their genes."

"I'm not using Luke! How can you say that?"

"Do you like his strong arms around you? Do you like his warm body in your bed?"

Fran blushed and turned to walk toward the bedroom.

"Did he take care of you and bring you food?" continued Dora. "Then you were using him. Men are the natural hunters and protectors. It's the way of the world."

"I had no choice! I would never use another human being for any reason."

"All I'm saying is there is no reason a girl can't find a man to help her get through the rough patches, and fall in love at the same time. I remember when Gram used to say, when she was young, girls went to college for the sole purpose of finding a man. It was the place they could find someone who would provide for them for the rest of their lives. Most women never had any intention of working after marriage. She said the thought was, it was just as easy to fall in love with a rich man as it was a poor one, so why not put yourself in the place where there were likely to be rich men? College."

"Gram said that?"

"She sure did. Of course she fell in love with a man who never became rich."

"That's because they became hippies, flower children, and they gave up the idea of striving for material gains. I'm glad though, because what I learned from our grandparents helped me survive here."

"Well, now you'll have to teach me, because I never cared much for being poor, so I didn't pay any attention to them. I always planned on marrying a man with money."

"If you stay here, you'll learn soon enough what is important in life. A nice bath for one thing."

"How *do* you bathe, by the way?"

"Sponge bath only. I don't have a tub and no room for one anyway. In the summer you can bathe in the creek, but I never had the courage to do it. The water is getting too cold now, though."

"Oh, Fran, I don't think I can do this. Doesn't anyone have a bath tub?"

"You can buy a bath at the boardinghouse. Mercy Brody has a bathhouse now, but it costs five cents to bathe. Believe me, that's costly. You will think twice about it when you see how little money there is to go around."

"Oh, money! I brought some." Dora ran to her carpetbag.

"Where did you find that bag?"

"Well, I spent a lot of time on eBay and other Civil War reenactment websites. You can buy any kind of dress you need. Those people are fanatics when it comes to accuracy. It's how I got most of the things I brought with me. But I also scrounged around in antique shops a lot. That's where I found a man who specialized in Civil War memorabilia. He had some coins and bank notes from the era. They were expensive, but I thought you might need some money. Look what I brought."

Dora laid out her dollars and coins on the bed. She beamed with the pride of her accomplishment.

"Oh Dora, you are a life saver! We can really use this. But we must spend it wisely. I won't get paid for teaching until the end of September. I hate to tell you this, but I don't think a bath is in the cards for you. But don't worry, we'll haul in some water and heat it on the stove. I was given some lye soap, but I'm afraid to use it except for the laundry."

"Ta da!" exclaimed Dora, as she pulled out two bars of soap; one was French lavender and one was goat's milk and honey.

Fran inhaled deeply. "This is a true treasure. What else do you have?"

When she pulled out the brush, mirror, and comb set, Fran squealed in delight. She marveled over the beauty of the jewelry and ribbons. "Why, you've thought of everything."

"It was difficult, because I tried to get things that were not only appropriate for the time period, but also made with natural materials and fabrics. But there was one thing I wasn't too sure about. Let's see if it made it okay." She began to poke around in her clothing, pulling one thing out at a time, taking inventory of her items. When Fran saw Dora's look of dismay, she had to ask.

"What's missing?"

"Feminine supplies. I tried every kind I could think of. Not one thing is here. I knew you would not need it, having damaged your ovaries when you were young, but I do. What will I do? I can't stop mother nature."

"I have friends who can help you with that. Don't worry, we'll figure it out. But you know what that tells me?"

"What?"

"Nothing can go back in time unless it is of that time period. Look, all of your clothes survived because they were made with cotton and wool and the proper buttons and thread. The soap was handmade, I'm guessing."

"Yes, they are all natural scents made with herbs and flowers. And the scarf I brought was made with wool yarn that was handspun from sheep and goats. They don't use any dyes, only natural colors. But then how were we able to come through?"

"Because we are connected by DNA to the Clarks. Our DNA is the ticket. I'm curious, you said you could not read anything on the back of the envelope I sent."

"No, it was blank. And I sent you a letter, too. I told you what I was trying to do. Did you get it?"

"No, nothing. I never knew if you were seeing anything I sent. So that must mean we can't alter history. Your letter could not survive here in 1875 because the paper and ink did not exist, yet. I wonder if a proper paper stock and a fountain pen or quill that uses an inkwell would have worked."

"I think you're on to something," said Dora, "but what about your message? You used a pencil or something from this era, didn't you? Why couldn't I see it?"

"Yes, I did use a pencil that Luke gave me. I think the writing disappeared because the letter originated in 1875. The letter was meant for Sarah and William Clark, the owners of this cabin, and it told the reason why the school teacher would not be coming to Holton and Twin Lake. The person in Canada who was writing didn't know the Clarks had already moved, so I got the letter instead. The other Mrs. Clark, the one from Canada, really did lose her husband and child, and, due to sickness, she lost her own life soon after. I don't think I was allowed to alter that letter or envelope after the fact. I still have it though, here in the trunk."

"How can it be here and there in 2019 at the same time?" Dora was getting very excited by this whole thing. She had read so much about time travel, but this was different for her because it was real.

"That's something we'll never be able to figure out. But it looks like I don't have to worry about upsetting history. It can't be done."

"What does that mean for you and Luke?" asked Dora, knowing this question was going to upset Franny.

Fran's normally light blue eyes turned dark as her mind was turning over Dora's question. "I guess it must mean I can never be with Luke. I mean, we know I can't be my own ancestor, right?"

"Maybe you can still be with him. You can't have children. There's no chance of upsetting the family tree."

"You're right. Maybe something good has come out of that horrible bike accident. But I'll always worry about Luke. Does he ever have his own children? And with who? Does that mean I should go back and leave him alone to carry on his own story the way it was meant to be?"

"Maybe you were always meant to be for him. Ever think of that?" Dora hugged Fran. "There are too many questions we can't answer. Let's take it one day at a time. Shall we? I want to experience everything I have ever read about, good and bad. Don't worry about me. I'll get a bath one way or another." The sisters laughed and hugged and began sorting through Dora's clothes. When Luke returned he heard nothing but girly chatter.

Chapter Eight

1875

It was already the third day since Dora had first arrived. Fran was pleased with how well she seemed to be adjusting, but she was worried that when the novelty of 1875 living wore off that Dora would miss her old way of life. When that happened Fran would have to make a choice as to whether to follow her back or stay, but for now she was happy to push that thought aside. They were sitting on the front porch in the rockers, casually talking about people back home and sharing childhood memories. It felt good to Fran to have a companion from her own time.

Francine stopped a moment from snapping the green beans she had recently picked. "Oh Dora," she laughed, "If you ever want to have butter, you have to put some oomph into it."

"What do you mean? I'm turning it."

"I mean you have to keep it going at a steady pace. You can't stop and start with every sentence. You never could walk and chew gum at the same time."

Dora laughed. "I guess you're right. I was not blessed with the coordination gene like you are. I do want butter though, so I'll keep plugging away. I can't wait to try some on that sourdough bread of yours. It really smells great."

"You're going to love it. Sorry, I ran out of butter right before you came, and with all of the excitement, I forgot all about churning up some more. Maybe later we can go out and pick some berries. I found a raspberry patch next to a path in the woods. We can top our bread with some berries. I wanted to pick some anyway, because Luke loves raspberries. And in another few weeks we'll be able to make apple butter, your favorite."

"You remembered! I couldn't get enough of Gram's when we were kids."

"I'm so glad you were able to find those antique cookbooks, Dora. I was getting embarrassed about asking my friends how to do things. They must think I was an awful wife in Canada."

"Tell me about your friends, again, so I remember their names."

Fran nodded. "That's a good idea. We want it to seem like I have written to you about where I have been living. Well, Rebecca Yoder lives just down the road on the opposite side – she's Amish. She's real sweet and always willing to help. Jessica Grainger is Luke's mother; they live next door you might say, although their house is about a half mile away. And Esther London is Ned's mother. They live closer to Twin Lake, near the depot. Both Esther and Jessica practically run things around here. Between the two of them there's always a gathering of some kind or a fundraiser going for the church and school. As a matter of fact, it was at the box lunch auction, when Luke and I had a sort of 'first date.'

"What's a box lunch auction?"

Fran smiled as she recalled that day only a few months ago. It already seemed like a lifetime. "Well, Luke bid on the lunch that I brought to the church that day, and he won the right to eat with me. We sat on a blanket on the top of a hill and looked over the wildflowers. We were completely out in the open, so there was nothing improper, but we managed to hold hands and lock eyes. It was so romantic."

Dora laughed at her sister's face. She had never seen her so in love before. "But I'm guessing from the body language that I have seen between you two that something very improper has occurred since then. Am I right?"

Fran blushed to the roots of her hairline. "Oh, stop, you're not getting any more out of me now. Keep that churn going; you should be almost done."

The sisters had been so involved in their conversation that they never noticed when a buggy pulled onto their lane, but the sound of the wheels on dirt and stone and a horse whinny brought it to their attention.

Dora jumped up and waved. "Look! It's Ned."

"Whoa, girl. Caution. Women here are much more reserved."

"You're right. I'd better mind my manners," she giggled.

When Ned got down from the Sunday buggy, the scene was all too familiar. He carried a bouquet a fresh sunflowers, picked from his mother's garden, no doubt. He had done something similar when Fran first arrived.

"Good morning, ladies," he called, as he approached them. "I hope I am catching you at a good time."

"Why yes, you are, Mr. London," said Dora flirtatiously, but she soon felt the sharp jab of Fran's elbow in her side.

"I see that you are busy making butter and snapping beans. I left a similar scene back at home myself. Ruthie and Ma were hard at work on the porch, too."

"It's a lovely day for porch sitting. Would you care for some coffee, Ned?" asked Fran.

"No, thank you, Francine. I was coming by to offer Miss Clarke a ride through our lovely countryside – the same as I did for you when you first came here." He blushed a little as memories of his crush for Francine returned. He could see clearly now, that he had been yearning for the wrong sister. It was obvious to him that Dora was the one he needed as a wife. She was much more fun loving and more youthful. Her beauty haunted his dreams.

"Why, thank you, Ned," Dora said, with a sweet smile. "I take it you are not working at the blacksmith shop today?"

"I decided to take a day off. I have no pressing orders, and we'll only take a short ride, if you're willing, that is. Then I'll be right back at the forge, in case someone loses a shoe."

"I would love to go with you, if it's okay with Franny – Francine, that is." Dora looked at Fran's face and saw a bit of worry. She knew what Fran was thinking, so she gave her a nod of assurance.

"Okay, then, but don't be long. We're going to pick berries. They're best picked in the morning before the sun hits them."

Dora hugged Fran, and her sister said, "Be gentle with him."

Dora giggled in her ear. "I wouldn't think of anything else," she whispered, with a toss of her head.

"Let me grab my bonnet, Mr. London. I'll just be a minute."

Ned beamed. He was sure this was going to be one of the best days of his life.

∞

A short time after Ned and Dora had left, Luke came in from the small field he had plowed and planted in back of the barn. He had put in a few rows of corn to help feed the chickens and cows, but he also made sure there was a variety of what he called 'good eatin' corn. He carried several ears in his arms, and deposited them on Fran's table. No one was around so he had walked in unannounced, as had been his habit when Francine lived alone. He assumed the girls were out taking a walk, but Moose was here, and Francine would not have gone without him.

Luke stooped to scratch Moose behind the ears. "Hello, big boy. Where's your mistress?"

"His mistress is in here," called out Fran.

He followed her voice to the bedroom, and was pleasantly surprised to find her in a new chemise. "My, my, don't you look pretty." His heart beat rapidly at the sight of her. How he ached to hold her. "Where's your sister?" he whispered. "I'd better step back into the kitchen. I don't want to ruin your reputation."

"Don't worry. Dora's gone. She went on a buggy ride with Ned. And as far as my reputation goes? I'm afraid you're too late," Francine said, with a devious smile. "There's a certain farm hand that I can't seem to keep my hands off of. Why don't you step in here, and see if you measure up to the competition."

"I'd be more than happy to oblige, ma'am."

Fran had not seen him grin this big since before her sister had arrived. He threw his hat on the dresser, and dropped his suspenders. Then he picked up his lover and tossed her on the bed, as she squealed with delight.

Chapter Nine

1875

"Where are you taking me, Mr. London?" asked Dora, demurely.

"Please, you must call me Ned; we know each other quite well now, don't you think?" He smiled as he remembered holding her in his arms.

"Why, I'd be happy to call you Ned. You're right, you were my hero, catching my fall the way you did. You're very strong, Ned." Ned blushed and looked away, not used to a woman giving him such an outright compliment.

Dora was enjoying this game. It was almost too easy. The men in this era were so polite, at least in this small town where they had not yet met different women of the world.

"If we're going to be on a first name basis, we must consider ourselves friends; shouldn't we?"

"I'd like to be friends, Dora, very much."

"Fine. We will be, then." She was pleased to see him look as happy as a little boy with a new puppy.

The horse's hooves made a steady clip clop sound. It was very relaxing, almost like a clock ticking. The buggy dipped and rocked as they passed over grooves in the road. Bird calls could be heard loud and clear. The scream of a blue jay, the caw of a crow, the sweet song of an oriole and the subtle warble of the robin. It was nothing like when Dora was riding in her new Camaro back home. Even with the windows down, the sound of the traffic and radios blaring from other cars drowned out everything but the sirens in a hurry to pass or the illegal Jake brake vibrating loudly from the semi pulling up to a stop light. Today she was able to take in the smells of the newly mown hay, and the surprisingly enticing smell of cow manure. The air had a fresh cool feel on her skin – moist but not oppressively heavy, due to Lake Michigan's nearness and all of the small lakes and rivers in the area.

"Where are you taking me, my new friend Ned?"

He smiled at her use of his name. "Just into town. Actually, we're going back where you came from but beyond the train depot. I did the same for Francine when she first arrived. She wanted to get her bearings, so I thought you might like to do the same. It's difficult to find your way in a new place, don't you think?"

"Well, there's not much to find here, is there?" When she saw his perplexed look, she changed her tone. "I mean that it seems like you are a close-knit community, by what Francine has told me. And most of you live fairly close to each other, so I suppose there's really no chance of getting lost."

He perked up when he realized she was actually making a pleasant observation. "That's true. We are close. We all help each other, and that's true throughout all of Dalton and Holton townships." Deciding to turn the conversation in another direction, Ned asked, "Do you like to fish, Dora?"

"Not particularly, but I have been known to catch a nice perch or two in my time."

"Perch? One of my favorites. Maybe we could go fishing sometime. I'd love to take you out on Twin Lake in my boat. Or if you don't want to fish, we could just take a Sunday afternoon row."

"I'd enjoy a row around a lake, Ned. Thank you for asking. Now where are we? I see some buildings coming into view."

As Ned went on to point out the businesses in the area, much the same as he had done for Francine, the two chatted like old friends. They were actually a very compatible couple, but just as Dora was leaning into Ned's arm at a joke he had told, she caught the look of a man getting off of a horse. He was taller than most men in the area, perhaps five ten or eleven, and although she could not see anything of his face, due to his hat which had been pulled over his eyes, she sensed a sexuality that was impossible to deny. His broad shoulders tugged at his shirt as he wrapped the horse's reins over a post. When their buggy came near, he raised his head as if he could sense she was there in the buggy with Ned, even though she was pretty sure he had not known about her, but, then again, word probably traveled quickly here. The man had a small cigar in his mouth that he clenched between his teeth, but he managed to get out a half smile and nod at the new lady in town. Dora was shocked to see a similar face to Luke's, only younger, and where Luke's eyes were light blue/grey, this man's eyes were dark. Where Luke could have a brooding look at times, this man seemed to be making fun of her even before she met him. She felt as if he were mocking her for flirting with Ned while keeping him dangling on a string. It was as if he could see right through her and her motives, and it was quite unsettling. Dora's heart skipped a beat when they moved closer and Ned pulled to a stop. Suddenly uneasy, she didn't know where to look. It was the first time ever that a man had put her ill at ease.

"Why, I can't believe it!" called Ned. "When did you get into town, you old scallywag?"

"Mornin', Ned. Miss. Haven't been here but two minutes. I just rode in. Pardon my dust, miss."

"Oh, sorry, let me introduce you. Dora, this is Wade Grainger, Luke's wayward and younger brother. Wade, this is Miss Dora Clarke. She just got into town, too. Dora is living out at the Clark cabin with her sister Francine."

Wade tipped his hat. "Nice to meet you, Miss Clarke. It *is* Miss, isn't it?"

"Yes, it is. And you, Mr. Grainger? Do you have a family of your own in town?"

"Just the Grainger clan waiting for my return."

Dora felt Wade's eyes boldly traveling over her form. When they returned from his inspection, moving from her bosom to her face, she felt herself blushing, something she rarely ever did. Their eyes locked for what seemed an eternity, until Ned cleared his throat.

"Does Luke know you're in town?" asked Ned, in order to start the conversation up again.

"Not yet, but he will soon enough. I'm pickin' up a few things to take home to Ma. I'd like to surprise her, if you don't mind."

"Sure. Not a problem. We won't say a word." Ned would be sure never to let the name of Wade Grainger cross his lips again when he was in Dora's presence. She needed to be protected from the likes of him. All through school whenever Ned liked a girl, Wade had a way of taking over and off she went with him instead. The Grainger men held an attraction for women that was hard to explain. Ned was extremely disappointed that Wade had taken this particular moment to return to town.

During the time the two men had been exchanging words, Dora had had a chance to study Wade Grainger. She had met men like him before -- cocky, sure of themselves, magnets to women, the bad boy, she supposed -- but she had always been able to tame them to her own desires. This one seemed different. While he had been talking to Ned, he had never taken his eyes off of hers. She knew he was interested in her, but she felt he was fire, and she didn't want to cause any problem for Franny. Her sister had a good thing going with Luke. Ned was one thing. A little flirting never hurt anyone. But this man could be dangerous, at least for her heart. Dora's hands were shaking; her heart was racing; she felt her breath quicken when he moved his eyes away from hers, almost as if she were wishing him to come back to her.

"Ned, I think we'd better continue with our ride. Francine will wonder where we've gone," said Dora, breathlessly.

"Yes, you're right. We have a few introductions to make yet. It was nice seeing you again Wade. Don't be a stranger. Ma and Pa will love seeing you, too."

"I'll stop by in a day or two and say hello. Give your folks my best regards." Wade shook Ned's hand, then turned his head towards Dora, tipped his hat, and winked.

'Why, the nerve!' she thought. She sat up straight, and said, "It was nice making your acquaintance, Mr. Grainger. Now, let's go, Ned, or we'll be late."

113

"Late?"

"Just go, please."

As they drove away, Dora heard a deep chuckle follow them, and she knew Luke's brother was laughing behind her back at her discomfort.

∞

Moose's friendly barking alerted the napping couple of Dora and Ned's return. They hastily got out of bed and pulled on their clothing, but not before a long leisurely kiss, skin to skin. Even with the hour in bed together, it was still not enough to satisfy Fran, and by the moan that had just escaped Luke, it wasn't enough for him, either.

Francine pushed him away and laughed, "Quickly, they'll be coming in soon."

"Okay," said Luke, stealing one last kiss, "but we have to solve this little problem of ours soon, Franny. I don't want to wait for you any longer."

Fran straightened the last few wayward strands of hair, and looked over her back to make sure all pieces of clothing were in place. "There's so much to talk about and work out."

"You make it sound so difficult." They moved to the kitchen, and he took his usual place at the table.

Fran slipped the apron over her head and began fussing at the sink. "Well, it is complicated, you have to admit."

"What's complicated?" asked Dora. She was happy to see that everyone was in their 'proper' place, because Ned was right behind her.

"Oh, you're back," said Fran, acting surprised. "How was the ride?"

"Very pleasant," answered Dora. "We saw the whole town and met some interesting people." 'One in particular,' she thought.

"We surely did," piped up Ned. Never enjoying always having to take second place to the Grainger boys, he decided to let the cat out of the bag. A little one-upmanship, so to speak. "We met someone of interest to you, Luke."

"Ned, we promised not to tell!" Dora chided.

"It's okay. We only said we wouldn't tell his mama."

"Whose mama?" Luke asked.

"Why, yours. Your brother Wade just got back to town."

"Wade's here? Why that whippersnapper!" Luke jumped up from the table. "Where'd you see him last?"

"In front of the mercantile," added Dora. "He said he was buying something for your mother."

"I'd better head home, then. Sorry, Mrs. Clark, I really have to go. We can work out our problem later, if that's okay."

Through this whole conversation, Fran had been listening in shock. She had no idea that Luke had another brother. She had met his little sister Ruthie, and his twin brothers, Zeke and Jake, but they were still in their teens. She had never heard about a brother who was not living in town. She wondered why.

"Sure, we'll tackle that problem real soon," she responded in a rather formal way. How Fran longed to kiss him goodbye, but for now she would have to be content with a nod of the head. Her sigh, as he went out the door, was audible and did not go unnoticed by Dora.

Even though Ned was now interested only in Dora, he was still a man who would always be willing to help someone in any way he could. "Is there something I can do to solve your problem?"

"I don't think so, Ned. Thank you for asking. We were just talking about the fact that school is going to start right after the harvest dance, and I don't really have a way to get to school every day, but walk. It would be quite a hike carrying papers and books."

"You're right. We need to find you a buggy."

"Luke was working on the old one that was left behind by the Clarks, but the tornado destroyed it."

"Tornado?" This was the first Dora had heard of a tornado.

"Yes, we had two, one after the other, right after I first arrived, but they never touched down. They did a lot of wind damage though, and the buggy Luke was working on was completely ruined."

"What does a buggy cost?" asked Dora.

Ned contributed his knowledge. "I can get a discount at the general store, I'm sure. I buy them on occasion to keep at the blacksmith shop. I rent them out sometimes to visitors. They retail for seventy-five dollars, but I should be able to get one for sixty-five."

"Well, that's out of the question for me. You know I don't have any money except for what I make selling eggs, and I need that to eat."

"I have money," added Dora. "I'd be more than happy to help. Then, on weekends and at night, when you aren't in school, we would have transportation."

Fran raised her eyebrows. "You brought that much?"

"Yes, I did. I saved up before I came," she said, glancing at Ned. "And I have some jewelry to sell, too."

"Oh, no, Miss Dora, that won't be necessary." Ned turned to Fran and said, "Let me talk to Ma and Pa and see what they suggest. There's no need for you to deplete your funds. We might have something we can loan you, Mrs. Clark, until you can buy a buggy of your own, without using every last dime that you have."

"Well, if I have to I will. And I know the store will give me credit. I have been good about paying off my bill."

"So, see? All is not lost. Now we have options. I'll leave you two for now, and we'll talk about it soon." He turned to Dora and smiled sweetly. "It was nice spending the morning with you, Dora." He glanced at Fran to see what she would say to the use of her sister's first name. He was reassured by her smile.

"Thank you, Ned. I had a lovely time. Maybe we can do it again sometime."

Ned beamed. "I'd love that, miss." His smile broadened to a grin, then he awkwardly left the two sisters alone.

"Isn't he just the cutest thing? Now, tell me what you two were really talking about when we first came in," demanded Dora, the minute the door was closed, "because it sure as heck wasn't about a buggy."

"I'll tell you, but then you have to tell me about Luke's brother."

"Oh, him," pooh-poohed Dora. "He's nothing special."

Chapter Ten

2019

The young sheriff in Holton knocked on the door to the Clark house, but no one answered. He was puzzled by this whole situation and couldn't seem to let it go. Ever since old Mrs. Clark had passed away, strange things had been happening, but his sergeant didn't seem to be as worried by it as he was. When the first Miss Clark, Francine, had gone missing, Deputy Daniel Kent was on the case. After combing the grounds extensively and searching every inch of the house, he had found nothing. Sergeant Miles had only been interested in taking down the facts. He was convinced that the woman had left on her own account, but Deputy Kent knew better. Why would she leave her car behind, and why was there not one footprint other than the family members' prints outside? And no fingerprints that could not be accounted for? Those were questions he had never found any answers to. It was all too suspicious, so on his off time he would often stop in to check on things, always on the lookout for a new clue.

Deputy Kent, or Daniel as Dora had begun calling him, had taken it on as his personal responsibility to keep the remaining sister safe. Of course, it had nothing to do with the fact that he found her extremely beautiful and charming as all get out. And he had to admit that her trim body and beautiful sad eyes tugged at his heart. When he had heard that both her parents had passed away, within months of each other, his heart broke for the newest resident of the Holton house. She had stopped by the Sheriff's Department to tell them she was going home to Indiana for an indefinite period of time, while she sorted everything out. She had asked that they keep her informed of anything new they might find about her sister's disappearance. Deputy Kent took it upon himself to visit the empty house every so often to make sure there was no vandalism or any squatters trying to move in. That's what he told himself anyway.

Daniel Kent always behaved in a professional manner, but one day when he arrived to do his routine check, he was surprised to find Dora's car in the driveway. She was back! His heart did a little leap of joy. When he knocked and she opened the door, he was thrilled to see the smile of greeting on her face. He was afraid that he was beginning to cross a line, but he no longer cared.

Dora had just been through something she would never wish on anyone else, having buried her mother all alone, and after the recent passing of both her father and grandmother, which was followed by the breakup with her fiancé; she was very happy to see a friendly face. Dora was convinced there was foul play where her sister Francine was concerned, and Daniel admitted that he was beginning to think so, too. So the two had gone over and over the few clues they had, but Dora had always held back her suspicion of time travel. She would never tell anyone about that, for fear they would think she was not of sound mind and stop looking.

Just having a reason to be near the very vulnerable and sweet Dora again brought Daniel back time and time again. He always came when he was off the clock, so he had not reported his activity to his superior, but on this particular day he might have to do just that. No one was answering the door, but Dora's car was here in its normal parking spot, sitting right next to Francine's.

Worried that something had happened to Dora, Daniel carefully walked the grounds around the house shining his flashlight beam on the ground. He peaked in the windows, rapped on the glass, and called her name, but the place was eerily quiet. He tried the door but the house was locked up tighter than a drum. Puzzled, the officer stepped back to his car and called the station on his cell phone. It was not going to be fun explaining why he was here on his time off, but he had no choice. He was positive something unexplainable had happened once again, and he shook with fear for Dora. It was at that moment that he realized he had fallen hopelessly head over heels in love.

1875

"Come on, Dora, tell me," said Franny. She tugged at her sister's hand and pulled her to the bedroom, which was the only comfortable place to sit.

Dora glanced at the rumpled bed covers and then grinned. "Fran, I thought you made the bed this morning."

Fran blushed. "I did, but I guess I mussed it up when I sat down to pull on my boots."

The two sisters plopped down on the soft mattress. "Aw, Franny. You can't fool me. I interrupted something, didn't I?"

Fran laughed out loud. "No, you didn't interrupt; we were finished."

"Francine Clark. I'm ashamed of you."

"You are?" Fran raised her eyebrows in surprise.

"What is the young schoolmarm doing, carrying on with the farm hand like that without the benefit of marriage?"

"Well, it's complicated."

"How so?"

Fran sighed. "Apparently, schoolmarms are not supposed to be married. Luke and I have discussed it, but --"

"What? You're talking about marriage?" squealed Dora.

"Maybe. But you see, if we get married, I might have to give up my position, and I haven't even started yet. The people in the town have given so much to me, with the intention that I would be around for a while to teach their children. If I walk out on them, it would be such a betrayal, and a disappointment for the kids."

"I don't get it, why can't you be married?"

"It's the old-fashioned idea that married women are provided for by their husbands and are needed at home to take care of the house for him. Also a married woman would most likely get pregnant, in which case

126

she would not be allowed to work anyway. Pregnancy is hidden from children. And of course she would have to stay at home with her child to nurse."

"But they don't know you can't have children. You should tell them, then you can be married *and* be the school teacher."

"Well, I'm still supposed to be a stay-at-home wife."

"What about the lady at the boardinghouse. I met her today. She runs the restaurant, too. Mercy Brody, right?"

"Yes, that's right, but you see, she has no choice. Her husband died. There's no other means of support without that business, and it's still keeping house and cooking, basically, so it's accepted."

"There's a woman at the mercantile. She seems nice."

"But again she works side by side with her husband. It's a family business. The mores and proper etiquettes are quite specific here, I'm afraid."

"It's not like you to cave in to them," responded Dora. She had always looked up to her big sister for standing up for what was right.

"I have been afraid to rock the boat here. I had to survive, and I still have to. Trying to change generations of thinking is not going to work. I need to fit in and so do you, if you are to stay."

"I guess, but it sure will be hard to keep my mouth shut when I see someone treating a woman less than she should be."

"As far as I have ever seen, women are treated with respect. No man ever curses in front of a woman, and they are always very gentlemanly. I like that part of this century."

"Yes, I have to admit to being impressed with it, too. The men are ...

"Dora, did you just drift off?"

"Yes, well, I guess I did. I met the strangest man today."

"Was it Wade, Luke's brother?"

"Yes, yes it was. He was – he was – well, very unsettling."

"Why? How is he different? Tell me. I didn't even know Luke had another brother."

"He's cocky, flirtatious, probably dangerous, and very, very handsome. He looks like Luke but different. I don't know. There's something in his eyes. It was as if he could see right through me. He threw me off balance, you know what I mean?"

"Yes," chuckled Fran. "I do know. It was exactly how I felt when I first met Luke. He almost frightened me with his intense stares, but there was a chemistry I have never felt with anyone before, and I couldn't seem to stay away. And now here we are, not knowing where we'll go next, but still a couple in a way."

"Well, I intend to stay far away from Mr. Wade Grainger, I can tell you that. Ned is sweet and kind, and probably very reliable, but who said I needed a man anyway. I've only been here a few days, after all. There's no need to get tangled up in the bedsheets if I'm leaving soon."

"You are?"

"Well, not yet. I plan to stay a good long while. I want to experience everything, but Franny, don't count on me being a permanent resident here."

Fran's face fell. "I guess, I always knew that, hon, and I'm not even sure how I feel about staying. I'm still struggling with that. But school starts next week after the harvest dance."

"Dance? When and where?"

"I've been told they do it every year after the crops are in. A celebration of a good harvest and a chance for folks to get together after working so hard. It's held in the large sawmill barn. I've been told they move aside some wood, build a bandstand and a local band plays."

"I'm ready to hear music. I can't wait. I hope we don't make fools of ourselves, not knowing the dance steps."

"Blame it on Canada. That's what I always do." They fell back laughing until their sides ached.

"We need to do something about getting you some furniture," said Dora. "Two grown women rolling around on the bed can't be good, even though we are sisters."

"You're right about that!"

"How about we use my money to buy a sofa and a side chair or two. If a rental buggy is being provided, we'll just need rent money for that. Do you think my money would cover the furniture?"

"Good idea," said Fran. "I'm not sure how much furniture costs; we'll go shopping next time Luke takes me in with my eggs, but we have to be careful with whatever you have. We can't spend it all at once. Life is precarious here."

"Shopping in the nineteenth century. How fun! That should be a hoot."

Chapter Eleven

2019

It just so happened that Sergeant Richard Miles was still at the office when the call from Deputy Kent came into dispatch. He was puzzled why the young deputy would be calling in something on his time off, and he was a little perturbed. It wasn't like Holton Township was a hot bed of criminal activity. Miles was eager to go home himself. His son was playing pee wee football for the first time, and Richard Miles was a very proud papa. He wanted to be there to cheer his son on.

The Sergeant sighed and reached for the paper that had just come across his desk. It seems that Deputy

Kent had been driving by and decided to check up on the pretty young Miss Clark. Sergeant Miles rolled his eyes. He was done with this 'so called missing persons' report. There had never been a clue as to the whereabouts of Francine Clark. Richard Miles could not afford a misstep, because he was testing for Lieutenant soon. He did not want a blot of any kind on his record. Since solving the Clark case was not going to happen, he had decided to drop it. Miles was convinced she had left of her own accord. But here was Kent saying that the sister, Dora Clark, seemed to be missing, also.

"What in the ...."

Miles threw his pen across the room, reached for the phone, and called home. Kent may have just placed an obstacle in his path to becoming Lieutenant *and* to missing his son's game. Kent had better have a good reason for this call, because now he was obligated to check it out. If Miles didn't follow up the report, that in itself could go against him. "Missing sisters," he muttered. "I'll be the laughing stock of Muskegon County."

When Sergeant Miles arrived at the scene in his unmarked car there was a patrol car there already with flashing lights.

"Turn those damn lights off, for Pete's sake!" he barked. "This isn't a murder case."

Daniel could see that his Sarge was riled up and he felt responsible, but it wasn't his fault that Dora was missing. He was worried, terribly worried, but he could not let that show, or it would be viewed as a lack of professionalism.

"Evening, Sarge," he said, as his boss approached.

"What have we got going here, Kent?"

"Well, I stopped by about an hour ago, to check up on Miss Clark, and --"

"And why did you feel the need to check up on Miss Clark?" interrupted Sergeant Miles.

"You know I never thought we finished up out here, and it's always worried me that she was living here alone, so -- "

"So, you thought you'd come to a pretty lady's defense. Be the hero, so to speak. Am I right?"

"Not exactly, Sarge, it's just that nothing ever seemed to make sense. And maybe I was right all along, because, now Dora – Miss Clark is missing, too."

"And how do you know she's 'missing'?" asked Miles, with a sarcastic snarl.

"Because she's always home at this time. She doesn't like to be out after dark."

"Always? Dark? How many times have you stopped by?"

"Truthfully? Dora and I have begun somewhat of a relationship. Nothing sexual, I promise you that. I've just become her friend, and lately a bit more. I stop by on occasion and we have coffee and cake, or sometimes we watch a movie together, that's all. She said she feels better when I'm around at night."

"So, the knight in shining armor, eh? Well, I don't want to hear about your love life," he growled. "I've got somewhere to be tonight. Tell me what your suspicions are."

Daniel went on to explain how no one seemed to be home, and how he had searched the property, but found no foul play, but combined with the fact that her car was still in the driveway, things didn't seem right.

"And just like before, there are no noticeable footprints or disruptions of the grasses or plants around the windows."

"Did you go inside?"

"Yes, I finally unlocked the door. She told me where she hid the key, just in case, she said. I've never used it before, I wouldn't do that, but I was afraid she might have passed out or something and was on the floor where I couldn't see her through the window."

"And?"

"Nothing. No disturbances of any kind, no notes, all of her clothes are still here, along with her purse and cell phone. What woman these days goes anywhere without her phone?"

"None that I know of." The sergeant sighed. It looked to him like it was going to be a long night, the paperwork alone would kill all prospects of seeing his son make his first tackle.

There's two of us now, well sometimes three, and if we have company, we'll need more seating."

"Okay, that's it then. Lizzy," called Fran, "we've made our decision. Can you place our order, please?"

The women were huddled together as Lizzy Foster wrote up the order and collected the price in advance, when the sound of a man's boots caught Dora's attention. She turned just in time to see Wade Grainger exiting from the hardware side of the store. He carried a heavy hay hook in one hand and a pulley and some chain in the other. She watched as he easily tossed his items in the back of his wagon. His pants fit him snuggly, hugging his nicely rounded bottom, even though his suspenders hung loosely at his side; it was a rather pleasant view. Most of the other men in town wore loose clothing for ease of work in the field. She guessed he was not usually a farmer. He seemed to sense her staring at his backside and turned with a crooked grin. Dora blushed, but she was unable to move, frozen like a deer in headlights. Wade watched her discomfort for a moment before tipping his hat, and then he jumped up on his wagon. As he drove off he took one quick glance over his shoulder, and he was not surprised to see her still watching him. Dora heard him whistle a tune as he drove away. It sounded familiar, but she was not sure of the title.

"Dora? Dora! Do you agree?" asked Fran.

"What? Oh yes, whatever you want."

"Okay, then let's get going. Luke will be picking us up in another minute or two. Thank you, Lizzie, for all of your help. We'll be anxiously waiting for our new furniture."

The storekeeper's wife waved them off and promised to notify them the minute their order came in.

Chapter Twelve

1875

Luke was frustrated. He never seemed to have any free time with Franny anymore. Her sister Dora was a nice enough person, but she was always around. He worked furiously with pent up frustration as he mucked out the stalls, tossing the horse droppings in the wheelbarrow a little more forcefully than necessary. He also held in some anger, but not toward Fran or Dora; it was more towards his younger brother.

Wade was the light of his mother's life. Jessica Grainger had had her trials in life with her children, as all mothers do, but for some reason, Wade could do no wrong. It had always irritated Luke, because he was the one who had been here through thick and thin to help out the family, except for the years when he was away at war. When he returned, mentally beaten and still healing from his physical wounds, he felt he had an obligation to make up for lost time. He needed to be there to help out his father in the fields and with the animals.

It had been difficult for Luke to come home after all that had happened; he would have loved to turn tail and run the opposite direction, but that's not who he was. Instead he buried all of the painful memories of what he had experienced, and he came home to his family. He had expected to be met with exclamations of joy that he had survived, but instead he found grief and sadness for the loss of another. His mother and father *were* very happy to see him, but all he could see was the disappointment and agony in their eyes, because instead of two sons coming home, there was only one.

Wade was just a kid then; he was only fifteen when Luke returned in 1865. He was all starry-eyed and full of questions about the war, but Luke was not in a mood to talk about any of it. He pushed Wade and his twelve-year-old twin brothers, Zeke and Jake, away. He became quiet and moody; he became someone no one wanted to be around, and it was all because he was afraid that one day he would give away something that he had been holding in for such a long time. He was afraid that he might tell the truth, and then no one would be able to look at him in the same way again.

But then one day, out of the blue, Francine had arrived and changed him forever. She was sweet and vulnerable, and she looked to him to solve all of her problems. He loved being her protector, and he loved that he had won out over that kid, Ned London. For the first time in many years, Luke felt like a new man, someone who was worth knowing. His parents had begun to respect him again for his hard work and dedication to the Clark farm. That's the way Luke felt, anyway. He had no idea that they had always respected him for his time served in the war and for what he had given to the family since he had returned. He only saw

143

the sad look in his mother's eyes. He never understood that after she was through grieving, her heartache was for him, because she sensed he was carrying around a heavy burden. When the Canadian teacher, Francine Clark, came on the scene, the light in Luke's eyes returned, and Jessica Grainger had her son back again. Luke had begun to smile and sometimes even laugh.

It seemed perfectly normal for Jessica to dote on Wade. He had been gone for such a long time, and she was thrilled he had finally decided to come home. Wade had always envied Luke's experiences in the war, even though he had heard how gruesome it had been from other returning heroes. Still he had wanted to experience something other than Holton, Michigan before he was required to settle down with a family, so he took off to work on the Pere Marquette Railway as soon as he turned eighteen; this week was the first time he had been home in seven years. Wade had seen a lot of sights all over the country, and he had met some very colorful people who had changed him in many ways, but he was still the same person he always was – cocky and full of himself. No one had been able to dampen his spirit.

Wade was the light of his mother's heart, they had always had a very close bond, but she knew his handsome good looks and flirtatious ways were bound to be his downfall. Jessica worried about her next son just as much as she had about Luke, although she knew Luke did not see it that way. Now that she had seen Luke get through his trial, whatever it was, she had set her sights on straightening up Wade. Jessica did not want him to be a bad example to her perfectly well-behaved set of twins.

∞

Later that day, Fran made an excuse to go out to the barn. She said she needed to milk the cow, because Luke had been too busy to do it earlier. The truth was she wanted to see Luke; she ached for his touch.

Dora saw right through her reason for going to the barn, but she didn't care. Let Franny be happy while they were here, she thought. Soon enough they would have to leave, and it would all be nothing but a wonderful memory. Dora settled herself in the rocking chair on the porch and began to shell peas for their supper. She hummed a song that had been stuck in her mind recently, Love Me Tender by Elvis Presley. It kept repeating in her mind, an earworm they were called in the 21st century. She had no idea that it was the very same tune that Wade had been whistling on his way out of town. Moose settled in at her feet feeling a little lazy after a long run in the woods. He was torn between following his mistress and sleeping on the porch in the sunshine. Sleeping won out. Dora called out a warning to Fran not to forget the milk, then she laughed, knowing full well that milk was the last thing on her sister's mind.

Fran waved the silly comment away. She didn't care anymore what Dora thought. She didn't even know why she made lame excuses when she wanted to see Luke. She needed to see him daily or she felt like she couldn't breathe. Her heart raced as she neared the barn. Stepping into the opening, she was surprised to see that Luke was shoveling manure with a fury she had not seen on him before.

"Something the matter?" she asked

He jumped at the sound of her voice. He had fallen down into a shadowy place in a world of his own making, and he had learned a long time ago that hard work was the only thing to chase away the darkness he found there. But as soon as he looked upon her face, his mood softened. Fran could see the change; she loved that she could do that to him. It made her feel powerful, and that made her feel sexy.

"Hi, stranger," he teased, "where have you been hiding?"

"Just in the house with Dora, doing, you know, 'house things.'" Fran slowly moved forward into the dimmer light. By the looks of his shirt he had been working hard for quite some time; he was damp under the arms, and he was breathing heavily; there was a sheen of perspiration across his brow. "Is something wrong?" she asked again.

"What? No, not at all. Just working. I have a lot to do today."

"Like what?" she asked, as she slowly moved closer.

Luke's breathing was quicker now, but it was not the heavy breathing of hard labor. His eyes followed the sway of her hips. Her top two buttons were undone, begging any man to complete the task in a downward manner. He had never seen this look in Franny's eyes; they smoldered with desire. It was intoxicating to know that her longing was for him and him alone. She tossed her head back to move a stray lock away from her forehead, but the movement only alerted him to her soft neck. He wanted her right here and now, in the middle of the day, in a barn. God help him.

"Truth is, Franny, I have nothing important to do at the moment," he said huskily. Stepping closer to her, he added, "What about you?"

"Well, there's always something a person can find to do, right?" she said suggestively.

"That there is," Luke responded, coming yet another step closer. "I've already accomplished quite a bit. I broke up a bale of straw over there in that stall, to get it ready for Traveler's area. It's fluffed up quite well, don't you think?" They had finally come close enough so he could take her hand. He entwined her fingers in his, kissed them, and led her to the opening of the empty stall. He heard her suck in a quick breath at his touch.

Franny stepped inside, looked around as if she were inspecting his work. "Yes, Luke, this seems to be very satisfactory. It almost looks like someone could bed down here." Fran tilted her head flirtatiously.

Luke could not hold back any longer. "That was my thought, exactly." He pulled Franny to him, wrapping her arm behind her back. She curled the free arm around his neck. Their eyes held contact a moment as they studied each other's soul, their lips close but not yet connecting. Luke's breath was ragged; Fran's heartbeat quickened.

No longer able to contain himself, Luke moved his lips to hers, claiming her as his own. They locked in a passionate kiss, neither one ready to separate, but finally Fran placed a hand lightly on his chest. "The door," she whispered.

"What about the door?" he said, as he went for her neck with nibbles.

"It's open," she panted.

"It's never bothered you before."

"Never had company before," she gasped. "Dora." It was all she could get out. Her breath was too short for more words. His roaming hands were finding places that were sending sparks through her whole body.

"Don't move!" Luke commanded, as he raced to pull the barn door closed. He was back so quickly that Fran barely knew he had left. When they made contact again, it was electric. Nothing could stop what was about to happen next. Luke scooped her up and lowered her to the fresh new straw, kissing her face and hair on the way down. When he heard her soft moan, he was lost.

"Franny, I love you, I love you. I need you so."

This time when Francine heard him say those words, she knew without a shadow of a doubt that she could never leave him. She could never consider going back again. She wound her arms around his neck and cried with the release of their joining, she cried for her lost past, but mostly she cried with joy for the hopes of yesterday in her new future.

Chapter Thirteen

1875

An hour after their arduous union, Francine heard her sister calling her name. They had both fallen asleep; it felt so natural to be together like this that it was difficult to move. Dora's call was not frantic, but it did seem like she needed something, so Fran raised herself up and began to dress hastily. Even though Dora most likely knew what had just happened here, she really did not relish being caught red-handed.

"Luke," she called softly, "Luke, wake up. We fell asleep. Dora's coming."

"What?" he said drowsily.

Fran admired his bare chest and his tousled hair. How she wished she could lie down beside him again, but that was not going to happen today. "Hurry. Dora's calling. We have to get up and look presentable."

"Oh, okay," he said, rubbing at his eyes. Fran was standing next to him, smoothing down her skirt and trying to pat her hair back into place. He slowly stood up, stark naked and pressed his body to hers. How he would love to pull her down to the straw once again.

"Hmmm. Woman, you must have cast a spell on me. I want you again right now."

"Please, Luke," laughed Francine. "Not now. We'll figure something out for next time, but hurry, now. Put on your clothes." She kissed him quickly on the mouth, as he groaned with desire.

Once everything was in place, they opened the door, Francine holding her still empty bucket. A man was standing next to Dora by a wagon. He was laughing, but she did not seem amused.

"Who's that?" Fran asked Luke.

"It's my brother, Wade."

"Ah, the one I knew nothing about. Well, come and introduce me. I want to know all about your family." Fran stepped out into the sunshine, squinting a bit. From what she could see from here, he was a carbon copy of Luke, only a bit younger. Dora gestured for them to hurry.

"Fran, Luke, we need your help. The furniture has arrived," she called excitedly.

As Fran and Luke approached, Luke said, "Mrs. Clark, this is my brother, Wade Grainger. He's been away for quite a spell."

Standing before Francine was a very handsome man, but then from what she had seen all of the Grainger boys were good-looking. Now that she was closer, she could see the distinct differences between Luke and Wade. Luke was about five foot ten where Wade was a tad bit taller, closer to five foot eleven perhaps. They both had the same chestnut brown hair, but Luke's eyes were steel grey, and Wade's a warm brown. Wade had a nice charming smile much the same as his mother, Jessica; he appeared to be more at ease with himself than Luke. Fran's instant impression was that there was something very likable about him. "Nice to meet you, Wade. Luke's been working for me all summer. I know your mother and sister Ruthie quite well. You have a lovely family."

"Thank you, ma'am. It's nice of you to say so."

"Why did you bring out the furniture, Wade?" asked Luke.

"I was in the hardware store when Lizzy asked Hank if he could deliver the pieces. I volunteered, since it was out our way. I knew how excited Miss Dora, here, was to get it." He looked at Dora and winked, although she was the only one who could see the bold gesture.

"Now, how did you know Dora and Fran had ordered new furniture?" asked Luke, with a puzzled look.

"I was at the store the same time they were ordering it. I overheard, you might say."

"Well, thank you for coming out. These ladies sure do need someplace nice to sit. Let's get this unloaded." Luke was pleased that his brother had done something for someone other than himself for a change. He had no idea that if Dora had not been in that house, Wade would not have put himself out so readily.

The brothers worked in harmony, obviously having done many a job together in the past. In a few short moments, Francine and Dora had a new sofa, two chairs, and a footstool in their so-called living room, as small as it was. The sisters laughed with joy at the beauty it brought to the room. They both sat down immediately to test it out, but when the men made a move to try, they were quickly stopped in their tracks.

"Uh, uh, uh." said Fran, shaking her finger. "You men are dusty and sweaty. These will be used only when you are fresh and clean."

Wade looked puzzled. "I thought Luke was the farmhand, here. When would he have an opportunity to relax in your fine parlor?" As soon as the words were out of his mouth, he saw the blush and discomfort on the face of both his brother and Mrs. Clark. A sly grin slowly spread across his face. "Oh, I get it. Pardon my ignorance. Good for you, old Luke."

"Wade! How dare you insult a lady like that! Get out! Now! Before I kick your sorry a--" Luke made a quick check of his language.

"I didn't mean anything by it. Please excuse me, ma'am. I'm so sorry. I guess I've been away from civilized society for too long."

"Thank you, Wade, I accept your apology," said Fran. She felt a little bad for him, because he was correct in assuming there was something between her and Luke, but since they couldn't make it known just yet, Luke was forced to act insulted. The fewer people who knew the better.

"Well, if you'll excuse me, I'd better get home. Pa is waiting for the supplies I went into town for. We're fixin' a fence. Miss Dora, Luke," he said, as he tipped his hat.

Fran was aware of her sister's tension. Something had been going on between the two of them before she and Luke arrived. She'd want to hear all about it later.

Luke cleared his throat. "Well, I'd best be getting home, too. It's late in the day already, and if Pa needs help on the fencing, I should pitch in." How he longed to get one last kiss goodbye.

"Oh," said Francine, "I forgot my bucket of milk. I'll be just a moment, Dora." She followed Luke out, and the moment they stepped around the house, out of view of both Dora and Wade, she melted into his arms as he crushed her to him. Then she quickly ran out to the barn to milk the poor cow, who had been patiently waiting as their passion was extinguished.

∞

"Okay, spill," said Fran, when she returned with the milk bucket. "What were you and Wade talking about before we came out of the barn?"

"Nothing," huffed Dora. "He's a real piece of work, I'll tell you. He seems to think a lot of himself. I couldn't tell if he was coming on to me or teasing me into an uncomfortable embarrassment."

"Maybe both. Men are not much different here in 1875 than they are back home. Just read the signs."

"Well, the signs say he wants to take liberties that no proper lady would allow. Isn't that so, Franny?" teased Dora.

"Oh, hush. You know things are different with Luke and me. Thanks for giving us privacy, by the way."

"I figured you two needed it, since I was the one who came barging into your lives."

"You didn't barge in," laughed Fran, glad to have an open discussion about Luke with Dora.

"Well, fell in, then, onto the train depot platform," she chuckled.

"That's all behind us now. We have a nice home, food to eat, and a new sofa! Let's enjoy this new life."

Dora ran her hand over the horsehair fabric of the sofa. It was exactly what they had ordered. "Let's have a sit, shall we?"

"Yes, let's give it a good test, then we'll put on supper. Have you heard any more talk of the barn dance coming up?"

Dora perked up at the talk of having some fun. "No, when is it?"

"Luke said it's this Saturday. We need to make sure our best dresses are ready to go. Maybe we can go into town and get a new ribbon or something."

"I have the jewelry still. We can wear a piece or two. There's a nice cameo in the group."

"Okay, after supper we can look them over and decide. It will be like the old days when we were getting ready for our dates."

"You've been here almost four months, Franny. Do you miss home?"

"Once in a while, but this is home now. I'm very comfortable here. How about you?"

"I long for a hot shower, and a flushing toilet, oh, and maybe electricity, but I'm okay for now. I know it's not forever, so that helps."

"Yes, well, we need to talk, but let's save it for after supper. We really should get the food started before it gets dark. I don't like to cook in lamplight."

"All right, let's get started. What's for supper?"

"Luke brought me a pheasant. We can fry it up like chicken, and have those shelled peas. I still have some of those little pearl onions you like, too."

"Mmmm, meat fried in grease again, yum."

Chapter Fourteen

1875

Wade and Luke were unharnessing their horses and taking care of the wagons. Luke glanced at his brother. He knew him all too well. There was a reason he had delivered the furniture to the Clark cabin, and it wasn't because he wanted to help out Hank at the mercantile. Dora was a pretty little thing, beautiful actually. Luke was not blind to that fact, even though Franny held his heart in her hands. He decided it was now or never to say something.

"Wade, what are your intentions, exactly?"

Wade looked up from the rub down he was giving his horse. "What do you mean?"

"I mean, toward Miss Clarke, Mrs. Clark's sister."

"Yeah, I wanted to ask you about that. Why is Dora's name Miss Clark, while her sister's name is Mrs. Clark? Wouldn't one of them have a different last name?"

"Easily explained, but you're changing the subject. So I'll answer and then you will. Dora's last name ends with an e, C-l-a-r-k-e. Her sister married a man with the name of Clark without the e from another family; therefore she spells her name C-l-a-r-k."

"Interesting, and they're from Canada? That's what Ma said. Where's Mrs. Clark's husband?"

"He died in a house fire, along with her small child. It was devastating for her, and she was all alone, so the town hired her to be the new schoolmarm, but she arrived early. I guess she needed to escape the memories. We've been taking care of her ever since."

"I'm sure you have," said Wade with a smirk.

Luke lunged at his brother and managed to get in a good punch to the jaw. Wade laughed as he rubbed his hand along the jawline. "I never knew you could move so quick with that bum leg of yours. Sorry, I'm not used to being in a more polite society. Railroading is rough. The men are rough, so I had to be rough, also, to fit in. I'll have to learn to curb my tongue, but the fact remains that there is something going on between you two; am I right?"

Luke grinned. "You just might be. Now, you have to answer me. What were your intentions when you delivered the furniture?"

Wade took a moment before he spoke, considering how what he was going to say might sound. "Luke, I have to admit that I am more drawn to Miss Dora than I ever have been to anyone in my life. I only met her once actually, Ned introduced us, but there's something I need to explore with that one. She's a real spitfire."

"Well, be careful. There'll be no exploring. If you must get to know her more, do it the right way. I don't want you to mess up anything with me and Francine."

"Oh, so it's Francine, is it? It's progressed more than I thought, then." He grinned again, not able to resist teasing his older brother.

Luke grunted and waved him off, but secretly he was singing for joy inside.

∞

The sisters had finished their meal and were now standing next to the bed with the jewelry spread out. Their best dresses were laid out also, so they could compare and contrast colors and ideas. Their choices were limited.

"Dora, you did a fantastic job. If we ever get into dire trouble we can sell something."

"That was my plan, since I wasn't sure how the money would play out. I spent a lot of time in the antique shops, looking for just the right period. It cost me a pretty penny, too, but I didn't mind. I had one goal in mind and that was getting to you."

"Did you do all of this on your own? I mean since mom and dad were not around to help, who could you trust?"

Fran caught Dora's little smile before she spoke again. "You know how I told you that Mom and Dad had reported that you were missing to the police?"

"Yes, that must have been a terrible time for you. I'm sorry."

"It was, but there was a deputy sheriff who made it a little easier. He was the only one who believed that there was something we were missing, maybe sinister even. His sergeant was positive you had left of your own accord, but Daniel --"

"Daniel? This is the first I'm hearing about a Daniel," interrupted Fran.

"Well, he's actually Officer Daniel Kent, or Deputy Kent, I suppose. When his commanding officer wanted him to drop the case, he refused. He couldn't get past the fact that there were no clues as to your disappearances – nothing. He would stop by and check up on me after I started living in this house alone. He usually came after his shift was over, so I would invite him in for coffee and then later dinner, and we became friends."

"Friends? Just friends?"

"Yes, that's all it was. A few times on a Saturday, he went antiquing with me. He couldn't understand my fascination with this particular era, but he tolerated it. I never gave you away, Franny, I promise." Dora took her sister's hand in hers.

"Was there something more between you two than friendship?"

"Toward the end I was feeling quite an attachment, he's very sweet, but I was on a mission, so I refused to let him get closer. There was never anything physical between us, although I admit that at times I wanted there to be. He's quite attractive, and I was lonely after separating from Kevin. But I'm proud to say, I did not let it go that far."

"What do you suppose he's thinking about you being missing now?"

"I try not to think about it. I sometimes miss him a little, and I worry that he's tortured since I'm gone. I'm pretty sure his feelings were stronger for me than mine were for him. Anyway, I'm sure he'll still be there when I get back, and then I'll see where it goes. Our time to return won't be long now; right?"

Fran took in a deep breath and looked her sister in the eye. "We need to talk."

"About?"

"Going back."

"And?"

"I'm not." Fran was worried about how Dora would take her news.

"What do you mean you're not?"

"I like it here. And okay, I'll say it out loud – I'm in love with Luke, and he's in love with me. I can't leave him, I just can't and I won't. And face it Dora. We're not even sure we know how to go back."

"Oh, Franny," cried Dora, "you can't stay. I won't allow it!"

"Dora, you're a big girl. You can make your own decision, but I am not leaving. Luke and I plan to be together."

"But you'll be altering history!"

"Then so be it. I won't produce any children for him, so there's that, but so far, it looks like history rights itself, anyway. It's possible my plan won't work. Maybe history will send me back without my permission or help, but I'm willing to take my chances."

Dora sighed deeply. "I guess I understand. If I loved someone that much, I might do the same. While we're here let's see if we can figure this out, because I *am* going back, sometime after the dance."

"Can't you stay through fall at least, watch me start to teach school, and maybe even come to a wedding?"

"A wedding? Are you kidding?" Dora hugged Franny while kissing her sister on the cheek.

"He hasn't actually asked me, yet. Well, that's not true. He did one time before, but we weren't ready, or I should say I wasn't. So I'm confident we will be married shortly after school starts. It's what we've been waiting for."

"Then of course, I'll stay. I wouldn't miss your wedding for anything. Can I still be your maid of honor, like we planned?"

"Of course you can, if they do that here. Now if you're bound and determined to leave, let's see if we can figure out how you should do it, then we'll be prepared."

The sisters poured over everything they had as evidence of their time travel, talking well into the night. Dora pointed out the tearstain on the unfinished quilt and how she had seen her own teardrop land in that exact spot. When she recounted her version of it, it jarred Fran's memory and she remembered doing the same thing. They were then convinced that it all had to do with a DNA connection to Sarah Clark who had been working on the quilt before she left for Allegan. But they were not sure they could reverse the process. They finally decided to call it a night and work out more details in the morning. Fran felt secure that she would have Dora for a few weeks more anyway, so they snuggled under the covers, and dreamed of Grainger men. One sister slept with a smile on her face; the other with a frown.

Chapter Fifteen

2019

"Kent, have you let that Clark case drop like I told you?"

"Sir, I have as far as the department is concerned, but I'll never let it drop until I've figured out what happened to those two women."

"You're that sure there's something amiss?"

"I am, Sarge. I know Dora pretty well. She was very worried about her sister. She would not have done the same thing, and just left without letting me know without a call or a note at least. I know that for a fact."

"Tell you what," said the seasoned sheriff, "I'll let you continue to look into the situation, it's all yours, but don't pull any of the other men into your investigation. And if anything more serious comes up, you drop it until that case is done. Agreed?"

"Thanks, Sarge. I'm going to solve this, I know I can find out what happened to the Clark girls."

"Okay, then. Don't tell me anything else about it, unless you have a break-through. Now back to the streets."

Daniel was relieved that he could now work openly on this case, but he was terribly worried for Dora. He wouldn't rest until he figured it out. He prayed she was all right.

That night Daniel Kent took a pass by the cabin again, same as always. But this time he freely used the key to let himself in. He walked around each room looking for something out of place, but it was all the same as before. The quilts were laid out on the back of the couch and some quilt blocks were on the floor near an overstuffed chair. It was then that it hit him. Dora had put away the quilts after her sister had gone missing, and now here they were all laid out just the same. 'Was she trying to recreate the night her sister disappeared?' he wondered.

He wandered into the room he knew she used as a bedroom, the one to the left of her sister's. Everything looked okay, here. He felt a little strange going through Dora's things, but he began to open closets and drawers. He was used to going through people's property. He often had to search for guns or drugs and paraphernalia, but this time he knew the person in question. He had dreams about her. Now, here he was, poking around in her personal drawer. He stopped a moment to touch something lacy, and smiled. How he would have loved to see her in it. Instantly, shame came over him. He was on a job; he could not afford to let this be personal, or he could miss something.

Daniel opened her jewelry box, and looked without touching, but then something didn't look right. Several pieces were missing, all of the new ones they had purchased together at the antique store. He especially remembered a dragonfly broach, some dangly earrings, and a rope of pearls. He had commented on the amount of money she was spending on antiques. He remarked that she had not seemed like a girl who liked antiques. She said it was for a project she was working on. She told him she was getting props for a play back home that she was involved in.

Yes, they were all gone, but other pieces were here, items he had seen her wearing. He loved it when she wore those big gold hoops. He held them a second trying to think, then he walked to her closet. The door had been left open from the last time he was inside the house. When she had first gone missing he had checked it then, of course, but he had not been looking for any specific items. He had only noted that her clothes were still there. He pushed some things to the side and back, when he realized that the dresses she had shown him were not there. He recalled the prairie style clothing she had purchased. She had held up a camisole and pantaloons, and they laughed at how people used to dress back then. He had longed to ask her to model them for him. He was sure she had seen the longing in his eyes. That night when he left, they had kissed for the first time. Daniel pulled out the drawers of her dresser. The old items were missing, too. This was very strange. He searched for a box or trunk where they might have been stored but found nothing. He questioned why her modern-day clothes were all here, but the antique items were gone. Daniel was beside himself. He was glad the rest of the sheriff's department wasn't in on this, because Deputy Kent had to wipe away a few tears. He had never been so scared for anyone in his life, and especially someone he loved. That night Office Kent stayed in the Clark house. He fell asleep in the chair. He knew this was way over the line, but he was afraid to leave until he could get this right. There had to be a clue somewhere.

∞

1875

It was the night of the big barn dance. Everyone was so excited, especially Fran because she was planning on dancing openly in Luke's arms where no one would criticize their closeness. Ned had asked Dora if he could pick her up. The new buggy was ready, so he would bring it to the Clark cabin. Luke was going to use his family's Sunday surrey. At the end of the night, it was planned that the two men would each bring their partners home, and then Luke would give Ned a ride home since he would have to leave the new buggy behind. The women were looking forward to having their own transportation, finally.

The ladies fussed with their hair and pinched their cheeks, trying for something that looked like the blusher they were used to. They each wore gloves and carried a fancy lace-edged fan that Dora had brought with her.

Dora pinned on a dragonfly broach that Daniel had particularly liked. Her heart skipped a beat when she thought of him. They had been very close to starting a relationship. She hoped when she returned he was waiting for her. She would have a lot of explaining to do, but she had become quite good at lying, so she knew she could figure something out to tell him.

"Are we ready?" asked Franny.

Dora had never seen her sister so excited to go on a date. And a barn dance at that! "I am. I hope we can figure out the dance steps."

"Oh, it's probably nothing more than the two step, the waltz, and maybe a polka. If our steps don't match theirs, we'll--"

"Blame it on Canada!" they said together, then they broke out laughing. It was at that exact time that they heard a knock on the door.

"Well, at least one of our men is on time," said Francine.

"I'll get it," answered Dora. When she opened the door, she had all she could do but not laugh. There stood Ned, hat in hand, a bouquet of flowers, and his hair all smoothed out flat. It still looked wet or perhaps there was some pomade spread on it. She supposed this was what the men here did to impress a lady.

"Come in, Ned. The flowers are beautiful. Thank you. I'm almost ready. I have to grab my evening bag."

"You look very pretty, Miss Clarke." Ned blushed a deep red.

"Thank you. It's kind of you to say. And I can see that you spiffed yourself up, too. I'm looking forward to the evening."

When Dora returned from the bedroom, she was wearing her bag which was a small drawstring pouch; it dangled sweetly from her wrist. Ned sighed. He would have the most beautiful woman in the room on his arm.

"Franny, would you like us to wait here until Luke arrives?" asked Dora

"No, you two go ahead. We'll meet you there. Oh, look, he's pulling in now."

Dora and Ned waved to Luke as they passed each other on the lane. He was glad they were gone. He had planned to be a little late so he could have some time with his Franny alone. He was wearing his Sunday-go-to-meetin' jacket and hat. He had not had it on in a very long time, but he wanted this night to be special.

Fran did not wait for Luke to come to the door. They were past formalities. She kissed Moose on the head. He knew she was leaving him and he whined.

"I won't be long. You guard the house, okay?"

Luke jumped down and moved quickly to Fran. He stood back for a second and watched as she walked toward him. She literally took his breath away. Her white blond hair was wound up high on her head, and she had some baubles dangling on her ears. She had managed to arrange her fancy blouse to expose more of her chest than was normally seen in public. He had never seen her look more beautiful. When she came near him, he took her in his arms, and under the moonlight, with no one watching but the crickets, he kissed her until her toes curled.

"My, my, my," he said, when he came up for air. "Look at the new school teacher. Scandalous!"

"You think so? Should I change?"

"You'd better not, or I will be right there behind you helping you with the job."

Francine giggled. "I think we'd better leave, or they will wonder what happened to us."

"But I'd love nothing better than to stay here and remove all of those beautiful clothes."

She laughed. "Now mister, I did not spend hours getting ready for you to dismantle my efforts in a few minutes. We'll dance first, then later we'll figure out how to remove clothing."

Luke sighed deeply. She was quite a woman, always ready to take care of a man's desires. He felt like the luckiest man in town.

Chapter Sixteen

1875

Dora could hear the music and see the torches and lanterns from quite a distance down the road, the sounds carrying freely over the newly leveled fields. She was so excited that she reached over and squeezed Ned's hand. She was surprised when he squeezed back and held onto her hand a moment. She smiled happily at him. Maybe it was wrong to give him false hope, since she planned to leave soon, but then she thought, why not have fun while I'm here? And even if he was a bit young for her, he was so darn cute.

"Thanks for taking me tonight, Ned." she said sweetly.

"It's my pleasure, miss."

"Well, now that we are to be dance partners you'd better call me Dora. We've talked about this before."

He grinned at the thought of holding her in his arms. "All right, I will, Dora."

"You'll have to stay close by, Ned. I don't know anyone." Dora smiled again and leaned a little into his shoulder.

Ned was jarred by the physical contact. He was sure it must have been an accident, Dora would never be so bold, but he was pleased nonetheless. "I will proudly take you around and introduce you to all of the folks. There will be a mixture of Holton and Dalton Township people, but since we live so close to the border of Dalton which is where Twin Lake is, of course, you'll already know some of them. You've met most of the store owners in Twin Lake, and you already know Luke. His whole family should be there, including Wade. You met him the day I took you for a ride. Remember?"

"Yes, well, I have seen Wade, since, a few times. He helped Luke deliver some furniture we ordered."

"Oh, so he has been to your house, then." Ned turned his head away and frowned. A little jealousy crept in that she might be more familiar with Wade than he knew.

"Yes, just to unload the things and then he left. Oh, look how pretty everything looks!" exclaimed Dora, as they pulled up to the huge barn. It was truly one of the largest barns she had ever seen. There were so many buggies and horses in front of the open barn door, and people were milling all around, the women dressed in their finery.

"This here is the sawmill barn. It's one of the biggest barns in the area. All of the newly stacked lumber had to be left outside until the dance is over, then we'll all pitch in and move it back after the dance, along with the large tools." Ned parked the buggy and helped Dora get down.

The excited partygoers were calling out to neighbors they had not seen in a while. The excitement was palpable in the air. She heard things like, 'Hi Martha, did you get your pickles put up yet?' 'Hey Richard, are you needing any help with your fields? I can lend a hand.' 'Who's the fiddler tonight? Anyone know?' 'Let's get in there before all of the food is gone.' There was so much laughing and eagerness to be around each other, that it was contagious.

Ned led her inside where the music was going full force. People were already moving around the dance floor to a wild polka. One man kicked up his heels, then spun his lady around. She shrieked, then gave him a little smack of reprimand. The barn was lit with a hundred oil lamps hanging from the rafters. They cast a soft, lovely glow over everyone. She spotted a food table on the right, and a barrel that the men were dipping into to fill their mugs. Obviously, this was not to be a dry party. Dora stood there with a big grin on her face. This party was going to be a hoot.

The music makers were on the back side of the barn. Dora could not see them because she was too short to see over the dancers' heads, but she heard a fiddle, a guitar, a banjo, a bass fiddle, and some type of drum. She jumped when she felt a tap on her back. It was Franny and Luke. Dora thought Fran looked a mite mussed up, but maybe it had been the wind in the open buggy. Dora had to admit that her sister had never looked more beautiful. Joy was radiating from every pore.

"Hey, you two. Did you just arrive?" asked Ned.

"Yup," said Luke, "we pulled up right behind you. So what do you think about your first barn dance, ladies?"

"I say, let's dance," replied Dora, as she pulled on Ned's hand.

He grinned and happily moved to the dance area, joining into the new polka with gusto. Dora squealed with delight when Ned twirled her around, her blonde curls threatening to loosen completely.

"Whoa, slow down, boy, or I won't make it more than a dance or two."

"Sorry, I guess I got excited to be twirling you in my arms. You're so pretty, Dora." He settled down his

186

steps, and was rewarded with a sweet smile. Ned eagerly awaited the slow dance when he could pull her even closer to him. His heart was racing so hard, he wasn't sure he could make it through the night without attempting to kiss those luscious, plump lips.

As they rounded the dance floor, Dora could feel all eyes on her. She was the new person in town. No one knew anything about her except that she was Francine Clark's sister. It was obvious that not too many strangers ever showed up in the villages. Most had friendly smiles, so at least Dora felt welcomed. The next song was slower, a waltz that Dora actually recognized; it was called Beautiful Dreamer, and if she recalled from her music appreciation class in high school it was written by Stephen Foster in the south, during the Civil War. Apparently, music was immune to political differences. Or perhaps ten years was enough to put hard feelings aside. Ned led Dora in a wide circle, moving in tandem with the others. He was quite a good dancer now that he had settled down.

When they rounded the turn at the back of the barn, Dora saw the band for the first time. A few men were sitting on hay bales while others were standing. The fiddler had his head down in concentration, but something drew her to him. As they moved closer, he lifted his head, and she found herself looking directly into Wade Grainger's eyes. His look of surprise was obvious. Dora tightened her face and turned Ned so that she could not see Wade. What was it about that man that put her off so? Once they had moved to the opposite side of the barn, Dora asked to sit for a while. She could tell Ned was disappointed, but she wanted to collect her thoughts, because she had never once considered that Wade might be at the dance – or had she?

"Sitting one out already?" Francine asked her, as she and Luke sat next to her.

'Fraid so. Ned went to get me a drink. He is quite an exuberant dancer. I'm tuckered out already." She chuckled at her own vernacular. "What about you two?"

"Oh, we haven't started yet. Too busy talking to folks."

Dora leaned around Fran. "Say, Luke, I didn't know your brother could play a fiddle. I was surprised to see him up there."

"He sure does, and he's real good, too. Course a lot of folks play an instrument of some kind, for their own entertainment, of course. Wade's always had the music in him from the time he was young so he gets asked to play often."

"I see," said Dora.

"Here's your drink, Dora," said Ned pleased to be able to do something for Dora. "I hope it's satisfactory. I wasn't sure if you liked cider or not."

"Of course, I do. I love it. Is it hard?"

He grinned. "Sure is."

"All the better. Let me have a few sips, and then we'll dance."

"How about it, Franny? Want to take a turn?" asked Luke.

"I'll give it a try as long as it's a slow dance."

"Slow is my specialty. I like to take it slow the best; how about you?" he said suggestively.

"Luke, not here." she slapped at him playfully.

The couples rounded the floor to another familiar tune, called 'Long, Long Ago.' Dora was surprised to see that Luke was not embarrassed to pull his sweet Franny close. Ned tried to do the same, but Dora kept a respectable distance between them.

When the couples neared the band, Dora's eyes were pulled toward the music. Once again she caught Wade's eyes holding hers. He stroked the strings with his bow, his chin held down and his head bent over the instrument. This time she let their eyes hold until he had moved out of sight. Wade Grainger was an extremely handsome and charismatic man. Everything about him screamed male sexuality. She could feel the magnetic pull long after they were out of sight; Dora's hands were shaking and her heart pulsating wildly. Ned noticed the differences in her immediately, but taking it for a thrill she had felt for him, he asked hopefully, "Are you okay, Dora?"

"Yes, yes, I'm fine. I think I need a bit of air."

"Sure, I'll walk you out." But as they were leaving one of the single young men, named Joseph Crookshank, approached and asked for a dance. Dora did not want to be rude, so she accepted. She placed her hand in his and left Ned standing, giving him a look of apology over her shoulder.

Ned figured he would have to fight for the hand of the beautiful newcomer, but he had not expected it to be so quickly. He had only had a few dances and already she was out of his sight. He was feeling a bit out of sorts. He was the one who had brought her. She should have stayed with him.

It wasn't long before little Ruthie Grainger, Luke's little sister, saw Ned standing alone, so she asked for a dance. He agreed because she was only ten, and he didn't want to hurt her feelings. He guided her out to the floor, their height difference quite comical, but it was common for the older men to dance with the young ones. It was a way to teach them and get them ready for adulthood. He felt like a fool, but the little girl was so pleased, that he couldn't help but smile at her sweet face.

Her curls bounced with their movement, and they laughed together at a misstep. When they had trouble untangling their feet, he picked her up and twirled her around. He realized he was really enjoying himself, but when he caught a view of Dora in Joseph's arms, his heart ached.

One man after another claimed Dora for a dance. She hadn't seen Ned in many songs. She had danced to the Jenny Lind Polka, Oh, Susanna, and Old Folks at Home. It was surprising how many songs she was familiar with. When Dora was finally released by the last young stud, she sought out some cool fresh air. She needed a break away from all of the men, including Ned. She was truly enjoying herself; her cheeks were flushed with excitement, and she had become the star attraction of the barn dance, but every time she went by Wade she felt his eyes on her. It was quite unsettling.

When Dora walked out into the moonlight, the air was fresh but still warm and balmy. Crickets and frogs could be heard over the sound of the music coming from the barn. The smell of the night air was intoxicating.

Dora inhaled deeply and walked a ways away from the barn, but when she discovered some lovers kissing by a haystack, she changed course toward the back of the barn. She leaned against the barn, looking at the enormous amount of stars. She had never seen anything like this back home. The lack of city lights only made the stars seem closer, a never ending display of nature's twinkling lights. The harvest moon was low and very large. Dora wondered what Daniel was doing and if he missed her. Did he see the same moon she was seeing? Was the sky this bright and clear where he was? She chuckled at the thought that she now had two suitors each in a different century. She jumped when she heard a voice say, "A penny for your thoughts."

He was leaning against the barn, down a little bit from where she was. He was smoking a cigarette with one hand and he had a jug in his other hand, dangling by his side.

"Oh, my, I didn't know anyone was there." Of all the people here, she had to find Wade on the same side of the barn where she was.

"Been here the whole time. You don't notice much, do you?" He threw down his cigarette and ground it carefully into the ground with his boot, while he placed his jug on the window ledge behind him.

"What do you mean by that?" said Dora in a huff. "You're the one who should have announced yourself."

"No need to. I was here first. Besides, I enjoyed watching you. Just as I enjoyed watching you dance."

"Yes, I noticed. It was quite rude, as a matter of fact." Dora tossed her head, her blonde curls bouncing, much like Ruthie's had when she was dancing.

"Rude?" He threw back his head and laughed. "You loved every minute of it." Wade had inched closer and closer until he was next to her, looking her straight on. "I know your type, Miss Dora Clarke with an E."

"What type is that?"

"You're not like your sister. You have experience with men. You know what we want, but you like to pretend you are all sweet and innocent."

"How dare you!" She started to slap him, but he caught her hand mid-air. Dora's heart was racing; she

194

knew she shouldn't stay and have a conversation with him, but she could not make her feet move away. There was something about this man; she knew beyond a shadow of a doubt that he was pure trouble, but, unfortunately, she had always had an attraction toward the so called 'bad boy.' The pull toward him was so strong it was impossible to deny, so when he leaned in for a kiss, she responded.

Wade pushed her back against the barn wall crushing her tightly to his chest, and once Dora made contact with him, she was lost. She wound her arms around his neck and responded in a very unladylike way. The turmoil of the last few weeks tumbled around her as if she were once again in that whirlwind that brought her here in the first place. Thoughts of her grandmother, her parents, her ex-fiancé Kevin, losing Fran and finding her again, and then meeting Daniel, swirled around as she fell into an abyss with this new man. Her emotions were all over the place, and Wade was here at just the right time when those pent up emotions were ready to be released. Wade's hands began to roam over her body, moving quickly toward her breasts. Dora opened her mouth and gasped for air. A small moan escaped her lips, and she heard his moan match hers. Dora felt like she was falling, but she had no will power to stop it. She had never felt anything like it before -- never with any high school or college boyfriend, and certainly not with Kevin. Just as Wade's mouth began to demand more, the couple was startled by an indignant voice.

"What in the Sam Hill is going on here?"

When Dora came to her senses, she was shocked to see Ned at the corner of the barn. She pushed Wade away, and straightened her clothing. He had somehow managed to unbutton the top two buttons already. She was glad that it was dark, so Ned couldn't see her disheveled state. A deep blush of embarrassment spread across her face. And worst of all was when she heard Wade chuckle. He made no apologies to Ned for taking what he had wanted.

"I'm sorry, Ned. I – I--"

"It seems that I have truly misjudged you, Miss Clarke! But of course, I would expect nothing less of you, Wade. You're the same rake you have always been. Seven years away has changed nothing. You can find your own way home, Miss Clarke. I won't be coming around any longer." And he turned on his heels and exited as quickly as possible.

"Oh, Wade, what have you done?" asked Dora, as tears fell.

"What have I done?" he laughed. "I believe there were two parties involved here, my sweet one, and it seemed that we were both enjoying ourselves immensely."

"You misunderstood. I didn't mean -- I was confused. I...."

"You what? Aren't the innocent you pretend to be?"

"Well, where I come from --"

"Is that so? Then I'm going to have to travel to Canada, soon, if the ladies are all like you," he whispered, his breath close to her ear. Truth was, he didn't care a hoot about other Canadian girls. This one was going to be more than enough for him. Wade wanted all of her, and he was positive she wanted him, too.

Dora pushed him off her, leaving him alone in the dark. She could feel his eyes following her as she walked away. She sought out Franny, wanting to go home, only to find the school teacher and her farm hand were dancing much too closely together to be proper. Before she knew it, another young man had grabbed her hand and was spinning her around to 'Wait for the Wagon.' She got through that dance and was about to ask Fran if they could leave, when Wade cut in and took her hand. She stood stock still, debating whether this was a good idea or not.

"Don't you have to fiddle?" she asked weakly.

"We fiddlers take turns. I did my stint. That way we can each have fun dancing with pretty ladies like you. You have to dance with me, Dora. It's my right as the fiddler, part of my pay, you see," he lied. "They're watching us. You'll embarrass yourself if you turn me down."

"I think I've already embarrassed myself enough for one night, don't you think?"

"No one knows but us and Ned, and he's too much of a gentleman to tell. Come on, my favorite song is playing. It's the last one of the night."

Dora moved in his arms to 'Aura Lee,' the same song she knew as 'Love Me Tender,' by Elvis Presley. The love song was magical; she felt like she was floating, and try as she might to forget about what happened behind the barn, the song only intensified the magnetic attraction between her and Wade. She could hear Elvis' version in her head; she could sing every word. Dora feared that Wade was not capable of doing as the song says, to love me tender, and it frightened her. When the tune came to an end, she looked up into Wade's deep brown eyes, watching him as he studied her mouth. She knew he was close to moving in for one more kiss, but he glanced around at his surroundings, remembering where he was, and instead he bowed, kissed her hand, and they parted in a very respectable fashion.

"I'd be pleased to escort you home, Miss Dora Clarke with an E."

Before she knew it was coming out of her mouth, she said softly, "I'd be pleased to allow it."

Chapter Seventeen

1875

The ride home was awkward. There was a sexual tension that was undeniable, and the darkness only enhanced it. They exchanged pleasantries about the dance, the people who had attended, and the music, specifically Wade's playing. Then shortly before they arrived at the Clark's lane, Wade began to whistle Aura Lee; she now recognized it as the same tune he had whistled when he left the mercantile that day. Dora hummed along, yearning to sing the words she knew so well of Elvis Presley's 1950s version.

"Do you sing, Dora?" he asked quietly.

"I do like to sing, although I'm not a performer, like you are. I prefer to sing in the sho -- " Dora stopped herself just in time, when she realized her mistake. There were no showers here, and perhaps they didn't even know what one was.

"Sing where? What were you about to say?"

"I was going to say the shed, but I meant the barn. I sing when I'm alone."

"Well, it seems that you have a very nice voice. I would love to hear it, sometime. But unfortunately, we have arrived at your house, and it looks like your sister and my brother are already here."

Dora laughed. "I believe we may have put a damper on their goodbyes."

"And they on ours," Wade muttered under his breath. "I'll walk you to the door, and bid you goodnight." As they were walking up to the porch, Fran gave a little wave and stepped inside; Luke passed them on the steps.

"I'm not sure how you two came to be together, but I hope you had a pleasant evening, Dora," growled Luke.

"It was unusual, that's for sure. But I enjoyed myself. I did indeed," responded Wade.

As Luke passed his sibling he whispered, "Watch yourself, little brother."

They waited until Luke was in his buggy and well on his way down the lane, until one word was spoken.

Wade leaned closely to Dora and said softly, "I'd really like to see you again, Dora, if I may."

"I'm not sure that's such a good idea."

"Why not? Am I too dangerous for you?" he chuckled. "That's the label I have in town, you see, but nothing could be further from the truth."

"No, it's just that your brother and my sister are getting very close. I don't want to mess anything up for her."

"I can't see how that would be a problem, and I don't think Ned is coming around again, so you'll be without male companionship." He stepped in closer.

"I think I can manage." Her heart was racing out of control at his nearness.

"Do you now." Wade bent his head and captured another kiss, this one more gentle and sweet.

"So you *do* know how," she said out loud without thinking.

"Know what?" he asked in between nibbles of her soft lips.

"Love me tender," she sighed, as she floated away on the dizzying sensations he was producing.

"Why, I'd love nothing more, ma'am." And he took her in his arms and kissed her, but not in the rough way he had behind the barn. This time the kiss was long and deep and lingering, but gentle and tender, just the way she had dreamed of.

∞

"Do you want to explain why you left with one man and came home with another?" asked Fran, with her hands on her hips.

"Can we talk about it in the morning? I'm beat."

Fran recognized that look on Dora's face. She had been bitten by the Grainger love bug, but this time it most likely would lead to nothing good. "Okay, but we will discuss it. I have to get some rest. Luke's going to teach me how to drive the new buggy; school starts on Monday, and I don't have a clue what I'm doing. I'll need to go in early and prepare some lessons. I sure wish I knew how this one-room school thing worked."

"Don't you put the various grades in sections or corners of the room to work on their own assignments?"

"Something like that. But some assignments are done together, with all grades taking part. Of course, I don't even know how many children will show up. There's still more time to the harvest season. I've heard they sort of drift in when their farm work is done. Once we get deep into fall and winter the class size grows. Strange, isn't it?"

"It sounds to me like anything goes, then. I wouldn't worry about it. You'll be great. Let's hit the sack." Dora yawned and rubbed her eyes dreamily.

"I hope you're right." But Francine knew nothing would quell her worries until the first day had actually begun. She needed to make a good showing as a teacher, to prove to the town they had hired a professional, and that she was not just a woman looking for a man. Once they were assured of her competence, they might accept her as Luke's wife.

∞

Fran was quiet while she was making breakfast. Dora had just returned from her morning trip to the outhouse and was sitting at the table with her coffee, while scratching Moose's ears. He bent back his head and looked at her adoringly. His head almost reached the top of the table.

"Okay, are we going to talk about the elephant in the room?" asked Fran, holding a spatula in hand.

"I don't know what you're talking about," pouted Dora.

"Oh yes, you do. You left with Ned and came home with Wade. What happened?" demanded Fran.

Dora rolled her eyes. It was just like her sister wanting to know the details of her life. She was still trying to play mother after all of these years. "Okay, okay. Ned and I had a little falling out, so Wade brought me home."

"What kind of falling out? He's always such a gentleman."

"Well, if you must know, he caught me kissing Wade behind the barn. Well, I'm not sure kissing is even the correct word for what we were doing."

"Dora! How could you? You know the moral values are much stricter here."

"Are you trying to tell me that no one ever got pregnant before marriage? I doubt that's true. Besides we had not gone that far – yet."

"Yet?"

"We might have if Ned had not interrupted us. Franny, there's something very magnetic about Wade. It was like I was under his spell. I've never felt anything like it before. It felt like an out of body experience. You know I'm not a virgin, but I've never not had control of myself. Oh Fran, I'm hopeless, and I'm truly sorry. I hope I didn't mess anything up for you."

"I guess I can understand, but I don't approve. I seem to have that same thing with Luke. Now, I'm wondering if it's the Grainger charm, or is it because we were transported here."

"You think? No, that can't be it, or we'd be all over every man we saw. It was Wade. I felt the connection when we saw him at the mercantile, and even before that when Ned first introduced us."

"We saw him at the mercantile? I don't remember that."

"He was going out when we were selecting furniture. I felt his eyes bore through me, and when I turned around, he winked at me. That simple wink shook me to the core. I've been fighting it ever since."

"What was going on when I saw you two at the wagon, the day the furniture arrived?"

"He was telling me he had never seen anyone so beautiful, and asked if I would go riding with him someday soon. I turned him down, of course. Then he laughed. He's so maddening!"

"Dora, you have to be careful. We have no idea if we can stay here forever, or if we just disappear."

"What about you and Luke?"

"I'm taking my chances. I'm too deeply in love. I have to stay; I can't bear to leave him."

"What about history?"

"I'll worry about that later."

"Then you're no better off than I am," sighed Dora.

"I know Luke better than you know Wade. It's a little early for you to be worrying about loving forever, isn't it?"

"Yeah, you're right. He's a very confusing man."

"As they all are, right? Well, let's eat. If I know Luke he's already out there with the animals, and we'll be leaving soon. What will you do when we're gone?"

"Are you planning on being gone a long time? I thought it was just a short lesson."

"I think Luke wants to get me alone," said Fran, with a dreamy look on her face. "And I'm quite eager for that. We really weren't ready to part last night."

"Well, if the rest of the day is anything like what it feels like out there this morning, it's going to be a scorcher. A true Indian summer. It's hot already and very muggy. I might take a walk down to the stream you were telling me about. Will I get lost?"

"Not at all; it's the same creek as Gram's. Just stay on the path. It goes straight back. Without a horse, it's quite a trek, though, if you're walking. Take Moose with you for protection."

"Do I need it? I figured we were pretty safe here."

"Oh, we are, but he'll route out snakes, bears, and pumas."

"What? Maybe I'd better rethink this idea."

"Just teasing," laughed Fran. "You'll be perfectly fine. No one lives anywhere near us for half a mile, and the wild animals are afraid of humans."

"Sounds good, then. Let's eat. I'm starving; barn dancing worked up a powerful appetite."

"Oh, it did, did it?" The sisters laughed like old times, back on track as equals and not as one looking over the other.

∞

2019

After several nights sleeping in the chair, Daniel moved to the bed. He washed the sheets and towels and slowly began to make himself at home. No one questioned his whereabouts. He lived alone in a small apartment, and his only friends were on the force. His acquaintances were used to the way he completely absorbed himself in his work. When he was on a case, he would disappear from all social activities for weeks, so this was nothing new. And this time more than ever, Daniel Kent was a man obsessed. Obsessed with the case, but more so, he was obsessed with a woman. He had always been able to find a link of some kind to send him on a lead, but this time there was nothing, absolutely nothing, and it was eating away at him. Why were all of her clothes still here, as well as her cell phone and purse? He made a list of all of the items he could remember that she purchased in antique shops, he searched the history on her computer to see what she had ordered online, and he talked to dealers to find other things she had purchased when he wasn't with her. The big question was why was she buying items from the 1800s? The house did not reflect an interest in antiques, other than what had been in the family for years.

No longer worried about the proprieties of going through her personal things, he took everything out of the suitcase she had brought with her from Indiana. He cataloged each item so no one would accuse him of theft; he even took pictures of the open suitcase before he had disturbed it. The smaller one contained mostly things females would travel with, which included makeup, toiletries, one book, and some fashion magazines. He sighed. Nothing. He flipped through the pages of the magazine. It was nothing unusual, just models in the newest fashion – the fall line it proclaimed. He tossed it aside, then picked up the book and riffled through the pages, looking for any piece of communication between Dora and someone else. He knew from past experience that people used the oddest things as bookmarks. There was nothing in it at all. The pages were pristine. Nothing was turned down. It was as if she had not started to read it yet.

When Daniel tossed the book on the bed, he got a good look at the cover, he had dismissively passed over it before. Several clock faces and gears seemed to be floating in space with an old train in the background. It reminded him of the steampunk fashion. Was Dora into steampunk? She didn't seem the type. He turned the book over and read the back cover. It seemed this was the latest installment in a time travel novel by an author he had never heard of before, someone named Jane O'Brien. Time travel? Dora?

Daniel quickly went to the computer and typed in the series name. It was a bestseller, and this particular book was number four. It had only been released a few weeks before Dora's disappearance. If she cared enough to read to book number four and bring it with her, she was probably a fan of time travel. Could that be what she was trying to do when she was buying items from the 1800s? Daniel's hands began to shake. He knew he was onto something, but he was almost afraid to think it. His police officer's brain was trained in logic, and this didn't fit with what he knew as reality. But strangely enough, it was all starting to make sense. Not one item she had purchased was in the house, there were no footprints or tire tracks showing she had ever left, and there were no signs of foul play. It had been the same with her sister.

'Her sister!' he thought. He sat weakly on the bed, then said aloud, "It can't be, can it? Did she go after her sister? And is it even possible?"

Chapter Eighteen

1865

Francine was ready when Luke knocked on their door. She wore a practical but flattering outfit, one he had seen many times; her choices were limited, but with a sunbonnet that Dora had brought she felt like a new woman. Luke nodded and smiled his approval.

"Are you all set for your lesson?" he asked.

"Yes, I am. I'm actually quite excited." After saying goodbye to Dora and Moose, she stepped outside. "Don't get into too much trouble while I'm gone," she called out.

"I can't believe you have never learned to drive a surrey!" exclaimed Luke. Mrs. Francine Clark was full of surprises, one of which was her lack of knowledge in certain everyday tasks.

"Well, like I told you, there was never a need. I had a father and brothers and then a husband. And we never had a fancy buggy like this one." Fran was getting way too good at lying, and she didn't like it, especially to Luke.

"Well, come on then. Let's start with the basics. I'm going to teach you how to harness it up before we drive anywhere."

"Then where will we go?" she asked, a bit flirtatiously.

"I have the perfect place in mind. Don't you worry."

The lesson went very well. Luke was a patient teacher, and Fran picked up on his instructions quickly. Soon they were trotting off toward Twin Lake. The horse didn't seem to mind if he was hooked to a buggy or wagon, or who his driver was. "Good boy, Traveler," called Fran.

"You're doing great. Now just remember to avoid deep ruts and holes. They pop up after a rainstorm, and you can break a wheel. So always keep your eyes forward, looking out for trouble. If you ever do damage something, stay with the buggy. Someone will come along eventually to help. This is a well-traveled road, and neighbors are always ready to give you a ride if you need one."

"Okay, I think I've got it. This isn't too bad at all. Can we stop at the school? I'd like to make sure all of the books have arrived. There were a few geography books I was hoping would come, for the older children. The postmaster said he would deliver them if they came. I think everything else is ready."

"Are you excited?" he asked, mostly to keep her talking. He loved watching how she concentrated on her task, her blue eyes focused on the road. The bonnet seemed to be bothering her, so she pushed it to the back where it lay on her shoulders. A few tendrils of white blonde hair escaped with it. Luke reached over to tuck one piece behind her ear, then he let his hand linger on her neck. He had never known how having a woman, just the right woman, would change his life. It had been quite a while since his 'darkness' had returned. He was hoping Francine had chased it away altogether.

When he arrived at the school he did not offer his hand to help her get down. She looked at him questioningly, and he said, "You'll have to learn how to do it yourself. There will be no gentleman here to give you a hand on school days."

"Of course, you're right. Let's see. I'll put my hand here, and my foot there, then pick up my skirt."

"Whoa! Mrs. Clark," he laughed. "Not so high. The whole town almost saw more than a proper schoolmarm should display. Of course, I didn't mind a bit."

"Oops. I'll be more careful next time. The question is did you enjoy what you saw?"

"Is that a test, Mrs. Clark? I believe you know the answer to that one." He longed to lean in for a kiss, but there was too much activity around.

"Then Mr. Grainger, you have passed with flying colors. I will apply an A to my record as your grade."

"Thank you, teacher. Now let's go in, shall we?"

The moment the door was closed, Luke pulled her into his arms. She pressed her body to his, looked deeply into his slate grey eyes, and they shared a kiss that curled her toes.

"My, my, school was never this good when I was a boy."

"Okay, enough of that," she said, as she gently pushed him away. "Look there's a new box to unpack. Let me see if my books came in." And they had. They were the 'hoped for' geography books, and some McGuffy's Readers for each of the lower grades. Each book held stories and poems, and at the end of the lesson there were new words to learn to spell. There were fewer geography books than readers, but the children could share, and she would prepare a lesson on the chalkboard. She had already received the arithmetic books in varying levels. But the treasure was the World Atlas. Fran would have to brush up on the borders and names of some of the countries, as many had changed over the years. But by far her favorite books were the ones she would read aloud to the children. One was Aunt Louisa's Book of Fairie Stories, and the other was Aunt Louisa's World Wide Fables. The covers were brightly colored and the illustrations inside were wonderful. She had seen many books like this in antique book stores, but here they were shiny and new.

"I can see how you love books, Franny," he whispered, as he tried to nuzzle her ear.

"I really do. There's nothing like reading. I have borrowed a few books to read for myself from the quilting ladies, but there are not a lot to go around."

"Yes, my mother says reading is important, but there never seems to be enough time to get involved in a story."

"I can see that with this way of life."

"What do you mean by 'this way of life'?"

'Darn it,' she thought. 'I slipped.' "Uh, well, you know, being a mother has a lot of responsibilities. I'm sure I have more free time than she does."

"Oh, sure. Ma is always doing something -- baking, cleaning, and washing clothes. She says it never ends, but then Pa says the same thing about farming, and he has time to read the Almanac at night."

"That's because your mother is still working until her bedtime. Women always have more to do than men."

"Really, now. And who has been taking care of you since you arrived?"

"You have, of course, and I appreciate it." She kissed him fully on the mouth, and as he reached for more, she gasped, wanting to give him more but instead she said, "We'd better get out of here before someone walks in."

Just as they pulled apart, Mr. Porter, the postmaster opened the door. Luke and Fran looked at each other and held back their giggles at almost being caught.

"Oh, good, ma'am. You're still here. Good day to you, and to you, Luke. Here's another package that was left behind. I guess I hadn't sorted all the mail properly."

"Thank you, Robert," said Luke. "I appreciate you walking it over."

"It was no problem at all. Have a good first day of school, ma'am. My Duke is looking forward to coming, but I'm not sure he'll be your best student. He can't seem to sit still for more than a few minutes."

"I'll handle him, don't worry, Mr. Porter. I'm sure he'll do just fine."

"Well, if he causes any kind of ruckus, you just walk across the street and let me know. I'll box his ears for ya'."

Fran laughed, but sobered her expression when she realized he was serious. "I'm sure that won't be necessary. I have a few tricks up my sleeve when it comes to children."

"Good to know. You have my permission to do whatever you need to. Now, I must get back. I left the window unattended. Have a good afternoon."

"Whew, that was close," said Luke. "What do you say we continue our 'conversation' elsewhere?"

"I agree to that. Would you drive the rest of the way? I like to be treated like a lady."

"And I like treating you that way." He slipped his arm around her waist, but when they reached the door they parted. Luke didn't mind. He had plans that included more than a few kisses.

"Where are we going next?" Fran questioned. "This isn't the way home."

"I'm taking you to my favorite spot. My private fishing hole."

"But we don't have any poles."

"Who said anything about fishing?" He reached over near to her lap and squeezed her hand while his eyes blazed into hers.

Fran shivered with delight.

Chapter Nineteen

1875

Dora's chores were done. The kitchen was clean and the parlor was swept. Luke had taken care of the milking today, so that left only the egg gathering which she had completed in record time. She was anxious to get out on her own and walk the property. Fran had taken her out on horseback shortly after she had arrived, but she was dying to get back to the creek and cool off. The day had turned out to be a scorcher. She filled a small jug of water, grabbed a quilt, and wet down a kerchief to place around her neck, but first she dabbed at her forehead and cheeks.

"Let's go, Moose, and for Pete's sake, stay near me. I'm not sure if Franny was teasing me or not about the dangers."

The walk was a little longer than she had anticipated. It seemed farther than when she was a kid, but then they usually ran all the way. The trail was dry and dusty. By the time Dora arrived at the creek, she was hot and sweaty. Moose wasted no time in running in, splashing around trying to capture a frog he had spotted. Dora spread her quilt, sat down, and removed her boots and socks. She picked up her dress as high as she could manage and waded in along the creek's edge. The water was gently flowing, as it babbled over small stones and branches. The pebbles were rough on her feet, but she didn't mind at all, because the sensation of the cool water overrode her discomfort. She breathed a sigh of relief. It was exactly what she had needed. She had not taken a bath since she had arrived. She must encourage Fran to buy a tub, even though it took a lot of effort to fill one and then to empty it later. It would be worth the extra work, though, in her opinion. How could any female go without bathing?

The thought of being fully immersed in this wonderfully, fresh water was more than tempting.

"I can't. Can I?" she said to herself. "What do you think Moose? Should I bathe in the stream? Who would ever see me? Franny said we're a mile away from anyone's farm." She looked around. As far as she could tell she was completely alone, except for the occasional butterfly, dragonfly, and a frog or two.

"The birds won't tell, will they? Hey Mr. Cardinal, will you keep my secret? Yoohoo! Mr. Bluebird, mum's the word. Mr. Squirrel, cover your eyes. I'll be real quick, Moose. You just keep a good lookout."

The large dog had decided to nap already; apparently the walk here was too much for him in the heat, and now that his feet were wet, he was feeling very comfortable.

"See? If you can do it, I can, too; right?"

Dora quickly disrobed, taking everything off down to her camisole and pantaloons, and then at the last minute she realized if she didn't take it all off she would have to walk home in wet clothing. She carefully laid the rest of her underwear on the quilt.

"Guard it with your life. Now, turn your head away. I don't like you watching me, you naughty boy."

Dora moved down the creek a bit where the water deepened. At some point, someone had dammed the flow in order to make a little swimming hole, probably for some children. Over time it had deepened even more. She was able to lower herself all the way in and lay back, although she wasn't really floating. Her bottom was on the stony creek bed. Dora's honey gold hair fanned out around her, floating and moving with the waves. Her ample breasts bobbed to the top, pointing straight up.

"Oh, this is so wonderful. I can't believe how great this is. Why haven't we done this sooner?" Moose cocked his head while she talked, but suddenly he picked up his ears, got up, and ran along the creek's edge.

"Hey, come back. You're supposed to be my guard. Oh, well, there's no one here. Have a good time finding sticks. Aaah." She closed her eyes in ecstasy, having no idea she was being watched, and the voyeur was enjoying himself thoroughly.

Wade had been seeking relief from the heat also, so he had been walking the creek looking for a good fishing spot. It was common for the neighbors to fish on each other's property. No one owned the fish, and they were all friends. So when he found himself on Clark land, he never gave it a thought, until Moose came running up to him. Luckily, the big guard dog failed in his duties and never barked once. He seemed more interested in making sure he got a good scratch between his ears.

"Shh, my friend. Let me enjoy the view for a moment longer," whispered Wade, as he crouched down behind a bush. He grinned with pleasure. "She's more than I could have ever hoped for. Look, she's magnificent." Wade watched Dora as she splashed her arms and face with fresh water. He could barely breathe, but he knew it was going to be sticky getting out of this situation. He decided to face it head on. He was not new to seeing a naked woman, and by her response to him behind the barn, she was not new to showing her nakedness, either.

He stepped out away from the bush, and simply said, "My, my, my. What have we here?"

Dora squealed, and tried to dip under the water, but it was too shallow to hide. Her first impulse was to cover herself with her hands, but then her spunky personality surfaced. She had been a handful when she was a teenager, defying everyone in her path, which placed her in some dicey situations at times. She had learned fairly young when she was in a bad spot that the best solution was to fight fire with fire, so she looked Wade straight in the eye, held his gaze, and slowly rose from the water. Her heart was pounding with fear, since she was not quite sure what kind of man Wade was, but she would not let him know it.

"Like what you see?" she challenged, with a toss of her wet hair.

Wade was completely shocked by her boldness. He suddenly became embarrassed at being caught. No one had ever put him on the defensive before. He took a step back, and fell over a root. He heard her laughter, and he was ashamed. While he was down, Dora ran to the bank and retrieved some clothing to hold in front of her.

"How dare you sneak up on me like that? Aren't you trespassing?" she yelled.

"How dare you bathe nude in a public creek?"

"Public? This creek is on Clark land. I can do whatever I want," she snapped.

"Yes, it does run through Clark land, but all waterways are public. That's to preserve the water for every farmer's use, and allow any horse passing by to have a chance to drink."

"Well, no one explained that to me. Now please leave."

Dora turned her back to slip on her pantaloons, but Wade refused to look away. He was having too much fun. Her soft rounded bottom was simply delicious. She placed her camisole on next, then turned to lash out at him, completely unaware of how the thin fabric clung to her wet body.

For Wade this was almost more alluring than her completely nude form. "Miss Dora, it seems we have come to an impasse. I was looking for a fishing spot, and it seems I have found a perfectly good one right here. Yet, you refuse to leave me alone to tend to my task. I think I'll stay a while, until I catch something to eat."

"Well, I'm not moving! I came here for a relaxing day away from the heat. You can do what you like, but I'm going to enjoy myself as I planned!" Dora knew she should really pack her things and go, but she had to admit she rather enjoyed the way Wade had looked at her. She glanced at him sideways to see if he was giving in, but all she saw was a big cocky grin.

"I'm not too sure what kind of fish I can find since you scared them all away."

"Then go."

"And miss the chance to talk to you? I wouldn't think of it. Besides, that guard dog of yours is useless. You need a protector." He readied his fishing pole and tossed the line in as he rested his leg on a fallen log.

Dora had never in her life seen anyone so handsome. His dark eyes were like sweet chocolate as they caressed her body. She laid back on the quilt knowing she was exposed through the thin cloth, but then why worry? He had already seen it all, and she rather liked turning him on.

Wade could not keep his eyes off the picture before him. If he had a bite on the line, he was not aware of it. All thoughts had fled his brain except for one thing. He needed this woman. He had to have her, but he would never take what was not given freely.

Dora rested on her elbows and put her head back to dry her hair in a ray of sun that was peeking through the trees. She studied a woodpecker up above working at getting an insect for his next meal, and then her eyes caught a hummingbird who was perched up high. The little bird looked like a miniature bump on the branch. He was so small she could hardly tell it was a bird, and would not have noticed him if not for his movement as he scratched his head with a tiny little foot; then probably sensing he was being watched, he zipped away with the speed of lightning.

The sound of the moving water was hypnotizing. Dora closed her eyes and lowered her head and body to the quilt. She must have dozed, for the next thing she knew, Wade was sitting next to her on her left. She watched him through her lashes, so as not to alert him that she was awake. His eyes were riveted to her face, and they traveled every inch of her body, but he never laid a hand on her. The feeling was so intense she shivered.

Wade saw the goosebumps on Dora's arms, and thinking she was cold from the wet clothing, he reached over her for her blouse which was next to her on the opposite side. His plan was to cover her with it until she woke up and dressed completely, instead he was surprised when she reached up and pulled him down to her. He looked into her eyes and was thrilled to see they were full of desire; the invitation was evident. All gentlemanly thoughts went from his mind. He had no choice but to offer her what she wanted.

∞

Once again totally naked, Dora woke to find herself completely alone on the quilt. She assumed after their lovemaking and the passionate kisses that accompanied it, that they would talk about what just happened. Thinking Wade had decided to fish some more, she did a quick search up and down the bank, but it showed no sign of him. It seemed as though he had left.

"How dare that jerk, that no-good nothing of a man!" she shouted at Moose, who had been lying at her feet and was now watching her closely. "After everything we just had together, he left without a word. Well, I will not be a 'slam, bam, thank you ma'am.' I'm done with Mr. Wade Grainger. Never again!"

Dora gathered her things in a huff and called Moose to follow, then she walked quickly back to the cabin, working up the sweat she had recently tried to relieve. Once she was back home, she cried in humiliation. What had come over her, she wondered. Offering herself to a practical stranger like that. Well, not totally a stranger, they had shared kisses on a few occasions, but she really knew nothing about him, except he was exceptionally handsome and charming and could be quite sweet at times.

Once home, embarrassed and humiliated, Dora found herself screaming into a pillow. She decided she would never tell Fran about what had just happened. Her sister did not need to hear about the complications she had brought upon her life here in this century. Franny had gotten her out of many bad spots in the past without telling their parents. Dora would not let her do it again; besides she would only berate her by saying, 'What were you thinking?' And Dora would have no answer, because it seemed whenever she was around Wade, she lost all of her senses.

Chapter Twenty

1875

Fran's day had turned out to be delightful. Luke had taken the reins after they left the schoolhouse, and he drove her to nearby Twin Lake, not the town but an actual lake the town was named for. She had no idea it was here. It was a lovely body of water, a perfect setting for small houses and cottages to line the shore.

"This is beautiful, Luke. Thank you for showing it to me."

Luke was pleased that he was the first one to take her to his favorite place. He led her to a small house with several rowboats lined up next to a dock. "Would you like to go out?"

"On the water? How can we? You don't have a boat."

"Oh, but Mrs. Shellman does. She rents out rowboats. It's her only source of income, as her husband is an invalid now. We'd be helping her out; how about it?"

"Of course, I'd love to. It's so hot, and I'm sure it's much cooler out on the water."

"All right, then. I'll go talk to her. I'll meet you down at the dock."

Eager to spend as much time as possible with Fran in the public eye, Luke quickly made the transaction, and secured boat number three. He helped Fran step in as the boat bobbed on the gentle waves, and then he pushed off. They glided for a little while until they were clear of the dock, and then Luke began to pull on the oars. When he was far enough out that he knew they would not drift back to shore, he removed his jacket and rolled up his sleeves. Even though it was one of the warmest days of the year, he had felt it necessary to dress appropriately to escort the school teacher about town.

"Isn't this lovely?" asked Fran. "It's so calm out here. The water is like glass."

"Yes, you *are* lovely." He looked at her with love in his eyes.

"Silly, I meant the water."

"Yes, that, too," he laughed.

"Why is it called Twin Lake? Is there another just like it?"

"I guess, it was originally named Twin Lakes with an s, but the town folk just shortened it. There are four small lakes like this one close by. Twin Lake is the largest, then there's West Lake to the west of course, and Middle Lake is between Twin Lake and West Lake. North Lake is to the north of Middle Lake, but there's one more. Close to North Lake is a smaller lake called Fox Lake. All four of the larger lakes, except for Fox Lake, are connected by channels, so if you had a mind to, you could row through all of them."

Fran laughed. "We would be here all day and all night. I know you have nice strong arms, but you'd be tired for sure, and I would be of no help at all. I'll be happy to stay on Twin Lake for today."

They glided silently across the water, pointing out the ducks and loons and swans in whispers. Then Francine said, "Don't you just love beautiful water birds? They're so graceful. They don't seem to have a care in the world other than finding food and enjoying life."

"Somewhat true. They must fear being hunted. They need to always be on alert, so I don't think they are as relaxed as you might think."

"Is this where you hunt ducks?"

"Sometimes, but this lake is getting to be more for people. I try to go to one of the smaller ones so I can safely shoot."

"Did you learn to hunt from your father?" Fran was loving the fact that he was talking about himself, which he rarely did.

"I did. Well, I should say we did."

"Oh, you mean your brother Wade?"

"No, I taught Wade, and Wade taught Jake and Zeke. I was talking about my older brother, Carl. My Pa taught us together, and then we often went out by ourselves to bring food home for the family."

"You never talk about Carl. This is the first time I've heard his name."

Luke's face darkened instantly, and a frown replaced his previous smile. Fran wished she had not mentioned his brother.

"He's hard to talk about, and it hurts my mother."

"Do you mind telling me what happened?"

Luke stared at her a few moments, and then spoke quietly. "I'm not ready to talk about it yet, Franny. You'll think less of me."

"Oh Luke, that could never happen. You have been my savior and my protector. You have gone above and beyond the job you were hired for. I'm not even sure you're on the payroll anymore; are you?"

"Actually, my pay stops next week when you begin teaching." Trying to change the subject, he grinned wickedly at her, "I can always stay away from the farm anytime you want me to."

"But I don't want you to. I want you to continue your duties for a very long time," she said suggestively. "I love how you perform your duties. Will you stay on with me? I need you." Fran held his gaze, and they each knew what the other was referring to.

"I'll stay forever if you want me, Franny. If you'll take me as a husband, I can stay until the end of time."

Fran's eyes misted over. She reached forward to hold Luke's hand, not caring if anyone on the shore saw them. "The moment we are sure the town wants me to be their schoolmarm, I will marry you, that's a promise."

Luke's sad face turned to joy. They had discussed marriage before but this was the commitment he had been waiting for. "Does it matter if you are the schoolmarm? I will always take care of you. There's no need to work."

"But I love teaching, and I want the parents to have confidence in me. I'd say by the end of the week, once I meet everyone, I should know how they all feel. I know most of them already, so it's a matter of being introduced to the last few remaining children and parents. Ruthie is coming, isn't she?"

"Of course she is. You couldn't keep her away. And she already thinks you're wonderful. She's even whispered to me that I should make you my wife."

"Really? Why that little imp."

"She's a real matchmaker, that one. She matched up Wade and his wife."

"Wade's married?" gasped Fran, but she was able to gain her composure as to not show her shock.

"Well, sort of. He has a wife, but they don't live together anymore. I'm not sure what went wrong, but he came home without her."

Fran was shocked. She had a strong feeling that Dora was interested in Wade. She needed to know more so she could pass the information on to her sister.

"How was it that Ruthie was able to introduce Wade to his wife? Is she from here?"

"She lived here as a child, but when she was a young girl her folks moved to White Cloud. Ruthie used

242

to play with her sister. Myra is Wade's age so Ruthie made sure they met at picnics and such. Soon there was a romance blooming, but when her family took her away, that was the end of it. Apparently, Wade ran into her again when he was working the railroad line. He said they fell in love and married secretly without her parent's consent. They were only eighteen at the time. The Blooms never cared much for Wade. He was always a troublemaker when he was a kid. When her folks found out, they were furious. It caused a lot of turmoil for the two of them, so when the rail line moved toward Big Rapids, and he had to go, she refused to follow, said she wanted to stay with her folks. He told Ma they never saw each other again."

Luke had been rowing toward shore while he was telling his story, and they bumped into the dock just as he finished.

"That's really quite sad, when you think of it. Two young lovers, being separated by the adults."

"I'm not sure how much love there was. I think she was just trying to get some attention by going against her father's wishes. He's quite wealthy for these parts. I believe Myra is a bit spoiled."

"Yes, that can happen. So what will Wade do now?"

"What do you mean?" Luke took her hand and helped her out of the rocking boat.

"You know, he's married but he's not. How can he move ahead with his life?"

"I don't think he much cares. That's just who Wade Grainger is."

The couple stood on the dock for a moment holding hands, and gazing into each other's eyes. "Don't mistake my brother for me," said Luke. "I would never treat you that way. I love you, Franny. I'll be yours forever."

"I believe that's true, Luke, and I will be yours forever, also."

"Now, let's stop talking about my family, hop in the buggy, and get it moving so we can feel a breeze. I just happen to know a little glade with some very tall grass where a person can get lost. It's a perfect place to shed some of this hot clothing."

"Sounds perfect to me," grinned Fran. Her heart raced with the anticipation of the lovemaking to come, but she had not missed how he had steered the conversation away from the brother he would not talk about.

Chapter Twenty-one

1875

When Francine arrived home feeling very 'zen' as she used to say, she discovered her sister in a totally different state. Dora was working in the kitchen. She was making a racket as she banged around pots and pans. Apparently, the day had not gone well.

"For Heaven's sake, what has gotten you in such a tizzy?" Fran asked Dora, who had not even bothered to say hello.

"It's too darn hot! Isn't there a fan in this place?"

"Oh, you mean one that runs without electricity?" Fran countered with a chuckle.

"Yes, well, you know what I mean."

"I'm sorry I left you alone in the heat, but what could I have done?" apologized Fran.

"Not a thing. Not one stupid thing."

"Now, Dora, you're having some kind of meltdown, and I think it's more than the heat. Want to tell me what's bothering you?" Fran had now taken on the role of being a comforting mother figure, as she had her whole life when it came to any kind of problem Dora had.

Dora turned to look at Fran and the moment their eyes met, she burst into tears. "I have made such a mess of things."

"Let's sit down. Come to the sofa." Fran took Dora's hand and guided her to the new couch, then she opened the nearby window. "Why, no wonder it's so hot in here. You never cracked the window. We need to catch any cross breeze we can."

"I don't like bugs," pouted Dora. "When are screens invented, anyway?"

247

"About ten years ago. I asked at the mercantile about them, because the Londons have some in their windows."

"What? Then why don't we have them?"

"Because they are quite expensive, and I am a poor school teacher without a paycheck as of yet. I'll make sure to put them in my budget for next year."

"Oh, Fran, are you really going to stay?"

"I am. I can't imagine leaving Luke. I love him, Dora. I truly do." Fran smiled dreamily for a second, then remembered her original question. "Now, tell me what's gotten you so riled up?"

Dora wiped her running nose on her sleeve. Fran scrunched up her face in disgust. "Dora, you are such a child. Here, use my handkerchief."

"That's another thing. I miss Kleenex." And she sobbed again.

"Okay, enough! Spill it. This is more than a mood."

Once the tears were wiped and she had blown her nose, she went on to tell Fran about her walk to the creek.

"When I got there the water looked so cool and inviting; even Moose couldn't wait to go in."

"I can imagine," laughed Fran.

"Well, what came next wasn't so funny. I took off my shoes and outer clothes, and I waded in with only my pantaloons and camisole on."

"You didn't!"

"I did."

"But you can see right through that thin material."

"But you know how impulsive I am. Just the underwear wasn't good enough. Oh, no, I had to take it all off and submerge myself."

"Dora! I can't believe you. What happened next?"

"Only that Wade came by and saw me. Let's say after a little banter to cover my embarrassment, we found a way to ease the sexual tension, if you know what I mean."

"Oh, Dora.   Not with Wade!   Please not with Wade."

"And it was actually quite beautiful, on the shore of the creek and all, out in nature, and he is so -- so --, well, let's say he knows what to do with a woman."   At this point Dora forgot her troubles and sighed.   It truly had been magical.

"Dora stay focused.   If you enjoyed yourself, what is causing you this upset, then?"

"Because we fell asleep, and when I woke up he was gone.   He left me, lying alone and naked on the quilt. Can you believe it?"

"Actually, I probably can," muttered Fran to herself.

"And now, I've been thinking.   Fran no one uses protection, here, do they?   Will I get pregnant?   I couldn't bring any pills with me, since they weren't compatible with this time. And, of course, I had no plans on having sex.   I never once gave it a thought."

"Protection has been invented, but I doubt it's a common practice, with all of the large families everyone has. And I doubt it's very good protection, anyway. I'm so sorry, Dora, I never had to worry about pregnancy. I don't know how to answer that question. I suppose you could get pregnant, here. But honey, you can't ever be with Wade again."

"I don't intend to; he's a jerk, he's a no good, low-down, woman abuser." Dora stopped her rant when she realized Fran was not offering her advice because Wade was a jerk. "Why not? What do you know?"

Fran took Dora's hand. "Sweetheart, I just found out that he's married."

There was silence as Dora studied her sister's face, and when what she had just said set in, Dora's face changed from simply being upset to being furious. She got beet red in the face, and it wasn't from the heat.

"He's married? Married?" she yelled. "Then why has he been coming on to me? Has he no scruples? Where is his wife? No one's mentioned a wife," she demanded.

"I just learned of it today, actually. Luke was telling me about his family. It seems that Wade got married very young, and it didn't work out. He left his bride behind when he was working on the railroad. She lives in White Cloud. That's about all I know. But I do know they haven't been together in years. He might not even think about it, and goes about as if he were a single man."

"Well, not with me. I won't be used. Leaving me in the dust was one thing, but if there's a marriage certificate in this picture, I'm done."

"I don't blame you. I would be upset, too. But honey you have to calm down. Just put Wade Grainger out of your mind. It was a one-time thing, and you won't repeat that mistake again, right?"

"I absolutely will not repeat it. I never want to see him again. I've made a decision. I said I would stay until after harvest and wait for your wedding, but I have to leave before then. How could I go to your wedding and face him?"

"Oh, Dora, please rethink this. I really want you there. I'm pretty sure our wedding will be very soon. There are no elaborate plans like in the 21st. You just announce you're getting married and people show up. They bring dishes of food and drink, and then music breaks out and they dance. It's very casual, and fun, so I'm told. Luke filled me in on the facts."

Dora saw the disappointment in Franny's face, so she capitulated. "Okay, I'll just avoid Wade at the wedding, but then I'm leaving right after that. And I mean it. No more delays. There are some men who know how to treat a woman, and one of them is back home wondering where I am."

"I'll agree to that. But you know I will miss you terribly when you go."

"And I, you." They hugged and a few more tears were shed, but Fran changed the subject as soon as she could.

"Now let's look at this cookbook you have. What were you making?"

"I found a recipe for cornbread." Dora flipped the pages of the book she had brought with her.

"Oh, I always loved Gram's cornbread, but I wasn't sure about how to make it. I tried a few times, but it wasn't the same. Jessica Grainger makes good cornbread, but I've been hesitant to ask for her recipe. I think it's pretty basic, and it would make me look like I had not a clue how to cook. Women here learn how to cook from early childhood. It's expected."

"Well, it is pretty basic. And there are other recipes in here, too, that will help, like Apple Dapple Cake, and Sassafras Jelly."

"That sounds good. I've found lots of sassafras. It's beginning to turn color now so it's easy to spot. I planned on making sassafras tea. That's one thing I do know how to do."

"And here's a recipe for rhubarb jelly, too. Sounds, good, right? But you know what else I noticed?"

"What is that?" Fran was glad that Dora's mind was onto something else other than Wade Grainger.

"Look how clean this book is. I bought it because it was called Old Timey Recipes. When I checked the publication date, the last date shown was 1873, so I knew the recipes would have ingredients we could use, and it's a simple paperbound book, printed in black and white.

I assumed it would transport just fine, and it did. But when I bought it, it had some bent down pages, favorites of the owner, I suppose, and there were some dirty spots, like you see in cookbooks when the cook has sticky hands. But Fran, look. Now it's like brand new."

Fran took the book and flipped through the pages. They were stiff and crisp. "You're right, it's just like we thought. The universe rights itself. This book looks like we just bought it. Didn't you bring some other books along?"

"Yes, I completely forgot about them. One you should have, for sure. Let me get them."

When Dora returned from the bedroom, she had three more books in her hands. They were small, only about five by eight, and each one did not have more than seventy-five or eighty pages. One was a paperback and the others two were hardbound. The covers were brown cloth and the print was a fancy scrollwork in silver.

"This one is called 'Herbs Gone Wild, Ancient Remedies Turned Loose, by Diane Kidman.' It tells you how to use wild herbs and plants for medicinal purposes, like indigestion and mosquito bites, and such."

"That will certainly come in handy. I've seen some herbs that I recognize, like wintergreen, and St. John's Wort. There must be others I don't know about."

"These two are more about how to use herbs in other ways. 'The Book of Magical Herbs,' and 'The Meaning of Herbs.' There are sketches of what the herbs look like, so you can identify them.

"You went all out on herbs, didn't you?"

"It was all I could think of to help you with some medicinal needs, but of course, a lot of them are used in cooking, too. I had no idea what this area would be like 144 years ago. I didn't know if it was desolate open land with no one around, or if there was a town with a pharmacist nearby. All I knew was that the cabin was here. I was just looking out for you."

"Thank you, it was so thoughtful. And once again, these all look like new books, fresh off the printer."

"I remembered this one in particular, had pages that were falling out." Dora pointed to Herbs Gone Wild.

"So this helps us a lot. We now know that nothing old can come back to 1875 unless it predates that year. And we can't send anything to the future unless it is made with the proper fabrics and in the style of this era. Yet, we seem to be able to transport ourselves because of a DNA connection." Fran bit her lip in thought. "So, Dora, this means if you go back, just like before, I won't be able to communicate with you very easily, and you won't be able to communicate with me at all. It will be a one-way postal system. I can still use quilt blocks, but I might run out of ideas on that, unless we plan ahead."

"How can I ever know if you are all right?" Dora was worried already. "And can I even come back if I want to, or is this a one-time only trip?"

"We'll have to think about it. There must be some way to do it. But for now let's make some cornbread. I've made cornmeal muffins before but they were not the best. I knew I was doing something wrong."

"Bake in this heat?"

"There's no takeout here. It's cooking and baking every day. We'll pop some in the oven and sit on the porch in the rockers. Maybe we can catch a breeze."

"Sounds good to me."

Glad for the diversion, Franny took her sister's arms and they laughed all the way through the ten steps it took to get to the kitchen.

Chapter Twenty-two

1875

Francine arrived at the school early on Monday morning, so she could be there well before any of the children showed up. She was pleased with the arrangements of desks. Some were smaller for the little ones. She had kept those on the right side as she faced them.

There had been no sign-up required, so she wasn't even sure how many and what ages would come. The blackboard was washed clean, and she had moved items around her desk more than a few times. It was getting late and no one was here yet, so she paced a few times, feeling sick to her stomach. What if she wasn't accepted and no one came. But after a half hour, she heard some horses and the children's high-pitched voices.

Two little girls came in together, identical twins. She had no idea who they were. They wore their hair in long ringlets, but they each wore a different colored bow on the top of their head. It would help to identify who was who. A man entered right behind them.

"Mornin' ma'am. Are we late?"

Francine laughed. "No, as you can see you are the first to arrive. Come in please. I'm Mrs. Clark," she said to the girls, "your new teacher."

"Good mornin', Mrs. Clark," they said in unison. She was to discover later that they quite often talked at the same time.

"Who might you two lovely ladies be?"

Their father spoke up, saying, "This one in pink is Clara and the one in yellow is Sarah. Last name is Crowley. We're from a few miles away, but we don't have a school nearby. Their ma wants them to get an education. Can they come here?"

"Of course, they can. Just step over here and sign up. Leave their names and ages and where you live. That's all that's required."

"Oh, I don't write, ma'am. I'm hoping I can learn along with the girls."

"Okay, then I'll do it for you. It's not a problem, at all. I'm so glad to have them here today. Won't you take a seat, girls? How about right here?"

As soon as Mr. Crowley left, Ruthie Grainger came running in. "Mrs. Clark, I'm going to be your student."

"Good morning, Ruthie. Yes, you are and I'm so happy. Are you all alone? I need to sign you up."

"Luke's comin'. He's busy hitchin' up the horse. I couldn't wait to get in to see you." She grinned and gave Fran a big hug. "Oh, there's the twins. Can I sit by them?"

"You mean, may I."

"Yes, ma'am. May I?"

"You may." Fran's heart skipped a beat when Luke came in. He seemed very formal, as he held his hat. He stepped forward to shake her hand. Fran whispered,

"It's just me, Luke." Then louder, "Please sign up Ruthie over here."

"I didn't want to treat you with disrespect, but my, oh my, you look so good standing here with your hair up," he said out of the corner of his mouth. "I'd love to see you later, but I have to pick up Ruthie after school and get her home, then I'll help out at the folks house today. I haven't been there much."

"Let's try to meet at lunch sometime. Will you check up on Dora today? She'll be all alone for the first time."

Just then a mother and son came in. Luke raised his voice. "I surely will, ma'am." Then he turned to Ruthie, "You be good now, or you can't come back."

"Oh, Luke," Ruthie giggled.

The first hour kids kept drifting in, parents apologizing for not knowing the start time, and kids excited to see their friends. Francine ended up with ten kids in her class, all in lower grades. As soon as everyone was introduced, she began her first spelling class. She was very pleased with the children's behavior. They were polite and eager to learn. My, how things had changed in the 21st century.

∞

Dora wasn't quite sure what to do with herself, but she decided she couldn't go wrong with a little housecleaning. First, she swept the floors, and then she dusted everything in sight. Luke was usually here, but he had to take Ruthie to school. She wondered if that meant she would be alone every day, and responsible for more farm chores than before. She knew the eggs had not been collected, so she donned her apron, grabbed a basket, and headed out to the chicken coop. When she first arrived in 1875, she had thought she would not like collecting eggs, but it had become her favorite job. It was a little like a treasure hunt. How many were there and which nesting boxes had some? The chickens were always happy to see her, because they knew she came with food. They clucked merrily and followed her around like little puppies. She tried not to get attached, because she knew every one of them had a short life span. When the eggs stopped coming, they became dinner.

After collecting the eggs, Dora wandered out to the barn. She had grown to love the smell of the hay, straw, and even the manure. It reminded her so much of home when she was a child. She had never liked to scoop poop, as they called it, but Grandpa had insisted. She regretted now how she had pouted and made Franny do most of the work. She could see that she was a spoiled child, the baby of the family; she had everyone catering to her every whim. She hoped she had grown out of it, but it was difficult here not to throw a temper fit once in a while. Things were just so inconvenient. She wasn't always the best sister, she knew. This morning she had preferred to sleep in a bit, even though Franny had been anxious about school. Her sister had had to milk Laney before she got ready, so Dora made breakfast to make up for her lack of consideration. Of course, Fran forgave her. She always did. She promised herself she would never do anything to disrupt Fran's stay here. Fran was in love, she had a teaching job, and she was about to get married. She even had her grandparents' cabin to live in. It was perfect for her.

Dora roamed back into the house with her eggs, and then she grabbed the sprinkling can which Fran had left on the porch. She planned to work in the garden and pull some weeds. It was a perfect fall day, fresh moving air, but warm at the same time. The smell of the early fallen leaves was heavy in the air. Even though it was September there were still some flowers blooming. The zinnias had not stopped since they first started to show their color, and the cosmos were tall and graceful with their lovely shades of pink swaying in the soft breeze. The vegetables were coming in full force. The garden was rich with tomatoes, cucumbers, squash, potatoes, and onions. A huge pumpkin vine was growing along the edge, reaching to escape the confines of the garden area. It was such a hardy crop, that they had become vegetarians lately, eating whatever was ready that day. All thoughts of meat had gone out of their heads, unless Luke provided something.

When Dora realized that the hoe she needed had been put back in the barn, she sighed and walked back to get it. No sooner had she entered the building than a wagon pulled up. Thinking it was Luke, she didn't even bother to look out. It seemed strange not to see Traveler in his stall. He was on school duty today. Fran said he took to the buggy like a pro. He'd probably been used for that purpose in the past.

Looking around, Dora discovered that the hoe wasn't where it was normally kept. Luke was constantly berating them for not putting things back. Now she could see why. It was so frustrating not to be able find it where she expected it to be. She knew it was here somewhere.

Dora walked around the barn looking in every corner, and just when she was ready to give up, and turn to go, she saw Wade coming toward her. He must have been the one driving the wagon. She had no clue what he was doing here, but she was furious.

"You're not welcome here. Leave!" she called out.

He continued to walk to her. "Dora, I need to explain."

"I'm not listening to your explanations. Nothing you can say will change my mind about you. You're low life scum."

When Wade reached her, he placed both hands on her shoulders. "Let me tell you what happened. Look at me. I know you're mad that I left you, but there's a reason." He pushed her gently toward the barn.

She pushed back with force, but she continued to walk backwards, until they were through the doorway. He advanced closer, and she was forced to step back again.

"There's no reason you can give that I will accept. You left me naked on the grass after you had used me. How dare you!" She took a swing and connected with a good slap across the face. He had not been expecting the blow, so it was forceful enough to move his head sideways and leave an immediate red mark.

Wade rubbed his cheek. "That was some slap, but I guess I deserved it."

"Well, here's another one." Dora raised her hand again, but this time he caught it mid-swing.

"Now, what was that one for?"

"For being married."

"Oh, that," he said softly.

"Oh that? Is that all you have to say? You're married and you took advantage of me." Dora was so angry she was seeing red.

"As I recall, you took advantage of me," he said with a sexy grin.

Dora gasped, and then sputtered, "What? What are you talking about? I did not!"

Wade reached for her again. Thinking if he could only hold her, maybe he could calm her down, but she stepped away again and turned her back.

"Dora, there's an explanation for both. I need to tell you what happened."

"Talk, but I'm not looking at you."

"Look, when we were at the creek, it was one of the most special times of my life. Honestly. We fell asleep wrapped in each other's arms stark naked out in nature, and it was wonderful. And if you recall you were the one to pull me to you, not the other way around."

Dora grunted an agreement. She was glad her back was turned, because the blood rushed toward her face and neck with embarrassment at how aggressive she had been in their love making.

"It was so hot, neither one of us thought about covering up. It was perfect, wasn't it? Can you at least acknowledge that much?"

Dora turned and when she looked into his eyes, she began to cave a little. It *had* been wonderful. Without saying a word, she gave a slight nod of the head. She couldn't deny that it had been the single most romantic thing in her life, and even though she hated Wade Grainger, she would never forget it.

Wade went on with his explanation. "I woke up to my name being called. It was my twin brothers. Pa needed me for something, and they had come to fetch me. I didn't want them to find us. It would ruin your reputation and embarrass you. So I pulled on my clothes, grabbed my fishing pole, and ran so they would find me a ways away from you. I didn't even have time to cover you, but I assumed no one else would come by. I knew you would be upset, but what could I do? I was trying to save you. Really. Do you understand now?"

Dora was softening a little more now. He had not left her in the way she thought. He was actually trying to be a gentleman. But then the marriage thing came to mind. What gentleman would have her if he was already taken?

"So, you were worried about my reputation? What about the fact that you slept with me, and you're still married? What does that do to my reputation?"

Wade moved closer again. "Will you come and sit with me? I don't know how you found out, but I need to tell you about it." He pulled on her hand and gently moved her toward a pile of straw.

Dora resisted at first, but curiosity got the better of her. She wanted to hear what he had to say. She needed to hear it for the sake of her sanity.

"I'm listening. It had better be good."

"Myra -- that's her name -- we've known each other since we were kids. We got along just fine. We went to some dances together, shared a few kisses --"

"I don't want to hear it."

"Okay. Anyway, it was always assumed that we would be together someday, but then her parents moved to White Cloud. It's not that far away, but when you're a young kid, there's always another pretty girl nearby to take away your interest."

"Oh, I see. That seems to your MO. Love em' and leave em'."

"My what?"

"Modis – oh, never mind. Go on."

"So, I dated other girls and had a few flings, but when I joined the railroad to work, it took me all over the place on this side of Michigan. One day I found myself in White Cloud and there she was. Still pretty as a picture. Looking back, I think I was manipulated. She wanted someone to marry, and I was there. Her parents weren't too happy with her choice. They remembered me as a wild kid. I think that was what she was looking for, to aggravate them, and I fit the bill," he chuckled. "They threatened all kinds of things to stop us, but we got married anyway. We thought we were in love – or I did at least. It was a big mistake, and we knew it from the start. We fought all the time. When I was transferred to Big Rapids, she decided not to come with me. She wanted to stay with her family. She chose them over me. And that's the last I saw of her. Simple. See?" Wade boldly placed an arm around her waist and pulled her in closer.

"Not so simple. You never got a divorce, did you?"

"We did not. I never once thought of it. Divorce isn't that common, you know. I guess I was embarrassed at the failure."

Dora was too close to him now. She could feel the warmth of him, and it was so tempting to lean in. "I can understand that, but after a while didn't you want to start a new life?" she asked, hoping he would give the right answer.

"It never occurred to me until now. I never met anyone like you, Dora. You're sweet, but very strong.

You know what you want, and you don't let anyone get in your way. You challenged me, and I guess I liked it."

She turned to look him in the eye, her own eyes were betraying her by filling with tears. Against her will, she found herself moving toward him until their lips met. She wrapped her arms around his neck, and he pulled her in tight. Dora felt fireworks going off in her head. She was lost in a world that was meant only for her and Wade. The sun and moon and stars were all colliding at once, and she was falling through the universe. Before she knew it, she was reclining with him, and they were shedding clothing for the second time in a week. Dora would never think of a barn again without recalling this moment, because this time when she woke from her dreamlike state, he was still there with her, kissing her all over, and calling out her name.

Chapter Twenty-three

1875

By the time Fran arrived home, Dora was dressed and working hard in the garden. Wade had left quite a while ago, not wanting to get caught here at this time of the afternoon. Fran waved when she pulled in the drive. She was happy to see that Dora was smiling and hard at work. Apparently, she had worked her way out of her bad mood.

"How was school?" Dora called out.

Fran hopped down, and picked up some books she had brought home with her. "I'll tell you in a minute." She unhooked Traveler, then led him to the barn, making sure that his feed and water were refreshed. Dora had not mucked out the stall, so she would have to do it later, but at least her sister had accomplished some things today.

The sisters walked in the house together arm in arm.

"Were you lonely today?" asked Fran.

"Not at all. I kept plenty busy." Dora hid her little smile with her hand. "Look, I baked cookies. They're just sugar cookies, but I think they came out quite well."

"You stoked the stove all by yourself?"

"I did. And I collected eggs, swept the floors, and dusted. Then I started on the garden. I actually had a very good time. It was quite exhilarating."

Fran couldn't believe the change in her mood. She was very pleased with how her sister had come around.

"Now, sit and tell me about your first day." Dora put on the kettle and reached for some tea and cups.

Fran laughed. "Well, you said your day was exhilarating, and so was mine. I have never felt more alive. The children are wonderful, so eager to learn and very well behaved."

"What did you teach?"

"We worked mostly on geography and spelling. I had to be quite careful. The world certainly has changed a lot. Of course the continents haven't moved," she laughed, "but the younger children learned how to identify the larger masses, and then I had the older ones finding various countries. I assigned each of them one country to write something about. That way I can check their penmanship and spelling at the same time."

"Clever girl. I think the town will want to keep you. You're a shoe-in. So when's the wedding?"

"Oh, we haven't set a date yet. I'll need a few days in class before we announce it. Why? Are you eager to leave?"

"No, not at all. I've changed my mind. I'm staying for a bit, but I do think we should continue to discuss the 'what ifs'."

"What do you mean?" Fran fussed with her tea, blowing on it until it was cool enough to drink.

"Well, right now, all is well, but what if something goes wrong and one of us or both have to leave quickly? Shouldn't we have a plan?"

"What could go so wrong that that would happen?"

"I don't know. It just crossed my mind today." It was something Dora had thought about before Wade had arrived. And even though she was willing to stay longer now, she realized how vulnerable they were. "I think we should be prepared, that's all."

"Okay, well after supper, and once the cow has been milked – You didn't do it already, did you?"

"No, sorry, you know I don't like to."

"It's okay. It's a bit early anyway. I'll do it before I leave and when I come home, if you will take care of the chickens and the house."

"Good plan. Now what about my suggestion?"

"We'll talk about it tonight for sure. I need to go over some of these papers and make a plan for tomorrow. Can you start supper?"

"Sure, no problem. How about grilled vegetables, cucumber salad, and some scalloped potatoes?"

"Mmmm. Just like home except we don't have a grill."

"I'll brown them slowly in the frying pan in bacon grease. They just won't have that smoky flavor."

∞

After supper the girls sat down to talk about their 'escape' plan, as Dora called it. They discussed ways they could actually leave.

"I think we have to go back the way we came."

"You mean hold the unfinished quilt?" asked Francine.

"Yes, but we have to cry on it. The thing is, I'm not sure if we have to actually be sad or if we can make tears fall, say, with an onion or some other irritant."

"I see what you're saying. Here's the thing Dora, we can't give it a test run. When one of us decides to leave, and it won't be me --"

"That's fine, because if I try to go, you can watch me, and if it works, you'll know what to do if you change your mind."

"That's a good idea. The problem is," added Fran, "I won't know if you made it or if you're okay. What if it gets harder on our bodies each time?"

"That's something I had not thought about. It could happen, I guess, but what's the alternative? Neither one of us should stay here forever."

"I guess you're right, but I won't like it. I can't bear the thought of leaving Luke. My heart will surely break." Fran's eyes filled with tears.

"Don't think about that now. Let's work out some details."

"Like what?" asked Fran, as she wiped at her eyes.

"Like, how we can communicate?"

"That might be difficult. We know from the envelope that I wrote on and the letter you sent to me that I never got that things don't move between centuries unless they're meant to be there. I don't think you'll ever be able to send a message to me."

"That's what I thought," said Dora, with a frown.

"But I can communicate with you with quilt blocks, again."

"It's a possibility, but it will be difficult to find blocks that mean what you want to say, and then it's only a thought, not real communication."

"Okay," said Fran, "let's ask the quilting women if they have any other favorite blocks, and use their names as a sort of a code. We can create our own system for the meanings." Fran was excited now. "We'll each have a list for use on major events. I'll leave one in the trunk for you. It should be there when you get back, just like the letter was."

"Wonderful thought, but here's another one. If you can leave me a list, then you can leave me more writing than that. Why not keep a diary and always store it in the trunk?"

"Dora, you've hit on the perfect solution! I can tell you all of the details of my life as if I'm writing to my diary." Fran was excited now. With this plan she could tell Dora everything and combined with some quilt blocks, Dora would be well-informed on her life. "I'll get a journal, and I will write to you once a month, after you leave. As long as you are able to check the trunk and always put it back, you should be able to stay in contact with me."

Dora bit her lip. "I wish we could find a way for me to write back, but I see that the words would always disappear on the paper, because they had never been in the 19th century in the first place. So, you think it's true? We can't go backwards, only forward."

"I'm certain that's how it works."

"Then we'll make the best of it, and if you're ever ready to come home, you can write about it, so I'll be ready for you."

"I have one more thought." Fran took Dora's hand. "You can never ever sell the cabin. We're not for sure where you'll end up, but I assume it will be from where you left. Since we both arrived here at the train station, I'm wondering if you might show up at some odd place in Holton. The train station is long gone, both in Holton and in Twin Lake. So the cabin and all of its furnishings must stay intact."

"I agree. I'll never sell, and I'll make sure my children never do, either."

"Oh, Dora, I'll miss your new life and your children, but what am I to do?"

"I understand completely. Your tie to Luke is strong, isn't it? Those Grainger men sure are something." Dora sighed.

"I thought you hated Wade. What's this change of heart?"

"I might have been a little too quick to judge."

"What happened when I was gone today?" Fran got up to heat up some more water, and Dora followed her.

"Franny, he came here."

"Wade?"

"Yes, apparently Luke asked him to check up on me. Of course, he knows nothing about the two of us, does he?"

"No, I never breathed a word."

"Well, anyway, he was so contrite, and he explained everything. Fran, he was actually protecting me. His brothers were coming, and he had to move fast to steer them away from my naked body. He didn't dare stay around; that's why he left me alone."

"If it's true, I can see why he would have no choice but to abandon you. But what about the marriage thing? How did he explain that?"

"He said they were young, and it just didn't work out. He never thought about divorce, because he had no reason to."

"And you believe him?"

"I do, he's not the loser everyone thinks he is. He's really very sweet. So you don't have to worry about me leaving for a long time. I'm here to stay with you. This discussion was for emergency purposes only."

"I see, well, I'm truly happy you're staying, but be careful. We're treading on thin ice, here. We have no idea what happens when we disrupt the natural order of things. I am unable to get pregnant, but you do not have that safety net. Besides, both Luke and Wade might have married and had children, and we could disrupt that family line. And women are not treated very well when it is known that they have been sleeping with a man before marriage. I've been terrified of being discovered this whole time."

"I know," sighed Dora, "but I don't know what to do. I can't seem to stay away from him."

"I understand, believe me. Those Grainger men have a magnetism that can't be denied." Fran smiled wistfully as she patted Dora on the leg. "Now let's get some sleep. I'm exhausted."

Chapter Twenty-four

1875

Francine was up early to get ready for school. Getting up at this hour was not new to her, but now that she had added another element into her day, she wasn't quite sure of the timing. Dora promised to take care of the chickens and the house, but Fran needed to make sure she fed and watered Traveler before she hitched him to her buggy. She would unhitch him when she got to school and tie him to a tree giving him a little more freedom to move and some grass to chew, but she wasn't quite sure what she would do in the winter. She would have to find a way to quiz Luke without giving away the fact that she didn't know the standard practices, here.

The new teacher was pleasantly surprised to discover Luke at her door as she was leaving. He glanced in the house quickly and pulled her out on the porch for a lingering kiss.

"Good morning," she sighed.

"Mornin'."

"I – didn't – know – you – would be here." She said between little nibbles.

"I couldn't stay away. Franny, not seeing you every day is killing me." His hands began to roam; Fran was feeling weak with desire.

"Oh, Luke, please," she gasped. "You'll mess up my hair." But in reality if she had a choice she would disregard teaching today altogether, but then she remembered that Dora was inside.

"I need you. Can we take a trip to the barn?" he smiled wickedly.

"Luke, stop," she tapped him playfully. "You know we can't."

Luke placed his arms around her waist and held her back enough to gaze into her lovely blue eyes. Her white blonde hair was arranged austerely on top of her head, in a proper schoolmarm fashion, but to him it was only an invitation to take out the pins and carry her off to bed.

"I can't wait to marry you and wake up next to you every morning," he whispered.

"Me, too, but we have a problem. Dora. I can't kick her out, you know that."

"I have come with a solution of sorts. I have finally finished the bed for her room. Sorry it took so long, but harvest time took me away from the task."

"Oh, Luke, that's wonderful." She kissed him first, then looked at the wagon. "I don't see a bed in the back. Where is it?"

He laughed. "It's still in pieces, but it's ready to put together. If Dora doesn't mind, I'll carry it in and assemble it right in the room."

"That's perfect. Let's see if Her Highness is up and ready yet."

"Her Highness?"

Fran laughed. "That's what I used to call her when we were kids. We loved pretending that we were royalty. I was Her Majesty."

"Okay, then see if the queen wants a new bed."

Fran put her head in the door and was going to call Dora, but she was pleased to find her fully dressed and making coffee.

"Morning, Dora. Oh, that smells so good. Pour an extra cup. Luke's here; he has something for you."

"For me?"

"He's brought you a new bed."

"You mean I don't have to fight you for covers anymore?" They laughed, but it had been a comfort for them both in this strange place to have someone next to them in the dark of night.

Luke was already at the wagon unloading the first piece. He wanted Franny to see what he had made before she left. He carried in a side rail of white pine. It was scraped of all bark and smoothly sanded to perfection, then covered with a gloss of varnish. The golden color of the grain glowed; the exposed knots making it a thing of beauty. It was truly a work of art.

"Oh, Luke, this is beautiful," exclaimed Dora. "Does this mean you like me?" she teased.

"It means," Fran countered, "that he wants you in your own bed. We are to be married very soon." She kissed him right in front of Dora, something she had never done before.

"Ma'am," teased Luke. "You shock me. But I like it."

They had turned a corner on their acknowledgement of the situation. And although it had never been discussed, Fran now assumed they were to live in her house after marriage, and that was just fine. Luke would be here all the time to help with the farm, and keep the old Clark place running.

"Well, I'd better grab some breakfast before I leave. Are you staying today, Luke? Want some coffee?"

"Yes, I could have a cup. Wade is taking Ruthie to school. We brothers are going to take turns on that chore."

"What about Zeke and Jake? Don't they want to go to school?

"They're fifteen already. It's a little late for them. Besides if I live here, Pa will need the help. They can learn from Ruthie's books as she goes, if they have a mind to. Ma will make sure they know how to do their sums. They'll need that for buying lumber and such."

"Yes, I suppose you're right." It was no use arguing with Luke right now about why farm boys needed an education. She'd save that discussion for another time.

"All right, then. Dora, you stay out of Luke's way, and see if you can gather some bedding together and make a list of what we need."

"The mattress is my gift," said Luke. "Well, it's more of a wedding gift to myself," he chuckled, "to have Dora in the other room. It's in the wagon. I bought the ticking and Ma sewed and stuffed it. I'll bring it in as soon as I get the bed together."

"Thank you, Luke. That was sweet," said Franny.

Dora watched the two together. They were perfect for each other, and although she could see many similarities between the brothers, such as mannerism and coloring, it was apparent that Luke was more responsible. Even though he had a dark side that even Dora had seen at times, he would always be there for Fran. Dora wasn't so sure that was true with Wade. It was then that she knew that the warning Fran had given her about being careful with Wade should be taken seriously.

∞

Dora was in awe of her new bed. When Luke had completed it, she could see the true beauty in what he had made. In her day they would have thought of it as lumberjack style, but here it was just perfect.

"Luke, this bed is absolutely gorgeous."

"Thank you, miss, but it's just a piece of furniture."

"Oh, it's so much more than that. You have a real talent for woodworking. Does it run in your family?" Dora was searching for more details about Wade.

"No, can't say that it does. I've always liked working with wood. I started when I was young by whittling all the time. I love the smell and the feel of it in my hands."

"Well, you certainly are a craftsman."

"I take that as a real compliment. I'll be out of your way now. I want to get a fence repaired that I've become aware of, and I think I'll take a ride around and check a few traps."

"Traps? I didn't know you were trapping." Dora wasn't sure she liked this idea.

"I thought I'd try to catch a few rabbits for supper, and maybe I'll get a mink or two in my other traps. I want to make something special for Francine."

It was the one thing that Dora had not been able to adjust to – the killing of animals. She could understand it, even though she didn't like it. Killing animals was necessary to fulfill the need for food, her grandfather had impressed that much upon her, but she had not considered that Luke might kill just for using fur as decoration. It went against everything she believed in, but when she thought it over, the reality hit her. Luke was hunting one hundred and forty four years before she even knew he existed. It was his way of life and everyone else's who lived here. These people didn't give a second thought to it, and there was not one thing she could do to change their habits or beliefs. And when she left, the practice would go on for many, many years to come. Furs were prized for their beauty, and the minks, foxes, and beavers were one way to provide what mankind had always required in addition to food and water – beauty. Dora made a decision on the spot not to antagonize or even comment. She had no intention of upsetting the universe by going on a crusade to save the animals. She was in one small part of the world in the 19th century, and little Dora Clark was not going to change a thing.

"I'm sure she'll love whatever you give her. Now I need to find something to put on this bed. I know we don't have any extra sheets, but I can use a quilt for both top and bottom."

"I'll leave you to it then. Have a good day."

"Bye, Luke. Thank you again. I'm sure I'll get a lovely sleep tonight."

Dora spent the rest of the day sweeping up and making the bed the best she could, then she went back to the garden to finish a task she had not completed. She smiled to herself. Strange how she was beginning to enjoy playing in the dirt.

Chapter Twenty-five

1875

It was the last day of the school week. Francine was thrilled with the way her classes had gone and very pleased with the acceptance of the children for their new schoolmarm. She was falling in love with each and every one of them. Some of the boys were a handful at times, but that was to be expected. Not much had changed in the last two hundred years. And the girls had their little picky fights, but they soon got over them and continued happily with their play time.

The days were getting a little cooler but there was still a warmth to the air when the sun was shining, drawing people around town outdoors so they could savor every last friendly day. Francine had taken to sitting on the steps at lunchtime with her meager meal packed in a tin box, monitoring the children as she ate. She had adjusted to eating smaller meals at noon, but when she came home to supper she was ravenous. In the 21st century she was always snacking on something, as she satisfied an ancient urge to chew. But here there was no thought to eating all day other than at mealtime. There was just too much to do. Fran had never been an overweight person, but now her body was trim and her muscles were firm. She felt confident that her legs could take her wherever she wanted to go without the slightest bit of ache, as the muscles in her calves were rock hard.

"Mrs. Clark, Mrs. Clark," called Ruthie Grainger, "Ned London is coming." Ruthie ran to stand by her teacher as she beamed at the oncoming blacksmith.

"Why, hello, Ned. How have you been? I haven't seen you in quite a while."

"I'm fine, ma'am. I needed a walk in the autumn sunshine, and I thought I'd see how you are doing at school this week. Ma was asking after you."

"How kind of her. I'm doing very well, and can you please tell her so? Also, I'd like to invite the quilting ladies over. I have some new furniture now, so there's a place for us to sit," laughed Fran, "but I'm not sure what the best way is to get the word out."

"I can do it for you. Just tell me the day and time. Between me at the blacksmith shop and Pa at the train depot, we see most folks in town throughout the week. I'll let the postmaster know, also. If I tell one person, it's like a telegraph and the word passes right on to each and every one."

"I was thinking about next week Saturday afternoon. I'm ready for another quilting bee, and I want to return their kindness. I'll provide dessert."

"Okay, I'll tell them." Ned felt a little hand curling into his; he looked down to see Ruthie looking up at him in adoration. Her big bow on the top of her head only exaggerated her huge eyes. She had a smudge on her cheek from the playground, which only made her cherubic face look all the more innocent.

"Why, hello, Miss Ruthie Grainger. How have you been?"

"I'm fine thank you. I've been learning a lot from Mrs. Clark. You could, too. Would you like to come to school? You can sit at my desk, if you like."

Ned laughed. "Why thank you, Ruthie. That's real kind of you, but I already went to school, all the way through the eighth grade."

"You must be real smart then; isn't that so, Mrs. Clark?"

"I'm sure he is," answered Francine. It was obvious the little girl had a big crush on the handsome blacksmith.

"I've been practicing my steps, so I'll be ready for the next dance, but I'm not sure when that will be."

"Oh, there's usually something going on in the late fall. I'd be proud to dance with you then. We need to have one last gathering before Ol' Man Winter strikes."

"I hate Ol' Man Winter," she pouted.

"I'm not too fond of him myself. Which is one of the reasons I stopped by, Francine, -- uh, Mrs. Clark." He glanced down at Ruthie. It wouldn't be seemly calling the teacher by her first name.

"What reason is that, Ned?"

"I noticed you've been tying up Traveler in the shade all day, and that's fine, but I want to offer a stable for your use, on rainy and snowy days. I'm just across the street, and I always have an extra stable. I think we overbuilt my shop for this size of town. Anyway, it's yours to use, no charge. Just my way of helping out the school."

"Thank you. That is so kind. I was wondering what I was to do when the weather turns bad."

"You're welcome. We're just glad you're here with our children. Now, I'd better get going. I have some shoes to forge. It was nice to see you."

"And you too, and don't forget to pass along my message."

"I surely won't. Bye now, Ruthie."

"Bye, Ned." Ruthie sighed and turned to her teacher. "Isn't he just wonderful?" she asked dreamily.

"He is a very nice man." 'Oh, boy,' Fran thought, 'this little girl's got quite a crush.' She only wished her sister had thought the same. She picked up the hand bell to ring out its tones. Recess was over.

∞

Dora was pleased with herself. She had done the best she could with the bed, adding the oldest quilt on the bottom to use as a sheet and then adding another on top for the blanket. Luke had even brought along a small pillow. She was anxious to try out her new sleeping place, which was in the same bedroom that the two girls had slept in together when they were kids, and the room she had used right before she came here. It was the same but different. Such a strange sensation.

She had completed her garden work, and Luke had taken care of the animals, so she suddenly found herself with a little free time before Franny came home. Moose had been neglected lately, and she really wanted to enjoy the weather and stretch out her legs, so she decided it was a perfect afternoon to take a walk to the creek, but this time there would be no swimming. She was not going to put herself in that position again.

The walk was just as pleasant as she had hoped. The breeze across the open field caused her bonnet strings to dance around her face, so she had to tie them to keep them in place. Her honey blonde hair had begun to lighten up with the extra time in the sun, just like Fran's always had, but hers would always remain a more golden color. Her curls had gone wild in this place where there was no 'proper' shampoo or cream rinse to weigh it down. In fact, she noticed that most women had curly hair, and if it was straight, like Fran's, it had a healthy sheen.

Dora squealed in surprise when a pair of scampering chipmunks ran across her path. She laughed at their little chittering sounds. Off to her side near the tree line, she watched some squirrels chasing each other around and around a tree, then they leapt up to a branch to munch on a nut. Dora had a vision of herself as a child in this very same field. From her perspective, it had not changed one bit, it was still a perfect place for a child to play, as they discovered things about the world.

A loud scream overhead caused Dora to look up. She shielded her eyes from the sun, because with her head tilted that far back, even the bonnet did not do the job. She watched as a bald eagle soared and danced with his mate, his white tail and head flashing in the sun with every turn. He would climb high and then let himself fall with a display of his power and dexterity, then just at the last minute before he reached her, the two would change course with the wind current. It was a fascinating mating ritual. She had never seen anything more beautiful in her life.

Dora smelled fresh water as she neared the creek. Moose ran ahead, always eager to get his feet wet and see what he could catch. She remembered the last time she was here and how she had been discovered stark naked, and she remembered how she had dared to show herself to a man who was virtually a stranger. Her cheeks warmed, but at the same time her heart quickened. She was sure no matter what century she lived in, she would never meet anyone quite like Wade Grainger again.

As she came out of the clearing and walked into the small wooded area near the water, she could hear Moose barking. It did not seem to be one of warning, but rather an excited greeting. Dora feared he had treed a raccoon or something she would not be able to handle, so she cautiously moved forward. What she found instead of a raccoon, was a fisherman.

Wade was kneeling beside the big dog, scratching his ears. He heard her before he saw her. A smile played on his lips before he turned around. His day had just gotten better.

"Well, if it isn't the little nymph from the creek. I brought special bait in hopes of catching you. It must be my lucky day. Although, I see that you are fully clothed this time. What a shame."

"Wade," was all she could manage to say. She hadn't seen him since the time in the barn, when she had sworn never again.

"That's my name. What a nice surprise to see you here."

"Well, it is our property. Are you poaching again?"

"Not so far. Haven't caught a thing," he laughed.

"What else do you steal from our land? Rabbits? Squirrels? Turkeys?" She moved closer to him but still kept her distance.

Wade stood up and quietly looked her up and down. "I have a habit of stealing fair maidens, and I have discovered one right here by this creek that I don't want to let go." His warm brown eyes darkened with desire.

Dora heard herself take a breath in a little too quickly. She was ashamed at how easily he had weakened her. She turned away, trying her best to avoid him. It wasn't right, this attraction she felt. He wasn't hers. No matter what story he gave, he was still a married man. Dora plucked off a leaf from a tree, stripping it down to the veins, then she said, "There are no fair maidens here, so you can go on your way."

Suddenly, she felt his strong arms around her. He had moved as stealthily as a cat; she had not even heard a twig snap. Without being aware of what she was doing, her head fell back to his chest. He kissed the side of her neck, and she was lost.

"Oh, but there is a fair maiden here, and she is right here in my arms."

"No, Wade," she whimpered, "we can't be together."

"Why not, Dorie? Why not? Give me one good reason."

She turned as he whispered words of love. He continued to kiss her cheeks, her nose, her eyelids, and when he saw her struggle to find a reason why they shouldn't be together, he moved to her mouth. But first he held her face in his hands, and looking deeply into her eyes, he moved ever so slowly toward the prize. Dora had never had anyone romance her in this way. It was intoxicating. When she moved to him, he pulled back a little, teasing her with his nearness until their lips were ever so close without touching. Dora could feel his breath melding with hers, and when he finally pulled her to him tightly, crushing their lips together, she could feel their heartbeat merging into one. At this moment she no longer cared who he belonged to. She wanted him all to herself.

Wade picked her up and lowered her to the grassy bank. Then he began the painstaking chore of undressing her. She wanted to help speed up the process, but he moved her hands away, taking pleasure in doing it himself. Before long Dora found herself in the same situation as before – naked under a tree on the side of the creek. There was no blanket beneath them, but she never felt the picky pine needles, or the little pebbles biting into her back. She only cared about one thing, and it wasn't until she heard herself cry out his name, that she even knew where she was.

"Oh, Wade, what have we done? This can't keep happening."

"It doesn't matter, Dorie, she's out of my life. I'm yours if you want me. I'll always be yours." He moved to kiss away her fears, and she cried in his arms until they found they needed each other once again.

After they had dressed, she sat on the bank while Wade continued to fish. He told her stories of his days on the railroad, as he helped to build the tracks of the Pere Marquette Railway through Michigan. She loved hearing him talk and watching him gesture with his hands, his fishing pole bobbing with his descriptions. At the end of the afternoon, Wade had caught several fish, which he happily divided up with Dora for their supper. They parted with no plan to meet up on another day. Dora was let down that he had not asked to see her again, but she knew one thing; she was going to make sure one way or another that they were together as often as possible before she had to leave after Fran and Luke's wedding. If it was an affair he wanted, she would give it to him, and she'd make darned sure he never forgot her.

Chapter Twenty-six

2019

The library was quiet as all libraries should be, but when a few children came in with their mothers for reading hour, the silence was broken by excited shrieks that echoed throughout. The little ones were herded or carried into a room that had been soundproofed for just this purpose, so the minute the door was closed, Daniel could concentrate again.

He was at the computer in the genealogy section, and he didn't have a clue what he was doing. He had tried to do some work from his home laptop, but he soon realized that he needed help. Hoping he would find it at the small library in Holton, he had decided to spend some time here on his day off.

Daniel worked on the Clark Sisters case day in and day out; he was a man who was obsessed. He was now to the point where when an actual case came in that he was required to devote his time to, he got annoyed. He knew the answers about what had happened to the girls was somewhere, but he just couldn't crack it. He had spent countless hours going through photo albums, searching for any clue about this house and learning about the girls when they were younger. Each time he found a photo of Dora, he fell more in love with her. The pictures of her as a little girl with dirt or cake on her face made him laugh. He especially loved the ones of her big grin when she first got her braces, the shiny metal flashing on her teeth. Daniel found the photos on her prom night, and he could begin to see the beautiful woman she would become. She was with a tall, geeky teenager, not yet filled out. He had his arm possessively around her; she looked so happy in her yellow dress with thin straps. Daniel was actually jealous of this young man who had known her when she was still in school — so sweet and innocent. But it was the photos of her as a woman closer to her age now that intrigued him the most. He could see that she had changed; there was a worldliness about her, a sexual awareness. She was often filmed with a man named Kevin, according to the back of the pictures. He was a person of interest he would have to track down, maybe it was someone from Indiana. She had mentioned a fiancé; perhaps this was the man. He frowned when he saw one of this Kevin with his arm draped around her while she was wearing a bikini. He longed to be that man. The one who would have someone like Dora love him.

He had spent quite a bit of time following her sister, Fran, also. There might be a clue with one of her acquaintances, since she was the first one to disappear. Fran was very pretty in her clean and natural way. She seemed sure of herself, like a woman who knew what she wanted out of life. She wasn't often photographed with a man, unless it was her father or grandfather. He found no one of a suspicious nature in her albums. But it was always Dora who caught his attention, the younger and more beautiful Clark.

Daniel sometimes felt like a squatter, because there was no way to pay rent. There was no one left in the family to offer it to. He fully intended to pay for the time he had spent here when he got the girls back, but for right now there was no way to do it, so he kept a journal of everything he used from the cupboards.

One night when he was going through more pictures and documents, he realized that this cabin had been in the family for a very long time. Dora had mentioned it to him, but he had not realized the extent of the family's ownership. His curiosity led him to look into this property and who had actually lived here. He spent some time in the county clerks' office looking at deeds and plat maps. He made copies of everything he found, then he would continue to look it over at the house. One thing he noticed was that the Clark name had not been absent from this cabin since the day it was built in the 1800s. Not knowing what significance this had, he made a list in chronological order. He soon had a chart of the names of the owners and how much acreage they held. For over 150 years the Clarks had had possession of this place, and now he, Daniel Kent was an intruder. Of course, no one really knew he lived here. He kept up his rent on his small apartment, but he had told the post office he was collecting any mail that was delivered for evidence of a crime. Everyone knew he was on the case; it was a small town to this day, and just like in 1875, the postmaster knew everyone's business. No one ever questioned seeing him on the grounds, but he kept the curtains drawn at night to prevent the light from shining through just to be safe.

Sitting in the library, looking for answers, he felt lost and out of his element. It was the building. He had never been one to use a library as a kid, and he felt out of place, but detective work came naturally to him, so he was sure he could figure it out. He knew how to work backwards from whatever facts he had. He would carefully take one step at a time, but this ancestry site he was using was a little confusing. He stretched out his long legs and rubbed his eyes.

Seeing the frown on the handsome deputy's face, the new librarian thought she could offer some advice, and maybe get reacquainted with him.

"How are you doing over here?"

Daniel looked up into some lovely golden eyes, framed by dark hair piled high on top of her head. It was Kathy Young. He had gone to school with her through grade school and junior high, and they had even had a few dates in high school, but nothing had developed more than that.

"Hi, Kathy. Honestly, I'm lost. I don't have a clue what I'm doing."

"What are you trying to accomplish?"

"I thought I would do some genealogy for my friend as a gift. Her family has a long history here in Holton." He thought it was better to not mention the Clark case. No reason for word to get around that he worked on it at night.

"Let's see what you have so far; do you mind?"

"No, of course not. I need all the help I can get."

Kathy smiled and sat down next to him, taking over the mouse, as her hand brushed his.

"Look, you already have a good start with your list of names, here. It looks like you're working on the Clark case; is that correct?"

Daniel had forgotten that he had his list laid out on the table. "Well, what I am doing is not for public knowledge. Can I count on you to be discreet?"

"Of course, librarians are not allowed to pass on any information that our patrons might ask for or discuss any books that are checked out. We have a Code of Ethics which protects your right to privacy and confidentiality. I take my oath seriously."

"Thank you, Kathy. Then you are the one I need to help me. I'm trying to track backwards through the family tree of the Clarks; they owned the cabin where the disappearances took place. Can you help me with that?"

"I'd love to. I'd consider it my civic duty. Here, in this space we'll put in the missing women's grandparents. Then we'll do a search for their marriage licenses and death records, because it shows their parents' names. Then we'll keep backing up, one generation at a time, through the census. See here? You can see the address in the sidebar, then you can match your names with the list you have from the County Clerk. Now you're on your way. How far back are you going?"

"I'm not sure. To the first owner, I suppose. According to my record, it's William and Sarah Clark, around the 1860s."

"Well, it will take a few minutes, but I'm positive we can get you there. Then we can print out the relationship list, and it will lay it all out in a very readable straight line."

"Nice. That's exactly what I was looking for. Thank you so much."

"No problem, Danny. Oops, I mean Deputy Kent."

They laughed together like the old friends they were. It felt right and easy. Daniel was glad to finally have someone to share his search with, because all of the cops on the job thought he was on a wild goose chase.

∞

1875

The first week of school was over. Francine was quite tired. She thought it would be a breeze but dealing with children was more trying than dealing with chickens. She didn't care about being tired because she had never felt more satisfied. She had mastered the buggy in no time, and now felt like she had been doing it all of her life. Traveler did most of the work, anyway. She had begun leaving him in the stable the last day or two, and Ned had been kind enough to even rub him down when he had time. They had come to an agreement as to payment; she had not wanted to take advantage of Ned. Francine wasn't sure if she could afford it or not because she had, as of yet, not seen her first pay. She assumed it would be soon but was afraid to ask, because the particulars had probably been settled with the proper school teacher before she was to leave Canada. For now she was content in the fact that she would be able to take care of herself, even if she never married Luke. But they both agreed that the extra income would be nice to start their new life.

Working had been difficult on their relationship though, because she had not been able to see him regularly. He would sometimes be at the farm while she was teaching, and then he often passed on messages through Dora. She was looking forward to this weekend, hoping Luke would stop by. Perhaps they could steal some time to themselves. Gathering her books to get ready to leave, she sighed with the pleasurable thought of what that might mean.

"My, my, my, look at the pretty teacher."

Fran jumped, and then laughed with joy. "Oh, Luke, it's you." Fran moved into his arms and they shared the kiss she had been yearning for all day. She wondered if she would ever get used to the sight of this gorgeous man. He had a way of carrying himself due to his bum leg that was so sexy, and his smile, when he chose to use it, shined like a beacon. His light grey eyes settled on her with a look that said it all.

"Come here, Franny. I have something I want to show you." He pulled her into a corner, and continued to kiss her and nibble her neck until her heartbeat was racing. She was breathless with his touch. She knew no one could see them in the corner where they were, but she was still worried someone would come in. The thought of being caught was as intoxicating as a drug. Luke's hands roamed down her side, but when he began to hike up her skirt, she came to her senses.

"Luke, not here," she laughed. He pulled back a bit and looked deeply into her eyes. They didn't talk for a moment. It was enough to look at each other and know that soon they could be together anytime they wished.

"Did you come by the schoolhouse for the sole purpose of ravishing the schoolmarm?" she teased.

"No, I came for a different purpose." His face began to crack a crooked grin, the kind that turned her weak in the knees. "I came to give you this." He handed her a small box wrapped in a velvet ribbon.

"What is it? It's not my birthday."

"It's something to remember your first week at school."

Fran pulled at the ribbon and opened the box to find a beautiful little gold school bell on a chain. "Oh,

Luke, it's beautiful. I've never owned anything so special."

Luke was very pleased that she liked it. She turned around and he clumsily hooked the clasp. He picked up the little bell to place it in the proper spot, and as he did so, his knuckles brushed her breasts. He left his hand in that position, wanting so much more, but knowing they could get interrupted at any moment. It was difficult to pull away, but he knew it wouldn't be long until they would become husband and wife. He would claim his prize then. "It's time, Franny," he said softly.

"Time for what?"

"It's finally time for you to marry me. You made it through a week and no one complained. In fact, all I hear are good things about you. You have been accepted by the community as one of them. It's time to make the announcement and set a date."

"Are you absolutely sure the town wants me?"

"I'm sure, and even if they don't, I want you, so what? I don't much care what anyone thinks anymore. I want you. It's you and me. We'll make a good life."

"Even without children in it?"

"Even then." His hands were on her shoulders now. He placed his palm on her cheek and then caressed her jawline. "I want you no matter what, and no matter where. I need you. You made my life whole again."

Fran's eyes filled with tears, as he backed her into the wall once again. He kissed her until she had lost all willpower. This time it was Luke who put a stop to it, by saying, "I'm going to follow you home, we'll have supper, and then we'll plan our life together."

"I like a man who takes charge. Let's go home."

This time they didn't care a whit if anyone saw them coming from the schoolhouse together. Luke even took her hand on the way down the steps.

∞

Dora was surprised when Fran and Luke came in together. They looked so happy that she almost felt out of place. This seemed like their house, and she felt as though she was a visitor.

"Hi, Dora, something smells good," said Fran.

"Afternoon, Dora. I hope you had a good day."

"I most certainly did," said Dora, recalling her time with Wade at the creek. She turned her head toward the stove so her blush would not be detected. After coming home, she had decided that she could not give Wade up. He was to be hers no matter what, but the trick was how, since he already had a wife, and they could not keep meeting at the creek. The nights were already turning cold, bringing on a colorful change in the leaves, with the crispness of the air at night. They might have an opportunity if Wade could get away from his father's farm during the day when Franny was teaching. But that meant this weekend was out for sure. She was jarred out of her thoughts when she heard a question directed at her.

"What's for supper?" asked Fran.

"Pork pie. We had some roast pork left over, so I thought I'd make use of it. It's nice to have pork for a change, isn't it?"

"But there's another familiar smell in the kitchen, not pork."

Luke piped up. "Could that be sassafras tea?"

"It sure is. I know that it's best in the spring when you can find early young roots, but I wasn't here then. There's quite a patch out by the edge of the field right before you get to the creek, so I pulled up a few small pieces. It's been boiling for hours."

"I love that smell. It reminds me of our childhood. Gram used to make it for us all the time." Francine inhaled deeply, taking in the root beer scented brew.

"I'm so happy you love to cook, Dora. You know it's never been my strong suit."

"Oh, so I'm to have a wife who doesn't cook?" said Luke, in mock surprise.

"I can cook, obviously; it's just never been my favorite thing to do."

"What is your favorite thing to do?" he asked, as he pulled Fran to him. Francine giggled as he cuddled her.

"Come on, you two, get a room!" The moment it came out, Dora realized her mistake in using that phrase. Luke raised an eyebrow, while he thought over what she had said, then he burst out laughing.

Fran covered by laughing it off. "We'll be using our room fairly soon on a regular basis. Luke and I are going to announce our engagement."

Dora put down her stirring spoon, and went to hug her sister. "I'm so happy for you. When will you get married?"

"We haven't decided."

"I think next weekend would be good, don't you?"

"Next weekend?" said the girls in unison.

"Why not? We'll have Ma tell all of her friends, that alone will spread the word, and between Duane at the depot and Mr. Porter at the post office, everyone in town will know by the following day. Folks are always looking for an excuse to have a party."

"But what about food for the reception after the ceremony?" Francine asked.

"That's not a problem. Everyone brings something. All we need is to ask Wade to get his buddies together for some dancin' music, and I'll check to see if the barn where we had the harvest festival is available. Everyone will come. They all love a good wedding."

"But -- but – aren't there to be flowers and decorations?" asked Fran.

"Well, sure, we'll pick flowers from everyone's gardens. It's the end of the season anyway. And there are plenty of sunflowers blooming. That's all the decorations we need."

"Are you sure we can do it? You make it sound so simple."

"Why, it is. When folks pitch in, many hands make for light work. We'll talk to the pastor tomorrow after school."

"What about a dress for me? It takes a long time to order a dress, let alone make one. I want to look nice for you."

"Ma has one that all of the girls in her family use. They spruce it up a little each time and pass it down from person to person. You only wear it once, right? Why get a new one?"

Dora and Fran laughed at the simplicity of it all. "Would she agree to let me use it? I'm not her family."

"But you will be the minute we say I do."

"Oh, Luke, life's so wonderfully simple here."

"Here?"

"Oh, sorry, I mean there's quite a bit more fussing in Canada." The girls giggled and Luke shrugged his shoulders, lost in their private sisterly communication.

Chapter Twenty-seven

2019

"Will you look at that?" exclaimed Daniel.

"It's amazing what you can do with a computer these days, isn't it?" said Kathy proudly.

She had managed to take Dora and Fran's family tree in a direct line back to William and Sarah Clark, pioneers and builders of the cabin in 1859. It had been relatively easy with the names Daniel already had from the deeds, and as they followed the census, birth records and marriage licenses, the connection was as clear as a bell.

"It's just as I suspected. There's a straight biological line from the missing women to the original owners of the cabin."

"What does that mean exactly?" Kathy had begun to get very curious about the Clark women. With her love of genealogy came an innate drive to solve puzzles.

Daniel grinned at her. "Sorry, I can't say or I would have to kill you."

Kathy giggled at his joke. "I understand. Police work. Well, I hope this helps a little."

"It does. It helps a lot – more than you know."

"Always glad to do my part for the Sheriff's Department." Then she thought to herself, 'and I'd love to do anything for you and to you.' Kathy stood up to go, and Daniel reached out to touch her hand. She felt shock waves, but he felt only a touch of a good friend. She was disappointed that her feelings were not returned.

"Thanks, again. I'll probably be bugging you if I need some more family tree information."

Kathy smiled wistfully. "I'm always here for you. It's my job. And Daniel?"

"Yes?"

"Thank you for not giving up on them. I know some people in the town have never been convinced it was not foul play, and they're worried that we have an abductor in our presence."

"Strange thing is, there is no evidence of any wrongdoing. I think it's safe to say you don't have a thing to worry about. Like you, I'm just doing my job and tying up loose ends."

"Well, come in any time. If it's around noon, maybe we can grab lunch together and catch up on old friends."

"I'd like that" he said, but he couldn't wait to get back to the Clark cabin and review what he had found. He felt like he was finally understanding things. The question was how did they do it?

∞

1875

Plans for the quilting bee next weekend had been put off. A wedding was taking place instead and the ladies in town couldn't be happier. Jessica was especially pleased because the wedding was for her oldest son. She had grown to love Francine, as had the other women in their quilting bee. She had a kind and loving disposition, and although Jessica wasn't sure what the teacher had seen in her surly son, she didn't care because he was a changed man. When Jessica heard the news, she was overjoyed and couldn't wait to pass it on to her best friends. The three quilters, Jessica Grainger, Esther London, and Rachel Yoder, put their heads together on how they could make this day special for their new school teacher.

Jessica got out her special bride's dress and after a quick once over, she decided it needed a little updating. They went to see Francine the next day and when she tried it on, it was obvious it was too big in some areas and too small in others. They all set about pinning and making suggestions on the alterations. With a tuck here, and a nip there, they decided there was nothing to do about the bosom but remove the lace on the scoop neckline. It was originally meant to conceal any hint of roundness and softness of her breasts. There was more décolletage than was usually seen around Holton Township, but this was the late 19th century after all, they said, well, all but Rachel, the Amish woman. She refrained from comment, but silently she agreed that it was the best solution to relieve the stress on the bodice. And once it was all pinned to perfection, Fran looked glorious in the buttery ivory satin, with the cap sleeves, the tucked in waist, and the roundness of the skirt with the many petticoats underneath.

"Oh, Franny," exclaimed Dora. "You look so beautiful. This creamy color is perfect for you with your light blonde hair."

And all the others agreed. "Dear, it looks like it was made for you. Are you sure it's okay to wear a dress that's been used a few times before?"

"Of course, it is. I consider it an honor that you offered it to me." Fran smiled and patted Jessica's hand.

"Well, you know once Queen Victoria got married in a white satin dress everyone seemed to think it was the only way to go, but you truly look perfect in the ivory. Now, let me take this home and get busy on the alterations. I'll be back in a day or two." She turned to the others, and said, "Who's got flower duty?"

"I do," spoke up Rachel.

"All right. Wonderful. I'm sure you'll find something we can use to spruce up that old barn. You have such an artistic eye. Just look at the quilts you make."

Rachel lowered her eyes, not used to accepting praise of any kind.

"I think we should come back here to *our* barn for the reception. It's plenty big, and it's more convenient. Esther, will you look after the food? I'm sure we'll have more than enough, but just double check to see how many dishes are coming."

"What about music?" Esther asked.

"Wade's already taking care of that. He's getting the boys together to practice tonight. So that's about it.

Luke is talking to Pastor Roberts now. I think we're all set. You're getting married, young lady!"

They all cheered, followed by excited female chatter. Fran and Dora grinned at each other. Fran thought of her future husband and Dora thought of the man who would be on stage with a fiddle in his hand. Would he have eyes only for her again this time? Would he sing her a love song?

∞

2019

Daniel had his papers laid out on the table. He could see a direct line of property owners back to 1859 when the Clarks first built the cabin, and he could trace Dora's ancestors through her family tree. No one other than Clarks had ever lived in this house. Next to him was the trunk of quilts which included a book of photos of the women who had quilted them, and there were a group of six blocks of matching colors looking like a quilt that had never been put together, or pieced as his grandmother had called it. There was also a quilt top that had never been quilted with the 'stuffing' and back fabric. He was not able to recall the proper words of 'batting' and 'backing' until he had researched quilts on the Internet. Then there was the puzzling envelope, which was addressed to the original Clarks, and dated 1875. There was no letter inside and the back was blank, but he could tell it had been sent from Canada. No clues there. He picked up one of the single blocks again and studied it. He had no idea what he was looking for, but maybe there was some little thing that would give him a clue. They were very old and had been in this trunk for a long time. When he looked carefully he was able to detect some faded writing. He grabbed his magnifying glass, but he really didn't need it, because he had spotted some initials with his naked eye. When he enlarged it, he was satisfied that it said *1875, F.C.* F.C.? He didn't remember anyone in the family tree with those initials; he quickly looked at the family tree again. No one even had a first name starting with those letters, and there was no one in the quilt photo book with a name that started with an F. It could be a daughter or grand-daughter who was not on the direct line he was following. Or was it possible that F.C. stood for Francine Clark? Had she been sending a message to her sister through quilt blocks? Because each one of the six individual blocks had the same initials on the back. And if so, what had the message meant? He took out his phone and took a picture of each individual block. He would have to look into this later. There were just too many questions he couldn't answer. His head was getting muddled.

Daniel sat back in his chair, took a drink of his beer, and tried to think. It was silent in the cabin, but even with the windows closed, he could hear the deafening sound of tree frogs merging with singing crickets. He walked to the door and opened it to get some fresh air, but instead he found the air to be heavy and damp. He could smell the fishy odor of the many lakes and streams close by. A screech howl called with its horse-like whinny, and farther away, deep in the woods, he heard a larger owl asking "Who? Who?" The night was pitch black; the moon was but a thin sliver, only a few stars were able to force their light through. For some reason Deputy Kent looked to the sky and asked for God's help in finding Dora. He was not a religious man and had never turned to God before, but this one was beyond him. He couldn't understand any of it, if he was thinking rationally, but somewhere deep inside him, he knew that the time travel thing was a distinct possibility. Could Dora really be with Francine in the 1870s? He was afraid to think it, let alone say it out loud, because if she was, he had not a clue how to get her and her sister back.

Chapter Twenty-eight

1875

With only a week to prepare, wedding preparations had been going full speed. It had been hard for Francine to concentrate at school, and of course, the children had heard the news and they were just as excited as she was.

"Mrs. Clark," asked Ruthie, with her hand raised straight up in the air.

"Yes, Ruthie?"

"Will we have to call you Mrs. Grainger after the wedding?"

"I suppose you will. I hadn't thought of that."

Ruthie grinned. "Then you'll have the same last name that I do."

"Yes, that's because we'll be sisters-in-law."

"Sister-in-laws? What's a sister-in-law?" asked Gordie, a little freckled face seven-year-old.

"Well, first of all, the plural – do you remember what a plural is? Anyone?"

Janie raised her hand, and wiggled in her seat, hoping to be chosen.

"Yes, Janie?"

"It's when there is more than one thing, so you add an s at the end of the word."

"Correct." Francine decided to take this opportunity to teach, so she turned to the blackboard and wrote out the proper form of the word. "Since Ruthie and I are more than one, we add an s to sister-in-law, but the strange thing with words that have a hyphen -- that's this line that connects more than one word together -- is that we don't put the s at the end. We add it to the first word. So we say 'sisters-in-law' instead of 'sister-in-laws.' Do you all understand now?"

"Sort of. But Mrs. Clark, what is a sister-in-law?" asked Gordie.

"It happens when I marry Ruthie's brother. I will be part of her family then, but I'm not a real sister to Ruthie. I'm a sister through marriage, so we call it a sister-in-law, because I will be *law*fully married. Maybe someday you will be a brother-in-law, Gordie. Does everyone understand now?"

The class said "Yes, Mrs. Clark" in unison. Francine marveled at how lovely it was to have such a polite group of children at her school.

The rest of the day went smoothly, but Francine found it very difficult to keep her attention on the children. What would it be like to be Luke Grainger's wife? Where would they live? Would they continue to farm? Would he contribute anything to the household with other animals, like his own horse, or did the animal he always used belong to the Grainger family? Her cow and horse were technically not hers. They belonged to William and Sarah Clark. What would happen if they came back? Where would Fran and Luke live? And what would they say when they did not recognize Francine Clark, their so-called cousin, because they had been writing to a *Frances* Clark in Canada? What would Luke say and how would he react if he knew she had been lying to him?

The last question was the one that bothered her the most. She had to find a way to tell him the truth, but she didn't want to lose him. He would probably look at her like a crazy delusional person. Francine decided it was best to wait until after the wedding. It went against everything she had ever been taught about being honest in a relationship, but she could not risk him leaving her. She had to find the right time, but she would wait until after the ceremony, and after they had had a few precious days together as man and wife. She was hoping he would feel so committed to her that he would not give up on her. It was a risk, but one she was willing to take.

∞

Francine's quilting friends were having a secret quilting bee. With less than five days to go, they had dedicated the entire day to quilting. This time they were meeting at the London's house, well out of view of Francine's path to school. They did not want to risk her seeing their buggies parked together.

"Is the coffee on?" asked Jessica. "I don't function well without my coffee."

"We know you well enough to know that," laughed Esther. "There's a pot already hot and one more ready to go, if needed. I had to take care of my men this morning."

"How long do we have before they come back?"

"Oh, Duane won't come home until dinner time, when he's relieved. Ned pops in sometimes for lunch, but he was told you ladies would be here, so he'll stay away."

They chatted as they brought down the huge quilting frame from the ceiling. Each woman was perfectly acquainted with how they went about lowering it, so it went like clockwork. "I hesitate to bring it up, Esther," said Rachel, "But how is Ned taking all of the wedding talk?"

"What do you mean?" Esther knew perfectly well what she meant, but she did not want to betray her son's feelings.

"Oh, Esther, honey, we all knew how Ned felt about Francine when she first came. The whole town could see it. Is it difficult for him now that Luke and Francine are together?" Jessica was bent over smoothing and tugging the fabric pieces to get out all of the wrinkles.

"Oh, no, he's long past that. I did get the feeling that he had someone else in mind for a while, but he never mentions it to me, so I stay out of it."

Rachel and Jessica looked at each other and laughed. The last thing Esther London ever did was to stay out of other people's business, especially her own son's.

Esther looked puzzled at first and when she caught on to what they were laughing at she said, "Seriously, I really did not ask him a thing. I have a feeling he was sweet on Francine's sister, Dora, for a while, but something changed after the harvest dance. He hasn't looked her way since. Maybe he's meant to be alone. Some men are, you know."

"Here's a chair, Rachel, and one for you, Esther. You might be right about Ned, though. Some men remain bachelors, but I can't imagine a lonelier life. I'll pray someone will come along who he is attracted to."

"And I will, too," added Rachel. "I'm sure the good Lord will provide a wife for him. A man and woman are meant to be together. It is the Lord's way."

"Thank you, ladies, I appreciate it. Now, enough about my son. Let's get busy. Time's a wastin,' as they say."

Jessica unfolded a quilt top she had had finished for quite some time. It was a lovely wedding ring pattern in various shades of reds and whites. She was pleased when she heard her friends gasp.

"Oh, Jessica, it's beautiful," exclaimed Esther.

"This is your finest work," added Rachel. "We've seen the blocks one at a time over the years, but put together like this it is perfect. Oh, excuse me Lord," she looked up to Heaven, "no one is perfect but Thee. But this is a close second."

Jessica actually blushed at their praise. "As you know, I have been working on this quilt a little at a time for several years. It was always meant to be the quilt for my first child to get married. I assumed it was for Carl and his bride." Esther paused to swipe away a few tears. "I honestly never dreamed it would be Luke. He's been so moody since the war. I couldn't imagine why any woman would want him, to be frank."

"He certainly has changed, hasn't he?" said Esther, as they tugged at the quilt to get it perfectly framed and ready for quilting.

"It is lovely to see him smile," said Rachel. Then she added, with a blush, "He is such a handsome man. Francine is lucky to have him."

"Why, Rachel Yoder, I'm shocked!" laughed Jessica.

Rachel's blush deepened. "I might be Amish, but I'm not blind. Besides my Joseph is the perfect man for me, so he would not worry if I commented on another man's good looks. Here, I have a needle already threaded. Who wants to start?"

As they arranged themselves around the quilt, each woman worked in the area in front of her. Throughout the day they stitched and talked, and as they finished a section, they shifted the quilt on the frame, exposing another area needing the tiny stitches used to hold the pieces in place. The only breaks they took were for lunch and quick trips to the outhouse.

"How long can we go, Esther?"

"As long as you two women can be away from home. I will continue after you are gone, to make sure the binding is on before Saturday."

"I'm good past supper time. I left food ready for Joseph. He can do without me for one time. I'd like to leave before dark though."

"And I did the same; besides, Duane has Ned for company. Sometimes those two get to talkin' about farmin' and the goings on around town, and they leave me completely out of it. I swear I am nothing but their servant."

"Aren't we all," Esther responded.

Rachel was humbly quiet.

Chapter Twenty-nine

1875

After dinner a few days before the wedding, Francine and Luke were sitting side by side on the sofa. Dora had politely taken Moose out for a walk to give them some privacy. Luke had his arm around Fran as she rested her head on his shoulder.

"Just think, Franny, in a few days we'll be man and wife. What do you think of that? Can you put up with me for the rest of our lives?" asked Luke, only half joking.

"I will put up with you for the rest of our lives and beyond. We were meant to be together, Luke. I truly believe that," said Fran, thinking about her life before she came here. "It was only a fluke that I came here in the first place, and if I hadn't, I never would have met the man of my dreams."

Luke was surprised she had used that term, since she had been married before. He smiled over the top of her head. "I don't bring it up often because of the pain it causes you, but I know I'm not your first choice. You had a man before me, and it must be hard for you to think about those times. I only hope I can live up to your memory of him."

"You have gone beyond anything I could ever have imagined," she said carefully.

"I never hear you say his name or that of your child. Don't you have pictures or anything you want to put out? It won't hurt me; I understand the pain of losing someone."

"You are so sweet, Luke, but I want this life to be yours and mine. We'll talk about my past some other time. Right now, I want to think about the joy of living with you."

Luke could not believe how lucky he was to have found her. She had suffered so much and was still so giving. He placed his finger on her chin and tilted her head up to his, where their lips met softly as they sealed their love.

Fran wound her arms around his neck and looked at this kind man, knowing she was deceiving him. She knew it would hurt him when she told him she had been lying all along, but it had to be done. She had been planning on discussing this delicate subject after marriage, but she knew in her heart that it was wrong to hold it back. She took a deep breath and began to tell the story that would change their lives forever.

"Luke, I have something to say." She caressed his cheeks and trailed her fingers down his neck.

Luke sighed at her gentle touch. He saw trouble in her eyes, and thinking he had brought it on by mentioning her husband and child, he wanted only to erase those thoughts from her mind. The need to comfort her turned into a need to comfort himself, because he too hid troubles. He pulled her to him in a crushing kiss, and he was pleased when she responded the same way. Their desire to go further was overwhelming, but Fran pulled back.

"Dora could come in any minute," she said breathlessly.

"Are you sure, Franny? I think we have time." he whispered.

"Silly, boy. You know I don't like to rush."

He laughed out loud. "That you don't, and I surely love that about you. But it does bring up a question we haven't talked about yet."

"What is that, my sweet?" she asked, with a little kiss and nibble.

"Now, Franny, don't start up on me again, or this time I will carry you straight to the other room, Dora or no Dora."

"Okay, I'll be good." Fran sat up straighter.

"I was about to say, what about after we're married. Can we go in the bedroom any time we want, or do I have to wait for nighttime? You and I have not been conventional in that way, and I really don't want it to change."

"Oh, so we are going to live here? I mean I assumed we would, since the wedding date came up rather quickly."

"Of course, we'll live here; won't we? I thought we would. There's nowhere else, unless you want to share a bunkbed with me and my brothers."

"I'll pass on that, thank you. It's just that I don't really own this place. My cousins could come back at any moment."

"You don't think they will, do you? It takes a long time to settle in a new place, and they only arrived in Allegan early this spring. I'd say we have enough time to figure things out."

"Where would we go if that does happen?" Fran had not given a thought to someone else living in her grandparents' cabin before. If they came back she would have to face that fact.

"There is a solution. It's a good backup plan. Ma and Pa have divided up their 400 acres into smaller portions. They had always planned on giving each of their children a piece. Of course, Ma kept having kids, so the parcels got smaller, but then we lost my oldest brother, so with me being the first to marry, they recently adjusted the lines again. She said I can have the lot next to your property line. It goes all the way back to the creek. That way if your cousins come back, we'll just build across the line to the south, just through the woods. We'll still be close to my folks, and you'll be next to your kin."

Fran was not sure she would want to live next to her ancestral family. She prayed they never returned, but she knew they most likely would at some point. The records show that the Clark name stays with the property all the way to the 21st century, but she would soon be a Grainger. She had not heard of any Graingers on the list of owners of this property. Her heart skipped a beat with fear. She must explain this all to Luke. It was so unfair that he didn't know and was making plans for their future.

"Luke, I have to tell you someth -- "

"Hi, you two. Did I give you enough smooching time?" Dora had walked in at just the wrong moment. Now Fran would not be able to talk to him. They had decided this was the last night they would see each other until after the wedding. The bed was just too tempting.

"Yes, of course, we were just working out some wedding details," said Fran, smoothing down her dress.

"Sure you were," laughed Dora.

"I need to get going anyway. It's late," said Luke. "Thanks for dinner, Dora."

"You're welcome. Hope I didn't scare you away. I don't mind a bit giving you two more free time."

"We're fine. Thanks, Dora. I'll walk you out, Luke. Let me get my shawl." Fran was hoping she could still find a chance to say something to at least get the needed conversation started, but she knew it was going to be way too complicated for a quick talk by the wagon.

As they walked out hand in hand, Fran clutching her shawl with one hand at her throat, Luke said, "Fran, don't take this wrong, because I like your sister, but how will we, you know, when she is around?"

"Oh Luke, my darling husband-to-be, do you only have one thing on your mind?"

"I'm afraid I do. I can't get enough of you."

"Well, there's always the barn, and thanks to you and the new bed, she has her own bedroom now, so we should be good."

"I kind of like our times in the barn, don't you?"

"I do, my strong virile man."

"Now you're being a schoolteacher on me. What does virile mean?"

"Just what you think." And she pulled him in for the kind of kiss he loved.

"What I want to know is, where did you learn to do that?"

Fran chuckled. "Right now, you're better off not knowing."

"Saturday can come none too soon for me. If only the women at church knew the kind of woman you are, they'd never attend this wedding."

She slapped him playfully. "Oh stop. They all have children, don't they?"

"You're right. That they do. Although I can't bear to think of them doing what we do."

"Lord help me, neither can I! Now, go. I'm getting cold out here."

Fran watched as he drove away. She had not been able to work anything into the conversation about where she had come from. Perhaps it was better left unsaid for now.

Chapter Thirty

1875

It was a wonderful day for a wedding. The sun gently warmed the October morning; the deep indigo sky served as a perfect contrast for the painted colors of autumn; their golds, oranges, yellows, and dark greens decorating the landscape. The air was fresh with the intoxicating smell of fallen leaves. The rolling hills of the farms resembled an artist's masterpiece.

The small church in Twin Lake held a single vase of sunflowers. It was to be a simple country wedding for immediate family only. The rest of the town would celebrate at the reception. Dora had helped Fran dress in her new/old dress which had been altered to perfection. A wreath of flowers was placed on her head and a new attached veil, which Dora had provided as a wedding gift, hung down her back.

The two women carefully climbed into the buggy making sure not to soil Fran's dress. Dora drove slowly so the air would not muss up the bride's hair. When they arrived at the church, the Grainger twins, Zeke and Jake, were on hand to help them down, because Luke was not allowed to see the bride. He was hidden away and waiting impatiently in the pastor's quarters.

The boys took their place in the second pew at the front of the church alongside Wade. Ruthie sat in front with their parents. Once Francine was in position at the back of the church, and Dora had taken her seat at the front, Luke was called out to stand with the pastor. The church organist began to play on the tall ornate organ, while a little boy from town pumped the bellows which forced air past the reeds, creating the sound used every Sunday for hymn singing.

Fran walked slowly down the aisle, wishing her parents and grandparents could have been here. She knew they would have been so happy for her.

Luke could not believe the beauty he saw before him. His eyes brimmed with tears. There was no need for a father to give Fran away, or for individual vows to be said. There was no need for a flower girl or a best man or a maid of honor. The pomp and circumstance and all the stress that goes with a modern day wedding was missing. It was simply a time for them to repeat the vows that the pastor read and close their eyes for prayer. He then declared them man and wife, and they shared a chaste kiss. On their way to the decorated buggy that Luke had arrived in, the family tossed some rose petals picked from a late blooming wild rose growing alongside the church.

"We did it, Luke. We are truly man and wife," cried Fran.

"Why the tears? Am I such a bad catch?" he laughed.

"Silly, you know what I mean."

"I only know one thing. You are the most beautiful creature on the face of this Earth, and I am the luckiest man alive." He pulled the buggy to a stop and kissed his bride the way he had wanted to in church, but this time he did not hold back. He kissed her in front of God and everybody passing them on the way to the reception. There were hoots and hollers and whistles, but they didn't care one bit.

"Luke," said Fran, when she could get her breath. "Everyone's watching us."

"So they are." And he went back for more.

∞

The barn was a bustle of activity, much like the harvest celebration had been. People called out their congratulations, some patting Luke on the back, others hugging Francine. Ruthie was the first one of the school children to run up to her and call her Mrs. Grainger. It sounded strange but nice.

"Are we sisters-in-law now, Mrs. Grainger?" she asked, making sure Francine noticed she had pronounced the s after sister.

"We are Ruthie, but let me whisper a secret to you. You can call me Francine when we are not in school. But only then. We're family now."

Ruthie hugged Fran tightly at the waist. "I love you, Francine."

"I love you too, Ruthie."

The child ran happily off to find her friends. Any party was a good time for them to run freely unsupervised. There were no helicopter moms here. When it got dark the mothers would begin to look for their children, but they weren't worried because they were certain they would come indoors when they were hungry or when the music started.

The barn was scattered with bouquets of sunflowers, but other than that there were no banners or streamers. The only thing festive was the hanging lanterns at the ready for the dark of the night which would come soon on this Michigan autumn day.

Wedding parties tended to last for hours and hours. Several meals were eaten and a lot of alcohol was consumed, but no one ever got drunk to the point of embarrassing themselves and others. Fran knew Luke was anxious to leave and have her to himself, but that would be very bad manners. After all the people had done for them, staying until the end was the least they could do. Fran had whispered to her sister that her wedding was the most stress-free, enjoyable wedding she had ever been to in her life. Dora was thrilled to see Francine's happiness.

Dora had spent most of the time alone, but she was able to keep herself occupied. She chatted with Jessica and Esther and Rachel, but she kept her eyes moving, always hoping to get a chance to talk to Wade. She had not seen him since they left the church where they had carefully kept their eyes off of each other, in case they gave away their attraction. She assumed he was out back with the men having a drink or two. He would be playing with the band soon, and then she would not get a chance to talk to him at all.

After an hour or so, the men began to tune up their instruments. When she heard a few notes on the fiddle, as the bow passed over the strings, Dora glanced toward the group, but Wade was not with them, someone else was playing it. A man with a guitar picked and strummed as he tuned up. The bass fiddle made a few deep thumps, and the drummer tested the skins with his brushes. The banjo player strummed a few chords as he nodded at the others that he was ready. At the last minute Wade stepped up, brushing back his hair as he placed his hat on his head. His eyes were a little glassy, giving away the fact that he had had a nip or two of the homemade alcohol that had been passed around, but when Dora looked around she noticed that he didn't appear any different than the rest of the men. She waited for him to acknowledge her, and she was pleased when he looked straight at her and grinned a crooked smile.

Wade stepped up front with guitar in hand; she had not known that he played guitar also. But before they started to play, he called the party goers to attention. He was weaving slightly, but Dora figured it would wear off soon enough when he worked it out with the lively music to come.

"First off, I'd like to congratulate my brother for catching the school teacher. She made a lovely bride and will make a wonderful sister-in-law."

The group cheered and clapped, and Ruthie beamed when she heard the term she had recently learned.

"Next, I'd like to say how proud we are to have a teacher in the family. Twin Lake and Holton have been eager for someone to come for a long time, and Francine, here, fit the bill. Let's greet the former Mrs. Clark. She will now be known to us all as Mrs. Grainger."

There was more applause until he held up his arm for silence. "At this time we would like to play a special dance for the bride and groom. You all know it as Stephen Foster's Molly, Do You Love Me? But I will be changing the words to Franny, Do You Love Me, as that is what Luke calls his bride." Francine blushed. She had no idea anyone else had heard him call her that. "Let the newly married couple begin, and then you can all join in." He pointed at Luke. "Brother?"

Luke took Francine's hand, and even though he was embarrassed to be the center of attention, he proudly led her to the dance floor. Francine and Luke could not keep their eyes off each other. After a few bars he pulled her close, and he even dared to kiss her tenderly.

Wade's smooth tenor voice sang the words that propelled them through the music.

Franny, do you love me

Can the morning beam

Love a lowly flowret

Living in its gleam?

Let one gentle whisper

All my doubts destroy

Let my dreamy rapture

Turn to waking joy.

Franny, do you love me?

Tell me, tell me true

Franny, do you love me?

Love as I love you?

Dora stayed focused on Wade. He watched Fran and Luke through most of it, but his eyes would quickly dart to her. One time he held her look just enough to give her the signal she had been waiting for. He was thinking about her through the whole song. Now she knew it. He heart swelled with joy. He wanted to be with her again. She would make sure that at some point this evening they found a moment to meet in the shadows.

Dora was kept more busy than at the last dance. She danced with both Jake and Zeke several times each, and Luke's father, Henry, even asked her to dance. It was obvious they were keeping her busy. She wondered if they had a hint of the passionate romance that she was having with the other Grainger boy, or were they just being polite to the single lady. A few other men also stepped up to the plate, including Ned. He was over his anger now, but he would never feel the same way about her again since the time he saw her behind the barn with Wade. He was polite, so he held her body away from his in a stiff fashion, almost as if she was tainted, and she thought perhaps she was.

Finally, Wade approached to ask her to dance. He was, after all, the brother of the groom, he said to his fellow band members. It was only polite. But first he requested that they play a special song for him.

Dora was thrilled when he came to her and held out his hand, and when the band played Aura Lee, she melted into his arms. She didn't care who saw how close they were dancing. Wade sang softly into her ear along with the band member.

> As the blackbird in the spring
> 'neath the willow tree
> Sat and piped, I heard him sing
> Praising Aura Lee.
>
> Aura Lee! Aura Lee! Maid of golden hair
> Sunshine came along with thee
> And swallows in the air.

Dora interrupted him on the next verse, as she sang her own words to that tune.

Love me tender

Love me sweet

Never let me go

You have made my life complete

And I love you so.

Love me tender

Love me true

All my dreams fulfilled.

For my darling I love you

And I always will.

Love me tender

Love me long

Take me to your heart.

For it's there that I belong

And we'll never part.

Love me tender

Love me dear

Tell me you are mine.

I'll be yours through all the years

Till the end of time.

"I had no idea you were such a good singer, Dora."
Wade looked at her so lovingly his feelings would have
been obvious to anyone watching, but the dance floor
was so crowded no one could see a thing. "Where did
you hear those words? They're perfect."

Dora smiled coyly, "Canada."

They separated at the end of the dance, but Dora
had all the confirmation she needed. Wade was hers.
She would convince him to tell everyone after Fran and
Luke's wedding had died down. No need to stir up more
gossip just yet.

After a time the band members needed a break; it
was time for them to refuel with food and alcohol. The
people in the barn quieted down along with them, even

though one man had stepped up and taken over the banjo plucking. He strummed some quiet tunes, giving the dancers a time to cool off, but at the same time not lose the momentum of the party. Chatter and laughter could be heard inside and out. It was a wonderful observation of the forming of a new family in the area.

The men all stepped out for a few more sips of their favorite brew. The drinking was heavier now that the evening was late. Wade worked his way to a group of his friends, and they passed the jug around more than a few times.

Dora grabbed her wrap and walked out into the now dark night. It was cool and fresh. A few people stood in groups laughing at jokes or talking quietly about the weather and farming. Dora hoped she might see Wade out here, but he was nowhere to be found. He was probably staying away so as not to arouse suspicion about them. She wondered how long she could remain in 1875, but if she got what she was hoping for from Wade, some form of commitment other than singing a song, she might continue to stay right here. After all, Fran was the only family she had left. The thought of sharing her life with Wade was not what she had planned when she came to find her sister, but now that she had met the most fascinating man she had ever known, she couldn't imagine not staying with him.

Dora leaned against a tree and hugged her shawl to her body. It was getting chilly and damp, but she needed a few more minutes alone. She had made arrangements to stay one night at the boardinghouse in town to allow Luke and Fran some privacy on their first night. There would be no honeymoon. That was for fancy people, Luke said. They had made arrangements for someone to drive her to the boardinghouse with his horse trailing behind the buggy, so she wouldn't be alone at night on the roads.

Some cloud cover had come in, and Dora found herself deep in the shadows of the tree with no moonlight to show the way. It felt good to be alone for a little while before she went back in to dance the rest of the night away, but soon her quiet time was interrupted with voices. At first they were whispers, but then she distinctly heard Wade's voice. Dora stiffened when she was able to detect that the other voice was a woman's.

"What are you doing here?" he said angrily.

"I came into town this afternoon, and when I heard there was a wedding at the Grainger barn, I had to see for myself if it was you gettin' married."

She talked as if she had honey dripping from her mouth. Her sweet tones were meant to tempt him. Dora longed to turn her head to see who the woman was, but then her movement would give her away, so she stood perfectly still.

"You know I can't get married. I'm still married to you."

"And whose fault is that?"

"It's yours. You wouldn't come with me. I begged you to come but you turned me down."

"I recall that I begged *you* to stay."

"You did no such thing, Myra. You rejected me for your family's money." He was getting angrier by the minute. His voice was tense, and his quiet tones were forced.

"Well, we see a different story, then."

"Why are you here?"

"I came to get you back, Wade. I love you. I always have; you know that. I truly do miss you."

When Dora sucked in her breath, she was afraid she had given herself away with the rush of air.

"You only think you love me. You threw me away like an old pair of shoes."

"I did no such thing, and you know it. We had a good night the last time we were together, right? One last time, we said. That quick roll in the hay was something, wasn't it? We're good for each other."

"Yeah, well, you lured me to bed and then turned me away all at the same time."

"I wanted to have something to remember you by," she purred. "You remember, don't you? How we were?"

"Get over yourself. It wasn't that good."

"Oh, really?"

There was silence. Dora heard some rustling. 'Were they kissing?' she wondered.

"Myra, stop," he said angrily, then more silence. And then his voice changed to a weak and breathless plea. It was muffled, but she plainly heard him say her name with a sigh, "Myra. Myra."

When Dora was finally able to step out of the shadows, she saw Wade with his arms around his wife in a passionate embrace, their bodies tightly pressed together. She choked back a cry and ran. When tears blurred her vision, she tripped over a root and landed face down next to where Ned was standing. He was quick to assist her up, and when he saw her crumpled up face, he pulled her to him, and gave her comfort. He knew without a shadow of a doubt that Wade Grainger was the cause of this, and even though he would never want someone like Dora for his own, she was much too worldly for him, he could not stand to see a woman in trouble. He held her while she sobbed into his chest.

"Take me, home, Ned, please," she begged. "I need to go now."

Chapter Thirty-one

1875

The bride and groom were finally home. Fran squealed when Luke picked her up and carried her over the threshold.

"Why, Mrs. Grainger, you're light as a feather."

"Thanks to all of the hard work around here."

They stopped at the doorway to share a kiss. It was a sweet kiss that conveyed their happiness in knowing they would be together forever.

When they pulled away from each other, Luke said, "Welcome home, Mrs. Grainger."

"Thank you, Mr. Grainger. I hope you'll be comfortable in my humble abode." They laughed at their silliness.

"Why look, Luke, there are vases of flowers everywhere."

Luke grinned. "And one reason why folks don't lock their doors."

"They're so beautiful. Do you think it was your mother?"

"And her friends. I'm sure they all had a hand in it. Now, Mrs., can I get to what I have been waiting for all night long?"

"What is that, Mr.?" They stood hip to hip with their arms around each other, until Luke turned her to him, pressing his body to hers.

With one swift movement he picked her up again and carried her to the bedroom. "I've been dying to get that dress off of you, pretty as it is. I hate to ruin the lovely creation you have made for me, but I need to see the rest of the beauty underneath it all. And I need to see it now." He began murmuring sweet words into her neck.

"Wait!"

"What?" Luke jumped, thinking there was some kind of danger.

"Look. It's a new quilt."

"It's just a quilt like any other, isn't it?" Luke asked impatiently.

"No, silly, you should know about quilts, being around a mother who does nothing else with her free time."

"I never pay any attention to them. It's women's stuff. Now come here."

"Just a minute, let's look this over and then remove it carefully. I think my quilting friends put this together just in time for our wedding night. The pattern is called Double Wedding Ring. Look how the two big circles entwine. That symbolizes our love and marriage, for an unending future together." As soon as the words came out, Fran felt guilty. How long would she have with Luke. Could she stay forever? And the next thought was when would she be able to tell him? But she had not a minute to spare before he ripped the quilt off the bed, threw it over the trunk, and tossed her on the soft mattress.

"We'll talk about the quilt later, Franny. I have some serious business to attend to, and there's not a moment to spare."

Fran's peals of laughter could be heard throughout the house.

After an hour of much needed alone time, and just as they were about to doze into a blissful sleep, they were roused by a loud tinny racket.

"What in the Sam Hill is that?" asked a startled Francine. She had been picking up more and more of the local vernacular.

"Oh, it's nothing but a little shivaree," laughed Luke. "Probably my brothers and their buddies."

"What's a shivaree? Should I be worried?"

"Nah, it's just the young men making a racket with pots and pans. They think it's funny to try to upset the merrymakin' going' on in here. They won't think it's so funny when it's their turn."

"How do we get them to stop," asked Fran, her ears covered with her hands.

"We have to give them something they want."

"Like what?"

"A kiss or two in public."

"At the door, in my nightwear?" shrieked Fran.

"Well, unless you'd rather do it without your night clothes," teased Luke.

"Grab me that thing, and let's get this over with. Your brothers are barbarians!"

"Not at all. It's common practice. A sign of approval."

"Well, they can approve of me in another way, or would you rather I give them a good show?"

"A good show will do just fine."

Fran almost backed down, but then decided if she was to truly fit in, she'd better give them what they came for. "Let's go, then."

When they opened the door, they found a group of ten young men all laughing and teasing with catcalls, but when they saw the new Mrs. Grainger, scantily clad, grab her man and kiss him like they had only done in their dreams, there was silence. They completely forgot to beat on the pots and pans. A few mouths dropped open in shock. This was much more than they had expected.

"There. I guess that shut them up," whispered Francine.

"And that, young men, is how it's done!" yelled Luke. Then he yanked her back in and slammed the door. "That was above and beyond the call of duty, ma'am, but I appreciate it very much."

"You're welcome. Now take me back to bed and warm me up. It was nippy out there."

"I'll say," he chuckled.

∞

By the time Ned and Dora arrived at the boardinghouse, Dora had calmed down a bit, at least in front of Ned. She was still seething inside. He had calmly tried to get out of her what had happened, but she had refused to talk about it, only confirming his suspicions that Wade had something to do with it.

Ned delivered Dora to Mercy Brody who had been waiting up for her guest to arrive. She could tell the minute she saw Dora's face that something was wrong, but with respect for her privacy, she did not mention it. Instead, she decided it was best to be upbeat.

"Welcome. How was the wedding?"

"It was wonderful. I'm sorry you missed it," said Dora softly.

"Well, unfortunately, it's the life of owning a boardinghouse. I had another guest arrive earlier, and I had to stay to get him settled. I really wish I had some help so I could get out once in a while, but other than a quick jaunt to the mercantile, I very rarely go away."

Dora nodded as if she knew what she was talking about, but her head was still back in those woods. Seeing Wade like that with another woman had just about killed her. Remembering her clumsy fall, followed by her quick departure, she turned to Ned.

"Thank you, Ned. You have rescued me once again. You are a very kind man."

"It was my pleasure, miss" then realizing what that sounded like he added, "well, it would have been under different circumstances. I'm sorry for whatever you went through. Send for me if you need anything. I'll be happy to help."

Dora smiled weakly at him, then she stepped forward and kissed him on the cheek. He turned a bright shade of red, then turned to leave the women alone. He was sure Dora would confess her problems to Mercy; she had a way with people.

"He's a nice young man; isn't he?" said Dora.

"He certainly is. Come dear, I'll show you your room."

"Thank you, Mrs. Brody."

"Call me Mercy. I'm friends with your sister, and now I shall be yours, too."

Dora nodded and followed Mercy up the stairs, carrying the lightweight carpet bag that felt like it was filled with stones. She was shown to a lovely room in a style she had only seen in magazines about antiques in 2019. It was pure Victorian elegance, but it was all new. The four-poster bed had a ruffled silk rust-colored canopy. The bed was covered with a white-on-white quilt that was stitched to perfection. There were oriental rugs on each side of the bed, their red and yellow threads, contrasting with the canopy color. Placed next to the window was a Queen Anne chair covered in navy blue horsehair, and beside it stood an ornate floor lamp with a gold velvet shade. The long fringe gently moved when Mercy stepped by it to turn back the bed.

"I hope you'll be comfortable. I gave you my best. You deserve it after giving up your own room for your sister's privacy, or should I say pleasure?" she giggled.

"Well, they needed time alone. But this room is way beyond my budget. I don't think I can pay for it."

"It has been pre-paid by the groom. He wanted to thank you for your kindness."

"How sweet. Luke is wonderful, don't you think?"

"He certainly is. He doesn't get enough credit for it, because he can be moody, but most men were after they came back from the war. He's had a harder time getting over it than most for some reason."

Dora took off her bonnet and set her carpetbag on the floor, then peeling off her gloves, she asked casually, "What do you think about his brother Wade?" When she saw Mercy's eyebrows raise, she quickly added, "I'm trying to get to know all of the Graingers a little better. They're family now, and I haven't been here long enough to figure them all out. I've gotten to know Jessica and Ruthie quite well, but I know nothing about the brothers."

"Yes, I see. Well, Luke and Wade are completely different. I love Luke, don't get me wrong, but Wade is – well, he's special."

"I heard he was a troublemaker and a womanizer," said Dora, trying to get as much information as she could.

Mercy laughed. "My goodness, will the rumors never stop? Yes, he was rambunctious when he was young, but he has such a pleasing personality. He just loves people, and they love him back. He used to cause all kinds of trouble, but it was all harmless. It was more like childish pranks, and he was always forgiven. He's never been in any trouble with the law, if that's what you're asking. And I think his reputation with the ladies comes from the fact that he couldn't help himself from flirting, even with the older ladies. But they all loved it. As far as I know he's only had one love, and that was Myra Bloom."

"Yes, Myra," said Dora softly. She turned her back and pretended to be busy with her carpetbag so Mercy would not see the tears begin to form. "I've heard of her."

"Well, she was never any good for him, but he wanted her. Had to have her, even against her parents' wishes."

"Why didn't they like Wade?"

"The Blooms thought they were too high and mighty for the Graingers, and such fine people Jessica and Henry are. But then Myra's family moved away. A few years later Wade tracked them down. And low and behold if he didn't up and marry her."

"Yes, so I heard."

"I surely don't know what happened. I understand he came home a single man, but just yesterday someone saw Myra in town. I guess I'll hear about it soon enough. All the gossip comes through here, usually around the breakfast table."

Mercy caught Dora's frown. "I'll leave you now, but if there's anything you need, just pull on the ribbon. The bell rings in the kitchen, and my room is right next to it. So anytime day or night, I'm available."

"You're so kind, thank you, but I'll be fine." And she expected she would be, once she figured out how to forget about Wade Grainger.

Chapter Thirty-two

1875

Morning came too soon for Dora. She had tossed and turned all night, the vision of Wade wrapped in Myra's arms had haunted her restless dreams. It wasn't so much the kiss, but it was the way they were kissing, the same passionate lovemaking she had thought was reserved for her. Now she knew that she was just the 'other' woman, and that had never been her intention. She had challenged him on his relationship from the moment she had first heard he was married, and he had assured her it was all over. But just like in the 21st century, men were men. She should have made sure there were divorce papers before she agreed to sleep with him, but looking back she knew she was too weak to deny him his pleasure, because it was her pleasure, too.

Dora rose from bed enough to get a cool wet cloth from the basin, which she placed over her swollen eyes, but it was going to take more than water to repair the puffy damage. Once she was sure that all the other guests had had their breakfast and were gone from the house, she dressed and ventured down the stairs. Hearing dishes clattering in the kitchen, she stepped inside to find Mercy elbow deep in dish water, the spots on her apron already showing a full day's work.

"Can I help?"

"Oh, my goodness no. You are my guest. This is my job, which I do daily, and have done long before you ever arrived. So please sit and have something to eat."

"But it looks like you're all through here. You're cleaning up."

"I am, but my restaurant next door is always cooking. I'll pop over and get something for you."

"No, please don't bother. I'm not hungry. Just some coffee will be fine."

"Okay, coming up."

"Is it okay if I sit in the kitchen with you?"

"You want to watch me work?"

"If you don't mind. You know, I used to work in a restaurant. I was studying to be a chef," said Dora.

"Studying? There's a class for grown women to learn to cook in Canada?"

"No, not to just learn to cook, but to make special meals – fancy meals."

"And women can do that there?"

"Yes, we are more progressive, I believe. You know, you said yesterday that you needed some help, and I'd like to give Franny and Luke more time to be together without having me in the next room. I'd love to help you out."

"Oh, no, I couldn't ask that of you."

"But I love cooking above all else. I've never been one for farming and animals. It would give me great pleasure to work in your kitchen. You have so much more room than our little space. Put me to work. I'll chop or clean or wash dishes. Whatever you want."

Mercy had an instinct about people. She had developed it over the years, watching the way a person moved their body or used their hands. She had a feeling there was more to this request than Dora was letting on; she was positive it had to do with the questions about Wade. And now that his wife was back in town, Dora most likely did not want to risk running into them if Wade came to visit his brother.

"Then I'd be happy to put you to work, but I must insist on paying you."

"No please, it will only be for a while. I just need to be busy."

"All right. We'll work something out. Would you mind stepping out into the vegetable garden in the back and pick me some fresh tomatoes? There's only a few left hanging on the vines."

"I would love to. Where might I find a basket?"

Mercy grabbed a woven basket off a hook by the door. "Take your time. It looks like you could use some fresh air."

"Thanks, Mercy." And with that, Mercy Brody got the first smile of the day from Dora, so she knew she had done the right thing by allowing her to help in the kitchen.

∞

Luke and Fran had three precious days all to themselves. Mercy had sent word that Dora was staying a while, and Fran had canceled school until Wednesday. With no substitute teacher to call on to replace her, she had had no choice but to give the kids some time off, which they enjoyed. But they would have to be all business after this, thought Fran. They had gotten off to a late start according to 21st century standards, because of the late harvest, and from what she understood, there was a lot of time off when the snow got deep, making it difficult for some of the children to get to school. She must cram a lot of knowledge into a very short amount of time. But for now she was content to lie in bed with her husband. They only got up to feed chickens and horses, milk the cow, or eat.

"This is the life," said Luke, as he stretched and scratched. "I could lay about all day long with you."

"Wouldn't you get bored?" asked Francine.

"Not at all, I would have my way with you, sleep to get refreshed, and do it all over again. I can't get enough of you, Franny. I love you more than life itself."

"And I you, but life goes on; besides, I have to teach school."

"You don't have to if you don't want to," said Luke. "I'll take care of you from now on. That's what a man should do. I'm your husband now."

"But Luke, the town is counting on me. I must honor my promise. Besides, if they had not brought me here to teach, then you and I would never have met. We owe them a lot."

"Right you are. And the kids need you. I'll allow it," he laughed, knowing this was one argument he would never win. "So come here, teacher. Teach me a few new things." She shrieked when he pulled her back into his arms.

∞

2019

Daniel had not had much time to work on the Clark case. There was a lot going on in the county. School was back in session and that meant duty at the football games, breaking up fights, and solving stolen goods from the lockers and locker rooms. They called him for every little thing. The principal liked to start out the year with police presence to show some of the punks that they were available. Once the snow started to fly, the kids settled down a bit. He wasn't fond of these menial tasks, but it was part of the job. The squad cars had to be on the roads making rounds, so until a murder case came up, which was rare, he was used in this way.

The best part of his day was at the end of his shift, when he could go home to the Clark cabin. So far no one had caught on that he was living there. In a way it made him feel bad that his friends weren't more curious of his comings and goings, but then he had disconnected from them to pursue investigating the disappearances. He showed up at a barbeque on occasion and went to the bar for a few drinks with some buddies, but other than that he was on his own. And since he had been spending so much time at the library, everyone thought he was seeing his old flame, Kathy Young. Kathy would love it if that were true, but she had not been able to detect any kind of attraction from Daniel at all. She had even gone so far as to change her hair style and buy some new clothes, but there was nothing, not even when she managed to brush her breast against his arm.

Daniel made a bowl of popcorn and sat down to watch TV. It was his favorite night of the week, Monday night football. How he wished this house had cable and a decent set, but luckily his favorite team, the Detroit Lions, were on a national network tonight. He did not dare to upgrade in any way. He had checked with the electric, gas, and cable companies to see how things were being paid. It seemed they were on an automatic withdrawal from the Clarks' checking account, so life merrily went on its way without them. Apparently they still had an active account that had a balance, so the bills were pulled out without him doing a thing. But if he made a change of any kind, someone would notice, so he struggled with what he had, just happy to be where Dora had lived.

He propped his feet up on the coffee table, settled in, and then sat straight up. Something felt different tonight. In the past he always felt Dora's presence. He knew she was near somewhere, that's why he had stayed on the case and close to this house. But tonight there was an emptiness in his chest, a loneliness. He had felt it before but only for a short time, but this time was different. If she was in another century like he suspected, she was gone from the cabin. He had felt the same thing yesterday, too. He prayed she was all right, because if something terrible happened to her, he would never learn about it.

∞

1875

It was Tuesday already and Dora had no intention of going back to the cabin. She was perfectly happy working here with Mercy. Mrs. Brody was a lovely woman, who had been more than kind. The two worked well together, and Mercy even took some suggestions on ways to hold her knife and how to properly clean a chicken for the most efficient and sanitized way. But most of the time Mercy privately thought Dora went overboard with her cleanliness. Once the chicken was cooked, no one would care what knife she used to cut it with. Dora insisted on using a clean knife every time. A knife was a knife. Dip it in the bowl of water to rinse it off and move on, Mercy said. But she let Dora do it her way to keep her happy, and she enjoyed the company.

By the second day, Dora had confessed to Mercy about what she had shared with Wade this fall, and then that she had seen Wade and Myra together. Mercy could tell the girl was in love and hurting badly. She had promised to never tell another soul. She herself had been in much the same predicament after her husband had passed away, she told Dora. It was lonely here, and she needed someone. A handsome man who came to the boardinghouse quite regularly, while passing through on business, had often slept in her bed. No one ever suspected, and when Mercy began to dream about marrying again, he confessed that he already had a wife and children in Kalamazoo. She had felt used, and ashamed that she had fallen for his lies. But Mercy Brody was a strong woman; she had learned how to go on and take care of herself. She would not tell Dora, but she had long ago decided that she would allow a man to come to her bed on occasion, but only after checking him out thoroughly, and he would always pay for his room. She would not exchange services and become a piece of property. And she always stuck to her rules. So Dora would not get any reprimands from Mercy.

On Wednesday, Francine stopped by to see her sister. She was shocked to see her wearing an apron, blonde curls hanging on her forehead from the steam.

"Franny, it's so good to see you." The sisters hugged and then walked into the parlor, where Mercy brought out some tea and cookies.

"How's married life, Mrs. Grainger?" laughed Mercy.

"Married life is wonderful. I couldn't be happier. I came by after school today to see if my wayward sister wanted to come home."

"Oh, Fran, I really like it here. And Mercy said I can stay and work for her for a while. She really needs me."

Fran laughed, "Then, I've lost my cook and housekeeper."

"It wasn't going to last forever, anyway," said Dora softly. "This way you can have Luke all to yourself. I miss Moose, though."

"Well, you must come for a visit soon, then. He misses you, too." Fran turned and smiled at her friend and boardinghouse owner. "Mercy, would you mind if I talk to Dora in private a moment?"

"Of course, I have some stew on the stove to attend to."

"Thank you." When she had gone Fran leaned forward and whispered, "What's going on?"

"What do you mean?"

"Are you avoiding Wade? He came by looking for you the day after the wedding and again yesterday. I finally told him you were still here."

"Oh, you didn't!"

"Why not?"

"Franny, I saw him locking lips at your wedding, and probably more, with his wife."

"His wife?"

"Yes, Myra came back into town looking for him. She showed up at the reception."

"No one said a thing to me about it." Fran was concerned about Dora now that she knew about the recent events.

"I'm sure Luke doesn't even know. Has he visited his folks' house since you were married?"

"No, he was going today. But why would Myra want Wade back? I thought she left him, or he left her, one of the two."

"I don't have a clue. I didn't stay around to find out. I'm not even sure Wade knew I was there. It was very dark; I'm sure he didn't see me. But Franny, they were really into it. There's a lot of passion there. I guess I was just a stand-in for her."

"I'm sure that's not true. He thought it was over. It's been a long time."

"Well, I've given it a lot of thought, and I've decided now that you and Luke are settled, it's time for me to leave, if I can."

"Oh, Dora, honey, I would miss you so much. I know we talked about it before, but I thought you had changed your mind."

"I had. I did. I wanted to be here for Wade. He sang to me, Franny. He sang me a love song, on more than one occasion. I feel something powerful for him, but I think, for him, it was just sex. I should have known better. I'm so ashamed." Dora began to cry silently, not even aware that tears were rolling down her cheeks.

"There's nothing to be ashamed about. It's over and done with, and now you can move on with your life. I just wished that didn't mean you were going back."

"Going where?" asked Mercy. "Sorry, did I interrupt? I thought you were done talking. I didn't hear any voices, so I brought more tea."

"We were finishing up. Dora's thinking about going home," said Francine. "To Canada."

"Oh, I didn't know. I thought I had a partner, here. I've enjoyed working with you, Dora. Maybe you'll reconsider when I offer you a full-time position. You can live here for free, and come and go as you please, as long as one of us is in the house at all times. Would you consider it?"

"That's so kind. I will consider it, thank you." Dora broke out a weak smile.

"Well, I'll let you two finish up. Sorry, I stepped into your talk. We'll get together later, Dora, and discuss details. What I have to offer might help make up your mind."

Chapter Thirty-three

1875

The next day after Fran's visit, Wade was waiting for Dora in the parlor. Mercy was surprised when he showed up at her door, since he was not a regular at the boardinghouse. She had seen him in town a few times since his return, but he had never come to her place of business. Nevertheless, she was thrilled to see him. He was one of her favorites, and so she had greeted him warmly.

"I hope you take your coffee black, but I can go back for cream or sugar if you like." She handed Wade a floral cup she delicately balanced on a saucer.

"Black is fine, Mrs. Brody." Wade seemed uncomfortable; not his usual easy-going self.

"Now to what do I owe this visit? I *am* glad to see you, but you haven't dropped by just for a chat since you were a kid, and then you were only hoping for a piece of pie."

Wade laughed. "Well, you do have the best pie in the county. I might stop by next door for a piece in a bit. Is apple on the menu?"

"Of course, it's the season."

"Actually, although I do enjoy talking with you, I came to see Dora. I hear she is staying here."

"Yes, she is. She's been working in the kitchen with me. She's a real joy, a lovely girl."

"That I know, I surely do." Wade turned his hat in his hand. He was very uncomfortable in this fancy parlor. "Could you tell her I'm here to see her, please? It's kind of important."

"I'll get her right now. You just enjoy your coffee. She'll be right out." Even saying those words, Mercy was not at all sure that Dora wanted to talk to Wade.

Something was going on between those two, but knowing what was not up to her. As a boardinghouse owner, she had learned to stay out of other people's business and to be very discreet over anything she saw or heard.

Dora was putting the finishing touches on an apple tarte she had baked. She was just about to put it in the oven.

"My, that looks beautiful. You make cooking look like art."

"Thank you, it's the first time since I arrived that I've had a chance to practice what I've learned."

"How long do you want to leave it in the oven? You have a visitor, so I'll watch it for you."

"A visitor? Oh, okay." Thinking it might be Fran, Dora took off her flour-dusted apron and wiped her hands. "Forty-five to fifty minutes should be good. Just until the crust is nicely browned. Thank you, Mercy. I'll probably be back before it's ready to come out, anyway."

When Dora stepped into the parlor and saw Wade, she turned pale, even though she was coming from the hot kitchen. She stopped moving, and stared at his big cockeyed grin. If she had known he was here, she would not have come out, or at the very least she would have cleaned herself up. She thought she must look a mess compared to the beautiful Myra. Of course, she had only seen her in the shadows, but she did look lovely. For the first time in her life, Dora questioned her beauty.

"Hello, Wade," she said stiffly.

"Dora, I" –

Wade jumped up and moved toward her. He had every intention of pulling her to him. He knew they could not be real familiar here, but he had expected something less formal from her.

"How have you been? I've been calling for you at Francine and Luke's, but I missed you several times, and finally they told me you were still here. Why was Francine keeping you from me?"

"You don't know? You haven't got a clue why I might not want to see you?"

"No, I don't. I thought we had something special. The way you sang to me, with those new words, why, it was a moment I'll never forget, Dora. I was hoping to meet up with you after we danced, but I couldn't find you."

"You were hoping to meet me?" Dora realized her voice was rising, and she did not want Mercy to hear, so she tried to compose herself. "What kind of a man are you? I heard stories, but it was not until that night that I believed one word."

"What are you talking about?" Wade seemed quite puzzled by her statement.

Dora moved to sit in a chair. If she was going to confront him with the facts, she had to sit down, her legs were getting weak, but she would not run from a fight. She never had and she was not about to start now.

"I was in the woods, getting some fresh air, when you met Myra."

"Myra? You saw us talking? I came here to tell you about her, actually."

"How dare you! She is the last thing I want to hear about. You were doing more than talking, Wade Grainger. I don't know why I snuck away like a thief in the night after I saw you. I should have come right out with it, but you *are* married to her, after all, and it was not my place."

"Yes, I am married, but Myra was the aggressor and I was very drunk, but I pushed her away."

"Not for long. You went right back in for more, and I heard you calling her name." Dora could no longer hold back the tears. They freely fell and dripped off her chin. She struggled to find her handkerchief in her pocket. What she wouldn't give for a few fluffy tissues right now.

"Call her name? I barely remember anything other than when she was kissing me, and I thought -- " Wade stopped as the foggy image of that night returned to the forefront of his brain. He had been with Myra, that was true, but at a certain point, when she began to caress him and her hands were moving over him, he had thought he was with Dora. He recalled now that he had been calling Dora's name, not Myra's, but the minute he came to his senses, he had pushed Myra away.

"Dora, I was thinking of you, and -- "

"Thinking of me? What kind of a cad are you? How dare you think of me when you are with someone else, even if that person is your wife?"

Wade reached for her hands, but she pulled back. It hurt him so to see her in pain over something he had done, but what's more was that he had more to say, and her pain would only get worse.

"Dora, please, I am so very sorry." Wade bent his head as he rubbed the back of his neck. "I came here to tell you something that will hurt you, I'm sure." He sighed with humiliation. "And I don't know where to begin."

"At the beginning?"

"Yes, well you know the beginning. You know how I married Myra, and then how we parted. You knew shortly after I came back that I was still married."

"And God help me, I didn't care," Dora admitted.

"But there's a new fact I need to add; I can hardly believe it myself." Now Wade was quite uncomfortable. He shifted in his chair, stood up, walked closer to her, and pulled her up to stand in front of him. He held her hands in his and began. "Dora, honey, Myra came back to tell me we have a child. I have a son."

"A child? Together?"

"Yes, he's seven already and his name is James. He was born eight months after I left her. Myra wants us to be a family, so I can get to know my son, and he can get to know me."

"A son?" Dora could barely breathe.

"I love you, Dora, truly I do. I know we've only known each other for a short time, but it works like that sometimes, doesn't it? I've never felt anything with anyone else like I do when I'm with you. It's true. I was looking forward to planning a life with you. I even consulted an attorney about getting a divorce, even though it's not something that's ever been done in my family."

Dora was pulling her hands back and sobbing, but he wouldn't let go. "You're staying with her?"

"I need to, for the child. I need to be a good father; I need to take care of him. I have to be there to teach him how to be a man."

"Yes, yes, you should. It's your duty. But do you have to stay married?" she demanded.

"What other way is there? I can't live with her without it. The child needs me in his home. Believe me, I'm torn apart by this decision, but it has to be this way. You understand, don't you?"

"Yes, I understand. I do, but leave me now. Just go away. I don't want to look at you any longer. I can't. Don't you see? I gave you every part of myself. You might have thought I was a so-called loose woman, but I'm not, not really. I only share my body when I, well, I couldn't help myself. I struggled every time after we were together, but I never turned you down, because I couldn't. I had fallen in love, and it was beyond my control. But you have destroyed that now. I have all the control I need."

"Dora, it's not my fault, please. Myra never told me about James, and her parents agreed to keep it quiet, because they didn't want me back in her life."

"Then why now?"

"Her father recently passed away; he was our biggest obstacle. Myra wants me to come back to help run their business. She said the two of them are finding things difficult to handle. She said if I came back it would help to keep the business going for our son's future."

Dora's face turned bitter. "I don't think she was thinking of your son's future when she was climbing all over you, was she? Tell me, did you sleep with her that night? Did you do to her the things you do to me?"

"No, my sweet," he held her close to his body against her objections, "we were not together, and I will not live with her as man and wife. Never. She betrayed me in so many ways. I can never forgive her."

Dora was sobbing into his chest now. She beat at him lightly with her fists out of frustration. The feel of him, the smell of his shirt, the sound of his voice as it rumbled in his chest, weakened her resolve. "Wade, Wade," she cried at her loss.

"Dora, will you meet me tonight after dark? Somewhere? Anywhere? I need you so badly. I can't let you go, but I know I have to. Can we be together one last time? I have to have you. I have to."

When Dora looked up, she saw tears streaming down Wade's face. She gently wiped them away and then kissed him softly. She intended to say no, but instead what escaped from her lips was, "Where?"

"Can you sneak out to the blacksmith barn? I'm sure Ned won't be anywhere around. It's too cold for us to meet outside now, but the barn should be warm enough with the horses inside."

"I'll be there," she said softly. Then they wrapped their arms around each other and kissed as if it were the last time.

When Dora returned to the kitchen, her eyes were red and puffy. Mercy didn't ask a thing about it. She didn't need to. She had been listening the whole time in the next room. Her heart ached for the young couple. Having lost her husband, she knew the pain of losing someone you love. She ran to the door and caught up with Wade. She pulled him close and whispered, "She's in room number five. It's at the rear of the house over the kitchen. Go up the back stairs. I'll leave the back door unlocked," then she kissed her favorite Grainger on the cheek.

Wade smiled in that way he had that tore at women's hearts, and then he hugged her tight. He was humming Aura Lee on the way out.

Chapter Thirty-four

2019

Daniel was exhausted. He had spent a very long day walking around a football field, watching the kids to make sure no one got into big trouble. There were always those unnecessary skirmishes between boys, usually over a girl. One kid got a bloody nose from a well-placed punch, but overall it was a quiet night, as high school football games go. The other detectives and sheriffs' deputies had asked him to go out for a beer, but he had declined. He was surprised at their invitation because they had been asking him less often, probably since he almost always turned them down. Daniel knew he should have accepted just to keep in touch with his fellow cops, but he wanted to be home – what he thought of as home these days. He needed to be there to think about Dora, and Francine, and how in the world he could get them back, if it was even possible.

Walking into the empty house was different this time. There was an immediate sense of disconnect from Dora, yet at the same time, there was a warm feeling of love and happiness. He was confused. When had he begun to feel so connected to a house? He had a crazy great aunt who loved houses. She said they had their own spirit. The family always said she was crazy, but what if they were wrong? She renovated old Victorian houses; they were a passion of hers. She said you could get a feel of the people who had lived there before, if you only listened. If it was a happy household, everything went smoothly in the renovations, but if there was turmoil in the house, she claimed the paint bucket would spill, or the wallpaper would not stick to the wall, or a broom handle would fall through an antique window and break it. Everything that could go wrong, did, she would say. She claimed she often sat down in a chair and talked out loud to the spirits, trying to reach the troublemaker that was giving her the problem. Once she had spoken and explained that she was just trying to make their beautiful home lovely again, things began to go right.

Daniel was beginning to wonder if she was onto something. Could you reach a spirit of a house by talking out loud? Was it just for those who had passed on? He was praying Dora was still alive. If he made a fool of himself, no one would know but him. Maybe it was worth a try.

He felt like an idiot, but with iced tea glass in hand, he looked around the room and said, "Hello Dora? Can you hear me? I know you used to be here, but I don't feel you anymore. Help me help you. Are you trapped? Send me a message. Please, Dora, I beg of you."

He sat very still but there was nothing. He rubbed his hand over his eyes, until he had a thought he did not want to face. Something had happened to Dora; he was sure of it. He took a shaky breath and tried again.

"Francine? Are you there? You don't know me. I'm the detective on your case, but I do know Dora. Actually, I'm in love with her. Maybe she's told you about me. We were working together to find you. Are you okay? Are you well?"

Once again he sat very still; he heard a cricket somewhere in the house. He would have to search for it later. Its rhythmic chirping was distracting his concentration. He remained still and soon he was almost in a trance. He began to feel warm and happy. The feeling of contentment was powerful. There was a strong feeling of love in the air, of sexual satisfaction; it was all around him. If it was Francine, she was happy wherever she was; he was quite sure this feeling was not attached to Dora. She was gone, not in the house. He prayed she was okay. The eighteen hundreds could be a dangerous place, plus their lack of medical knowledge would prevent most major illnesses from being cured. Had she taken ill? But if so, why would he feel such joy from this house when trying to reach Francine? Wouldn't Francine feel despair and sadness at losing her sister? Could it be that they had never found each other, and they were in two different worlds? Was that possible? He would probably never have answers to his questions now, with Dora out of the house.

∞

1875

It was well past dark. Wade had been waiting at the back door until he was sure the house was settled for the night. When he was ready to make the move, he slipped into the house as quiet as a mouse. It took all he had not to run up the stairs. He tiptoed down the hall, and when he came to the door marked number five, he turned the knob. Not knowing if he should knock or just walk in, he made the decision to go in unannounced. There would be less of a chance of anyone hearing him call her name.

It was dark inside. He was disappointed; he had expected her to be waiting for him. But the moon was shining brightly through the filmy curtains, and the moment his eyes adjusted, he was able to detect a rounded form under the covers. He stepped closer to the side of the bed, and there across her pillow, lay her lovely honey gold hair, spread out like an angel's tresses. She was sound asleep, and the loveliest thing he had ever seen. His heart swelled to bursting.

Wade reached out to stroke her cheek. She sighed, and whimpered a cry. Her eyelashes fluttered open, and he could tell she was about to scream, so he placed his hand gently over her mouth.

"Shh, it's me. Mercy told me to come to you."

She pushed his hand away, and whispered angrily, "What are you doing here?"

"Like I said, I got permission from your landlady. Were you not planning on joining me tonight at the blacksmith's shop?"

Dora sat up, and brushed back her hair. She neglected to straighten her camisole and the curve of one breast was exposed. It rose and fell with her anger. "I thought better of it when I returned to my room. What good will come of it?"

"This is what will come of it," he murmured. He leaned over and kissed her hungrily while at the same time crawling into her bed. He pushed her back gently, and lay down beside her, never breaking his hold on her lips.

The bed was the softest place they had ever been together. Dora sighed, cried out, and then she welcomed him into her arms.

It was a magical night, full of passion and sorrow at the same time. Dora was sure she had died and gone to Heaven. They whispered their love, and Wade swore he would never love another like he loved her. They slept for a few hours wrapped up in each other's arms, afraid of losing contact, but when dawn came, he was gone. Her bed was empty and cold. Dora was not surprised, because neither of them could bear to say goodbye.

Dora knew she had only a few options. She could stay here, and wait for the few days a year when Wade would visit his family. She was sure Mercy would continue to allow them to meet in secret, but then she would be nothing more than a mistress, waiting painfully for the day he would return to her. She knew she would end up alone in the end, because he would always choose his family. Her second choice was the one she knew she had to take – she would go home, like she had first decided. She would talk to Fran after school, and they could figure out how to do it without alerting Luke. Some story had to be made up about why she was going back to 'Canada.' And then they had to plan out how to do it. If it didn't work she would be at Wade's mercy for the rest of her life, and it would destroy her, because she knew without a doubt that she would never love again.

Chapter Thirty-five

1875

They had been married exactly one week, and Fran couldn't be happier, but best of all it was Saturday and she could spend all day with Luke. They had planned a picnic as soon as he was done with the chores. Soon, days of being outside would be few and far between, as the white winter encroached on the colorful fall, bringing the cold and bitter winds off Lake Michigan, and swirling snow from the north. Fran had hinted at some things she needed to say. She felt an outdoor environment might soften the blow of what she knew would rock his idea of who she was.

With an anniversary of a different type than their one week marriage coming up soon, Luke also had something to say. He had decided it was time to talk to Fran about why he had dark moods at times. He tried to control them, but every year, at least once or twice, something would remind him, and he would go to that dark place again. He wanted her to know it had nothing to do with her.

Francine packed a lunch, quite a bit better than the first one she had made for Luke. This time there was more food to choose from. They now had fresh vegetables and fruits, and pork was readily available, too, besides chicken and beef, and many other things Luke managed to hunt. It was a good life, and Fran was thankful every day for her wonderful husband and provider.

The ride out to the creek was extra nice today, because they took a long way around, walking the horses along the south fence line, so Fran could really get the lay of the land. Luke pointed out a spot on a slight rise that he had in mind for their very own house someday.

He told her his dreams of how he would build it, something much bigger than where she was living now, a two-story clapboard. They would have a huge barn, he said, and they would raise beef cattle, since working in the fields was not his favorite thing to do, although he would always have to grow feed for them. It would require more land than he had, so it would be a while before he could save up for the purchase.

"I had no idea you loved cows," said Francine.

"Always have. But not for milk; it doesn't get you anywhere except for your own household. People are eating more beef all the time, it's the wave of the future."

"Oh, is it now. You're a real visionary, Mr. Grainger."

"Well, it's true. I'm going to build a smokehouse, too, and make jerky. We should have a small one at our place now. I've put it off for too long. It's the best way to preserve meat for the winter. I plan on getting right on that next week."

"My, you're ambitious. I like that in a man," she teased.

Luke grinned at her, happy that he had pleased her, and hoping what he had to say would not tarnish her image of him. They rocked along in their saddles, just enjoying the day. Moose kept running ahead and coming back with his tongue hanging out the side of his mouth, happy to be leading the way. They rode in silence for a while, but finally Fran had to talk.

"Luke, I have something to talk to you about when we get to the creek. I hope you can listen with an open mind."

"Why, I was going to say the same thing. Is your news good or bad?"

"I guess, you could say both."

"Hmm, don't like the sound of that."

"How about your news? Good or bad?"

"I don't know how to categorize it. Informative you could say."

"I like information," she chuckled.

"Yes, well, you may not like this kind, but let's save it for after lunch. We're almost there, and I'm starving."

"Could it be that workout we had this morning?" she said with a wink.

"It surely could, Mrs."

∞

Dora had been sullen for days now. She knew there was nothing she could do about her situation, and that was the worst part. She liked to take charge and get things done her way. She felt so helpless, and she missed Wade terribly. She had heard by the grapevine that he had left to join his wife in White Cloud, but that they would be moving out of the county soon. They were going a little farther to the east, to Big Rapids. It was still on the rail line so he could come home to visit his family easy enough, but Myra wanted a new house and Big Rapids was promising to be *the* town to be in. There was talk of a new college to be built called Big Rapids Industrial School. Dora figured out that it would later be called Ferris State University in her time. It was only in the planning stages now and there was a lot to be done before they opened in the next ten years, but it would be a city of intellectuals, and she wanted her son to be brought up around fine people, so they moved their banking and loan business to accommodate the new arrivals.

Dora apologized to Mercy, explaining that she couldn't stay around any longer. There was always a possibility of Wade and Myra coming home, and with Luke being her brother-in-law there were bound to be family gatherings that she could not tolerate. She told Mercy she would be going back to Canada soon, so she wanted to spend a few days with Francine. Fran was going to take her home after school on Monday, and they would begin to plan when she would leave. She needed to contact relatives there and let them know she was coming. The two women hugged and promised to write. Mercy asked Dora to send her new recipes when she learned them at her chef school, as Dora said she was planning on going back to her studies.

Dora tried to put Wade out of her mind and for the most part she managed quite well, until she was alone in her bed where she recalled his warm body next to hers, and his sweet kisses and loving caresses. Then, and only then, did she let down her defenses and allow herself to cry well into the night, until exhaustion took over and offered her a deep restless sleep. This would be her pattern for the rest of her days. Every night she would fall asleep with Wade's name on her lips.

∞

"That was a mighty fine meal," said Luke, as he wiped his mouth on his sleeve.

"Glad you enjoyed it, but in the future could you please refrain from using your shirt as a napkin?"

"Napkin? That's for fancy folks. But I promise to try my best whenever a napkin is present, just for you, Franny."

"Thank you," Francine replied. "Now who's going first with our talks?"

"I'd like to, or I may not get it out if I put it off much longer."

Fran was worried by the look that had just darkened his face. He had been so happy only a moment ago, and now he looked like he was afraid of losing his best friend, and he had been.

"Okay, I'm all set. Are you comfortable here on the ground?"

"I'm fine, just a bit nervous, is all." Luke took a deep breath and looked down at the grass. He studied an ant who was trying to carry a morsel of food away. It was way too heavy for him and yet he managed. He decided if that little ant could handle that kind of misery, then he could too.

"I guess, I'll start by saying I love you."

"I know that already, Luke. Are you stalling?" Fran was worried now. This looked serious.

"I suppose I am. You remember how moody I was when you first arrived?"

"I recall that very well. It was hard to figure you out."

"That's because I go into this dark place sometimes, and I can't control it. You were the only one who was able to pull me out, and it hasn't come back, but I'm expecting it to very soon."

"Why is that?"

"Because it's almost the anniversary of my brother's death, and on that day, I remember things I'd rather forget."

"We're all unhappy when we remember a loved one we lost. Why do you get so depressed?"

"What I'm about to tell you, I have never told another living soul, but I feel you should know who you're married to."

"Go ahead. You know I would never say a word to betray you in any way."

"That's what I thought. You see, it all started when I had to join the war so I could be just like my big brother. I looked up to him so, and when he left for the army I was lost, so I begged Pa to let me go, too. I was too young then really, I was still only sixteen, but the minute I had my seventeenth birthday I signed up. I requested to be in the same unit he was, the 7th Regiment Michigan Volunteer Cavalry, it was called. I wanted to keep watch over him, so I could report back to Ma. As it turned out it was the worst thing I have ever asked for." Luke took a deep shuddering breath. He did not want Francine to see him this way, but he had no choice. He would be living with this woman for the rest of his life, and she had to know about his moods.

Fran reached out a hand and caressed his arm, giving him strength to go on.

"Carl rode as a scout. He would go ahead with another man or two, and they would check out an area before our whole unit came, to be sure we would not run into trouble or get ambushed. It was his job to keep the unit safe and give accurate information. When we neared Fairfax, Virginia, we were looking for a place to make our new headquarters, and we were told there was a large farm ahead that was abandoned by the Marstellas family. It seemed like the perfect place to bed down for a few days and get some rest. Carl asked if I could ride with him, and our commander agreed as long as one other man went with us. Carl told him I was good at hiding in the woods, and I could be a lookout for them.

"It all sounded good to me; I was excited to ride with Carl. As we neared the farmhouse, we found a ridge where we could watch for movement inside. We stayed there an hour or so, lying in the grass on our bellies, and we saw nothing. By now it was starting to get dark; Carl wanted to go in while it was still dusk. He wanted to be able to see well in case it wasn't clear. The unit had been moving slowly behind us, and they would catch up to us soon, so it was now or never."

Luke stopped. It was more difficult for him to go on from this point. He swallowed hard and proceeded with his tale. "I was just a kid, and had never pushed myself this hard before. It was much harder than anything I had expected. Food supplies were low; we were all hungry. It had been raining for days, so we were all wet through to the skin, and all I remember was how tired I was. I was getting sick, I'm sure, and I started to shiver. I think I had a fever, but that's no excuse. Carl told me to stay behind on the ridge and use the whistle that we used to use when we were kids if anything looked suspicious. They left cautiously down the hill and proceeded to the house. It took them over a half hour to get down there because they hid behind trees and bushes as they went. I was leaning against a rock, and I began to imagine I was home in bed, and I swear I don't know what happened, whether it was exhaustion or the fever, but I'm ashamed to say, I fell asleep."

Luke stopped talking, and Francine was shocked to see that he had large tears rolling down his face.

"Sweetheart, you were a kid, so young. You should never have been in a war at that age."

"It's no excuse, Franny, we were all young, and mostly untrained."

"What happened next?" she asked softly.

"I woke up to gun shots. Our unit had arrived and they had charged in to help, but it was too late. A small Rebel group had been lying in wait for us to show up. Carl never had a chance. When I looked down at the scene and I could see my brother's twisted body, I finally came to my senses, and I barreled out of there to help. I did my share of killing to get back at them for what they did to Carl. It was the first time I took a man's life, but that didn't stop me from what I had to do. We managed to take the farm, there were a lot of dead soldiers on the Rebel side, and both of our scouts were dead. And it was all my fault. If I had only stayed awake, I might have seen some movement or something. I would have been able to alert them. Carl was depending on my whistle, and I let him down. It's my fault that my brother is dead."

With this last sentence he broke down and sobbed. Even after all of these years, it still hurt him like it was yesterday. "The worst part is that I never told Ma and Pa. How could I tell them that their oldest son was dead because of me?"

Luke was finally able to look at Francine. He needed to see if she thought of him as a coward. He knew for a fact that she would never look at him the same way, but he was glad he had told her. At least in this instance he had finally done something right.

"Oh my baby, my poor baby," said Fran. She pulled her husband to her breast and rocked him while he cried. "It's okay. It's all over now. You aren't the reason your brother died. That horrible war is."

When his grief was expelled, Luke was humiliated with his behavior, but he was filled with wonder at the compassion that Franny had shown. He would forever be in awe at the amount of love she had given him. Because of her, he had been able to move on with his life. If not for Francine, he would still be wallowing in despair.

"I'm sorry, Franny. I know you have something to tell me also, but I don't have any strength left to hear it."

"That's okay. Let's go home and rest, and maybe I can talk to you there."

"That's good. I'd like to crawl back into bed with you. I need to hold you in my arms." He kissed her deeply with gratitude for not condemning him as a coward. "Now where did that dog go to?" He whistled shrilly and Moose came charging out of the woods, with a big stick in his mouth. He was so comical looking that it made them both laugh. They mounted their horses, and headed for home, where there would be yet another emotional conversation to come.

Chapter Thirty-six

1875

"Hmm. You always smell so good," said Luke, with a satisfied sigh. "I've never been in a bed so much in my life, except for one time when I was a kid and I got 'terrible' sick. Ma made me stay there for three whole days until my fever broke, but as soon as I could get some broth down, then it was off to the barn to do my chores, weak as I was. Didn't matter. They had to be done. Maybe that's why I don't care for milk cows."

"Poor thing, but we do need milk cows, and they don't wait for anyone, do they?"

"Ain't that the truth? Speakin' of such, I'd better get to it right now." He stood up and pulled on his pants, yanking the suspenders up with one swift movement. He stood there a moment to view his lovely bride. Her hair was messed just the way he liked it, the silken strands hanging down around her breasts, giving a man a good peek. She smiled an invitation and beckoned him back with her eyes. He was half tempted to crawl in bed again, but Moose nudged his leg and whined. He either had to eat or go out, but just like the other animals on the farm, he could not be denied.

With a crooked grin of appreciation, Luke said, "Don't you go away, Mrs., I'm not done with you yet."

Franny threw back her head and laughed. Could life get any better than this? "I'll have the coffee on when you come in. There's some leftover buttermilk pie."

"Now, you're truly tempting me. I won't be long for sure."

When Luke left the house, Fran got out of bed and dressed in only her chemise and pantaloons. These days, when they were by themselves, and since they were still on their honeymoon, there was no need to get formally dressed. Soon enough it would be over, and they could expect folks to pop in at random; then she would need to wear full attire from morning until night.

Fran fussed in the kitchen, putting a pot on and stoking the fire. On one hand she was as happy as any person on Earth had a right to be, and on the other, she was terrified for what she had to tell Luke. She was hoping that since she had shown him compassion and understanding for the story he had told her, that it would be returned. But she knew her story was so far-fetched that he might never accept it. What then? Would he ask her to leave? It was her house so he couldn't. Would he leave her? Or did he have enough faith in her to think that it could possibly be true? The more she thought about what might happen, the more nervous she became.

Luke returned in record time, and the first thing he did is move to her side and nuzzle her, whispering sweet naughty words. She giggled and pushed him away.

"Luke, don't you ever get tired of me?"

"Never. Why would I? I have the best wife in the entire world. Who would have ever guessed that the sweet schoolteacher was such a wild woman in bed?" He chuckled and shook his head.

"Luke, you're embarrassing me! It's just that I've never felt anything like what I do when I'm with you."

"Not even with your husband?" he asked softly.

Fran turned red. Her heart was racing. "Well, I think it might be time to talk about that. You told me something of your past, and I promised myself that I would do the same. I want us to be relaxed when I do, so let's eat our little snack and then go back to bed. What do you say? Sometimes stories are best told in a reclining position."

Puzzled, Luke looked at her a moment and could see how serious she had suddenly gotten. "Let's get to it, then. I'm ready to hear about your past." And with that he shoveled in a huge bite and washed it down with a gulp of his coffee.

∞

They lay on top of the covers in only their underwear. Luke loved seeing her in the thin see-through muslin. He began to roam his hands over her body once again, but when he noticed Fran shiver, he got up to light a fire in the fireplace. It was the first time they had had to consider heating the house, because as the sun lowered in the evening sky tonight, the chill was bound to turn colder once it became dark. He had no idea the shiver was not from the cold, but from intense fear.

He returned with a few smudges on his cheeks, but it only made him all the more desirable in Fran's eyes. He was her sexy he-man. A man who could do anything, who had gone to war as a kid and survived, and who had helped pull his family through hard times, but was he capable of hearing the truth, as unbelievable as it was? She was about to find out and it terrified her.

"It'll be warmer in a few minutes. I got a good fire going. Are you ready to tell me about your life?"

"I am." Fran raised herself up on an elbow as Luke settled into bed. "But Luke, once I start talking you must keep an open mind."

"What does that mean? You mentioned keeping an open mind before."

"I mean, I have some shocking things to say, and you cannot judge me until I can prove what I'm saying, because I know you will not believe me at first."

"I'll try my best, but I can't imagine what it could be that I would not believe anything you had to say."

"Okay, then, here it goes. I'll start by saying that I'm not who you think I am."

"What? Your name is not Francine Clark? Who are you then?"

"Yes, I am Francine Clark, or I was until you married me, but you see, there was a misunderstanding when I first arrived at the depot. I have since learned that the folks of the town were waiting for a Frances Clark, a schoolteacher from Canada."

"Aren't you a schoolteacher?"

"Yes, I am, that's how things got so confused, but I didn't come from Canada. I just happened to arrive at the depot when they were expecting her. She *is* a cousin of mine, though."

"If you're not from Canada, then where are you from?"

"Originally, I came from Indiana."

"What does that mean, originally?"

Fran was glad he was asking questions. It allowed her to ease into the truth. "It means I was born there, but I spent a lot of time right here in Holton."

"But then folks would know you, and no one recognized you."

"No they didn't, and here's where the story gets sticky. You see, my ancestors built this cabin. It's always been a Clark cabin, even when I grew up."

"Ancestors? This cabin was built in the 1860s, sometime just before the war. How could you have ancestors? William and Sarah Clark are still living. They built it by the sweat of their brow, just like the rest of us did." He sat up and tried to sort through what she had just said. Nothing was making any sense.

"Not in my world." She took a deep breath and forged ahead. "You see, William and Sarah are my four times great-grandparents."

"They're your what?" he said in shock. Was she crazy, he wondered? "But four times would take you back five, no six, generations, including your parents," he said counting on his fingers. "With at least twenty years per generation, that's one hundred and twenty years ago, not counting yourself. Why, that's impossible! That would go back to, if my arithmetic is right, 1755 for all the sets of parents. Michigan was nothing but Indians and woods, then. Am I missing something, here?"

"Yes," said Franny gently. "I am talking about going forward six generations. I am talking about me being born in 1989."

Luke went pale as what she just said sank in. He had never heard of such a thing. He must be married to a witch, that's why she was always so eager in bed.

"1989? Franny, this isn't funny! Explain yourself, right now."

"I'm dead serious. If you'll let me tell you the rest, this time without interrupting me, I can make you understand."

Fran very carefully went through the whole story about her grandparents living in this cabin in her time period, how her grandmother had passed away in 2019, and when she was going through her things, how she had come across the trunk, which was in this very bedroom, filled with quilts.

"This trunk? The one sitting right here?"

"Yes, the very one you made. I know I told you I would explain everything, but some things I can't. I don't know how you made this for me, and yet it was in the cabin 145 years later. In my time it is filled with quilts of all the women who have ever lived here; it has become a family treasure. Even the key is still with it there."

Once she was sure that Luke was ready to listen, she went on. "When I arrived at the station, Ned

445

brought me here. I recognized the cabin as soon as I walked in. Keep in mind, I didn't know where I was or how I got here. One minute I was mourning the loss of my grandmother with a quilt in my hands, and the next I was on the station platform in Twin Lake. I was afraid if I told them where I had come from, they would tar and feather me or something, so I stayed quiet and went along with their plan to house the schoolteacher. Then I read a letter about the one in Canada who was married. She had lost her husband and child in a fire, so I took on her persona."

"So, you've never been married, or had a child?"

"No, Luke, you are the only man I have ever truly loved." She reached out and caressed his cheek. It seemed to soothe him a bit, so she went on.

"I hated going on with such a deception, and I feared that the real teacher would show up, but then another letter came that said she had died, also. I knew then I was safe, unless William and Sarah came back and claimed their house."

Fran paused a moment to let Luke catch up with her tale. For now, he seemed to be listening to her, but for how long?

"Wait, what about Dora? Who is she? You claimed her as your sister."

"Dora is my sister, just like she said. When I went missing, she never gave up until she figured out where I was, but she still didn't know how I got here. And then one night, while holding the same quilt I had been, she suddenly found herself on the same depot platform. Ned brought her here to me, and the rest you know."

There was silence from her husband. She could almost feel the gears turning in his brain.

"So what's this about Dora's last name ending with an e?"

"That's easily explained. She quickly made up that story when she realized we both had the same last name, and I was supposed to have been married before, which would mean she should have my maiden name. She had already announced herself as Dora Clark, so it was the first thing she could think of."

447

"Franny, this is a lovely tale, but I'm not believing a word. I don't think it's possible for anyone to travel through time; otherwise we would have heard of it before."

"But what if others have done it and are just as afraid to tell people about it, as I was? Maybe, it's not so uncommon after all."

"No, no, it's not possible. It can't be. I never pegged you for a liar." He rubbed his eyes, and then moved his hand over the top of his head. "Why would you tell me this? We were so happy. How could you turn everything we have upside down? Are you looking for an excuse to go home to Canada? Do you want to leave me?"

"No! I love you, and I told you I'm not from Canada." She reached out to him, but he pulled away.

"But all those strange phrases, and funny words you use sometimes -- and you stumbling through life here. We all thought that it was because things are done different there. That you were a foreigner in our parts. We trusted you and took care of you. We gave you food and clothing and set up your house. All of us did. And all the time you were lying to us, just to get a free meal?" As what she had been telling him began to set in, he only felt the betrayal. The rest of the words meant nothing. She was not the Franny he knew. She was a liar, plain and simple, and so was her sister. They were free loaders, looking for a place to live without paying. And most of all she had made a fool of him, a fool in front of the whole county. She was teaching their children, and she was not even a teacher. That was probably a lie, too. Poor Luke, he thought they would say, falling in love with that woman – that witch.

"Please, Luke, I listened to you. Can you relax and listen to me?"

"What I had to tell you was nothing like this. I did betray my parents by not telling the whole story, I'll admit to that, but I never lied to them. If they would have come out and asked, I would have told them everything. What you did to me, and this town, was to fake a life to get something for yourself. Why, even my little sister Ruthie admires you so. She'll be crushed to find out you're a fraud."

He was at the bedroom doorway, pain and disappointment in his eyes, and Fran could tell she was losing him, just as she had feared all along. He grabbed his pants and his hat, and even though she begged him to come back, he turned away from her and left. She heard him stop to put on his boots at the door and then the door slammed shut. The only sound left to be heard was her sobs, as she called out his name.

"Luke! Luke, please!"

Chapter Thirty-seven

1875

Francine dragged herself out of bed, her eyes almost swollen shut from crying all night. She needed water to drink and to splash on her face. She had no idea where Luke had gone, but he had not come back all night. She prayed he didn't go home to his parents and relate her entire story to them. She had never felt this low in her entire life, even when her Joey had gone MIA. It felt like her insides had been ripped out. She had to find a way to convince him to come back; otherwise there was no reason left to live.

She walked out of the bedroom all disheveled from lack of sleep, her hair hanging almost to her waist now. It looked like a mouse had run through it and tried to make a nest. Her nose was red and still dripping. She sniffed a few times and swiped at it with the back of her hand. When she was able to focus, she saw a somewhat blurry image of Luke sitting at the table. His hands were on his chin and he was leaning on his elbows, while holding up his head, which was bowed low. He looked like he was praying. She stood silently, afraid to chase the vision away. When she heard him sob, she realized he was real. Was he crying? Was it for her or for his brother? It had been an extremely emotional day yesterday.

She cleared her throat to let him know she was there. "Luke?" she said softly.

Luke looked up at her, not knowing if she would accept him after he had walked out on her. Her pain and heartbreak was all over her face. She was a like a lost child; perhaps that was exactly what she was. Lost. He realized he had been so foolish not to trust her. He stood up and pushed his chair away from the table so violently it fell over with a crash.

"Franny!" He was at her side in an instant, cradling her head to his chest, as she found more tears to cry. "I love you, Franny. I don't care who you are or where you came from. I don't even care if you're a witch. All I know is I can't live without you."

"Oh, Luke, I'm so sorry I led you on. I didn't know how to – I didn't think -- I didn't" --

Before she could get enough air to finish her sentence, Luke was crushing her mouth to his. He covered her face with kisses, saying over and over, "I'm sorry. I'm so sorry."

Franny put her face in his neck and sobbed all the more. "You still want me?"

"More than anything. Look at you. You look like an angel. Any man who gave you up would be crazy. Nothing will ever make me walk out that door again, I promise you that." He stroked her hair and looked into her tortured eyes. "Once I had a chance to clear my head, I realized how hard it was for you to be here not knowing anyone. I don't care a hoot about your story. You were all alone, but you were so brave."

"Oh, Luke, do you believe me, then? Do you?"

"Let's sit and talk it out. I still have a lot of questions."

"Can I get some coffee first and maybe comb my hair? I must look a mess."

"I don't care about that. You are my beautiful mess. Can we go back to bed a bit? I need to hold you for a while, close to me. I need to make up for my foolishness. I need to beg for your forgiveness and show you my love."

"It's not necessary, but I would be more than happy to accommodate you," she grinned. "First, I need some water, and a trip outside, if you know what I mean." She took his hand and kissed it. When she returned, he was waiting for her in the bedroom. She had never seen such love on a man's face in her life.

∞

2019

Daniel had become an obsessed man. He knew something was wrong, but there was not one thing he could do about it. He wasn't bathing often enough and had forgotten to shave on more than one occasion. In fact, one of his fellow cops had told him he looked like death warmed over. His chief had called him into the office to see if he could get out of him what he was going through, but he had been unsuccessful, except to hear that Daniel had some private issues he was working out. It was suggested that he take leave until he figured it out. It wasn't good for anyone to have an officer walking around like he had been, lately. The other cops depended on his backup when they needed it, and that meant he had to be alert at all times. Daniel was anything but alert. It was agreed that he would take a well-needed vacation for a week, and if he had not worked out his problem by then, he would be put on temporary leave of absence, without pay.

Daniel ate a lot of pizza and drank a lot of beer, something he had never done before. He felt it was all so hopeless; he wished he had never gotten involved in this case in the first place, but then he would look at the gilt-framed photo of Dora, and he knew he would never give up. Somehow he had to figure this out. He knew beyond a shadow of a doubt that she was in another time and place.

He stayed close to the items she had left behind, including her clothes and shoes. The trunk and the quilts were still in the living room and the lid was left open. He stared at it constantly hoping for any kind of hint. He went over and over the ancestor list and the plat maps. Most nights he was too drunk or exhausted to go to bed. He would fall asleep on the couch, watching the door for the moment she walked in. He was worried about her, but also for himself, because he didn't know if she came back if she would want him. In the past, his dreams about her were vivid, but lately there was nothing. He was beginning to think she was dead, and that only caused him to drink even more. How could he be so in love with a woman who was not even here? They had barely begun their relationship, if you could even call it that. Dora was probably not even aware of the depth of his feelings for her. But none of that mattered, because there was no way now that he could ever tell her.

This particular night was no different than any other. He watched some TV with the drapes drawn, ate a frozen dinner, and passed out once again on the couch, arm hanging down, drool pooling around his mouth. He wouldn't move a muscle until morning, when he would start the whole routine all over again.

∞

1875

"Tell me about it, Franny. Tell me all about it. I want to know everything," said Luke, with his arms around his sweet wife.

"I will tell you everything, but first let's get dressed, eat breakfast, and take care of the animals."

"You're right. Work must come first. I'll get some eggs and milk while you heat up the stove. Start a fire in the fireplace, too. It's cold out there."

Fran grinned as she stretched. She had her man back, and he had promised never to run out on her again. She wasn't sure if he believed anything she said, but it didn't matter, because he said he didn't care. He wanted her in his life, he said, and if she believed what she said to be true, then he would go along with it. Her job now was to convince him it was real, so he would never tell another living soul. She had to be sure he would keep her secret.

Over breakfast Luke asked questions, but mostly he listened. She told him about electricity, running water, cars, telephones, and airplanes. He was shocked, and found most of it hard to understand. And when she got to television, computers, and smart phones, he simply shook his head. She decided to save space travel and the walk on the moon for another time. It was all too much to take in.

"All I can say if this is not real, you have one heck of an imagination. You mean, you can buy a complete meal that's as frozen as a lake in winter and put it into a box and it cooks in three minutes? Does anyone ever cook?"

"Yes, most of us do, but some women are too busy with their careers, and they find it difficult. Some of them never learned to cook. We also have what we call fast food. You drive your car up to a building where there is a -- um, clerk in the window. They take your order and give you the food in a minute or two."

"You eat it there?"

"No, you can eat inside the building, or go to a park in the summer, or take it home and eat it in front of the TV."

"What's TV?"

"That's what we call television."

"And that's a moving picture in a box, you said." Luke rubbed his head, his eyes wide with amazement.

"Yes, it was in most homes by the 1950s, I guess. At first it was black and white pictures only, but now it's so advanced that it's in full color and almost looks real."

"How big is this box you look at?"

"Over the years it's gone through many changes. In the beginning it was only about 15 inches and it sat on a table. But now it can be fifty to seventy inches, sometimes bigger, and most are hung on the wall. It's like watching a movie."

"Whoa. What's a movie?"

And their conversation went on all day long. They ate, they walked, they drank, they curled up on the sofa, but they never stopped talking about the future. If she was making it all up, Luke thought she must be the best storyteller in the whole world. He was beginning to believe every word.

"Do you miss your family? Will you want to go back and leave me someday?"

"Here's the thing, Luke. I don't have any answers. I know both my parents are gone now, Dora told me, and I had no boyfriend. Dora was really my only true friend and she's here. So I have no reason to go back. But, I don't know if this thing that brought me here wears out. Maybe I'll be snatched away from you someday. If that happens, please remember I didn't do it because I wanted to leave you. I will never leave of my own accord. But someday I might just come up missing, and I don't think I can contact you if that happens. Our days could be numbered."

"Then I will never let you out of my sight. I'll hold on to you for dear life, and you can take me along."

"You sweet, sweet, man." She wondered if it was possible to love him any more than she did at this moment.

They kissed and caressed and made promises they weren't sure they could keep.

Chapter Thirty-eight

1875

Everything was back to normal for Francine. She was back at school, teaching the eager children, and Luke was home at the house putting things right the way he wanted them to be. It was their house, now, she had told him and he could do whatever he wanted with the outbuildings and the animals, just leave her garden alone. Today he was finally working on that smoke house and after that he wanted to make a larger pasture for more cows. He planned to start building the stock in the spring and it needed to be ready then.

At the end of the school day, Francine was surprised, but pleased, to see Dora at the door with her carpet bag in hand.

"Hi, Franny, are you about through?"

"Yes, I was just getting ready to leave. I see you have packed up. Are you coming home with me?"

"That's what I was about to ask. I figure I gave you two lovebirds enough time alone. If you don't mind, I'd like to sleep in my old room until I go back."

"Oh, Dora," said Fran, taking her sister's hands. "I really wish you wouldn't."

"There's nothing for me here now," said Dora, her big blue eyes filling with tears.

"There's Luke and me. Isn't that enough?"

"Unfortunately, along with Luke and his family comes Wade. I couldn't bear family gatherings."

"But he won't be here very often. They moved to Big Rapids."

"Just once is too much for me. I couldn't stand seeing him with his wife and child."

"I get it, but what will you do back home?"

463

"I'll stay in the cabin, so I can keep in touch with you, and Daniel will help me get through this, if he's still looking for me."

"Come on, let's get in the buggy and talk as we ride. I'm ready to close up now." She grabbed a few books and dropped them in her basket, put on her bonnet, and they left.

"Okay, now tell me, how will you explain things when you get back? You've been gone for months."

Dora bit her lip and said, "I'll simply say I can't remember."

"You mean, like amnesia?"

"Yes, that's what I'll do."

"But what will you say about me? You can't give anything away."

"Oh, no, I promise. I will never say a word about you and where we were. Besides if I did, they'd lock me up," she laughed.

Fran was glad to see her sister laugh, but the subject was frightening. If word got out, she could be stalked and harassed by reporters, movie producers, publishing houses. Everyone would want her story.

"My biggest hurdle right now is Luke," added Dora. "How do we explain my absence to him?"

"That won't be a problem," said Fran with a grin. "He knows everything."

"You told him? And he believed you?" Dora's eyes were wide with surprise.

"No, not at first. We had a big upset. But he finally said he loved me, and he couldn't bear for us to part. He'd rather take me as I am than not at all. After that he was incredibly accepting. He is so curious, he's like a little boy. I tell him stories every night about my childhood and how life is there."

"So he knows about me, too?"

"Of course he does. He knows how we came, and he knows that you want to go back. But I didn't mention your involvement with Wade. You can tell him if you want. That's your business; I'll stay out of it."

"Thanks, Fran. I think I have to tell him, though, don't you?"

"Only if you want."

"Okay, I'll think about it. Now, how will all of this work? We have to come up with some sort of an idea, because we're not even sure it will work."

The horse slowly plodded along as the two planned how Dora would leave, and by the time they had arrived at the house, they had it somewhat figured out.

Luke heard the buggy come up the drive when Traveler whinnied, eager to get to the barn for his feed. He was pleased to see Dora. He had not wanted her to feel like she had to move out because of them. He had only intended for her to stay one night at the boardinghouse, but the week he and Franny had had alone was special and he would never forget her sacrifice.

"Hello, ladies, I see there are two of you today. Are you home for good, now, Dora?"

He helped them each get down, and Dora said, "Yes, and no."

"Now that's a curious answer."

Fran kissed her husband in a wifely manner, but all she wanted to do was give him the kind of greeting they both loved.

"She means," Fran said, "that's she's going home."

"Home? Oh, you mean your past home, or future home, whatever it is. Are you sure Dora? Here let me help you with that bag. We don't mind you staying here one bit. Franny likes to have you around."

"Thanks for being so understanding, Luke, but I have to. I'll explain when we're inside."

Luke raise an eyebrow. "Well, let's get going, then. I have a nice fire going to warm you up."

They went in, and like any normal family, they began the routine of getting supper on the table. The two women chatted about Fran's day, and Dora's stay at the boardinghouse, while Luke sat at the table with a cup of coffee. He decided he rather enjoyed having them both here. They were so much alike in some ways, but they were so different in other ways. His Franny was more settled and took most things in her stride, but Dora had a fire in her. She would be a hard woman to tame as a wife. He had certainly made the right choice between the two.

As they finally got to the business of eating their meal, Luke said, "Dora, let's get to the one subject we have been avoiding. Francine told me all about you two. I want you to know that I'm still not certain about it all, but I will accept what she says, because she is my wife. I understand that you want to leave, but I think it's best if I stay out of the planning of it. The less I know the better. Then I'm less likely to spill the beans, don't you agree, Franny?"

"You might be right," agreed Fran, "but you do know how to keep a secret, that much I know."

He smiled at her sweetly, and Dora could only guess at what they were talking about.

"Well, Luke, I don't want you to think I'm leaving because of you two living here together now. It's something altogether different."

"I think you should tell him, Dora," said Fran.

"You might be right, but it will be difficult. Please excuse me if I get emotional."

Luke put his elbows on the table. "Isn't that what women do?"

"I guess, we do. Luke, it's about your brother."

"Which one?" Luke asked in surprise. He certainly had not expected his brother to come up.

"Wade," she said softly.

"Wade? Now what has he done? Did he hurt you? If he did I'll whip him until he can't get up."

"No, nothing like that."

"Luke, relax, it's not what you think," said Fran.

Dora took a breath, then told him how she and Wade had fallen in love, that she had not known he was married when they first began flirting. She left out how far it had gone.

"It's so like him, not to tell you right up front."

"In his defense, he didn't know about his son at that time and that Myra would want him back."

"Yes, it had been many years since they were together."

"Honestly Luke, he broke my heart when he went away with her. I can't stay here. I don't want to be

469

around when he comes home for a visit with his family. I couldn't bear to see them together."

"I understand. But there's something about this whole thing that's not right, even Ma said so. I don't think it's going to last."

"But there will always be the child."

"That is true, and Wade should not let that obligation drop. He's been taught well, so I'm sure he won't."

"You see what I mean? It was difficult for us to part; he loves me as much as I love him. So it's to spare his feelings, also."

Luke took a moment to study his new sister-in-law. "You're a much different woman than I first thought, Dora. We will miss you around here. Now, I'm going out to the barn to let you two hash this out. Let me know if I can be of any help. The meal was great, Franny," he said as he kissed her.

"You truly found a wonderful man, Fran. I'm happy for you."

"That I have. Thank you, Dora."

∞

As soon as the dishes were done, the two women set about planning on how they would do Dora's return trip. Dora presented Franny with a beautiful hand-tooled leather-bound journal she had purchased in town.

"If you write something in this at least once a month and place it in the trunk, I should be able to read it, since it originated in 1875. I can try to write back, but from our experience last time, it probably won't work. At least I'll know if you are still okay. I'm worried though, because if you ever build that house you mentioned on your own property, I'll lose track of you. You can't take the trunk with you. It has to stay here."

"Luke has agreed to stay here as long as possible, especially now that he knows the truth. So what if writing the journal entries don't come through? We know the quilt blocks work. Let's get a list of blocks and make our own Underground messages. You'll have to memorize yours just in case the written list doesn't transfer with you."

"Good idea. I'm going to leave you with all of the jewelry. I'm afraid the money is all gone. Mercy paid me a little, but I spent it on this book."

"That's not a problem; we'll be okay. We're farmers like everyone else around here, and I'll have an income from teaching, so we might be better off than most."

"You'll have a wonderful life, I just know it. I'm not sure of my future, but I'll figure it out when I get back. I'll find a job somewhere cooking. Maybe not haute cuisine, that can't be found in Holton, but a diner will do me just fine. I'll make a life for myself. I don't want you to worry."

"I will worry, of course, I will, but I'll put my trust in God to watch over you. So when do you want to do this, and how will we explain your leaving to the folks in town?"

"I've already laid some groundwork with Mercy. I told her I wanted to go back to Canada to see my family."

"That's good," said Fran. "But what about Duane at the depot? He knows when everyone comes and goes."

"Oh, Duane. I forgot about that. Do you think I have to leave from where I arrived?"

"Hmm, let me think. Probably not, because we left from the house and arrived at the depot."

"Well, we'll try it from here, first. I really don't want to disappear in front of people at the train station."

"You're right, that wouldn't work. We'll try here in the parlor; it's also Gram's living room, and then if it doesn't work, we'll be back to square one. Do you mind if Luke watches? It would cement my story for him."

"That's a good idea. He should be with you on this all the way. It would be helpful to have someone to cover for you if you slip."

"Okay, let's make a list of the quilt blocks we want to use. I can think of a few. We'll give each one an assigned message. It doesn't have to have anything to do with the block name, as long as *we* know what it means. I asked my quilting bee to help me with some common block names. I told them I was going to do a class project with the blocks."

"Good idea. Grab a paper and pencil, teacher. Let's do our homework."

"Here are the names they came up with, basic blocks and easy to do.

Flying Geese

Bear's Paw

Pieced Tulips

Grandmother's Choice

Hole in the Barn Door

North Star

Broken Dishes

Drunkard's Path

Friendship Stars

During the time they were planning, they had as much fun as when they were kids planning an outing or plotting against their parents. But when they talked about what they were really doing, they cried at the thought of being away from each other forever, because as far as they knew, this might be a one-time thing. One trip back in time and then another back home. Maybe that's all that was allowed.

"Okay, that's nine of them. And our list looks good. We'll make another copy, but let's go over it and see if you can memorize it."

"I feel like a kid, Franny, it's like our own secret code."

"If anyone finds these they would never know what they mean, but if someone finds my journal, it's all over, Dora. I'll try not to be too specific, but you should still keep it safe."

"I will, I promise."

"Pinky swear?"

"Pinky swear," and the two sisters did the ritual that so many kids have done over the years to seal a promise.

"Now, when do you want to go?"

"Tonight. Now. I'm ready, and my courage is up."

"If you're sure, I'll get Luke from the barn. You get the unfinished quilt from the trunk. Will you have a problem crying? You'll need tears."

Dora looked at her big sister with an ache in her heart. "I'm crying already."

Fran sniffed back her own tears, then ran to get Luke.

Chapter Thirty-nine

1875

Luke wasn't sure what he was going to see, but he knew one thing. He had to be a part of this. It was the only way he could convince himself what they had told him about time travel was true. When he walked in with Francine, they found Dora sitting on the chair with the unfinished quilt in her lap.

"Now, tell me again, how this works," he said.

"We're not really sure, but we each had the same experience," explained Fran. "We were holding this particular quilt, which I believe Sarah Clark started and did not finish. She left it behind when they moved. It's one of the quilts we found in the trunk in 2019. Then as we both cried with grief, our teardrops fell on a stain."

Fran showed the mark to Luke.

"It looks like a watermark."

"It does, but I think it's from tears. It contains DNA."

"What's DNA?" asked Luke.

"Oh dear. I'm not sure how to explain it exactly. But every person on the planet is made up of DNA. The letters are for a big long word. It's what we call a genetic marker. Scientists can view the patterns and markers and tell who we are related to. So, for instance, these tears on the quilt carry Sarah Clark's DNA, and it matches both Dora's and mine, because we are direct relatives through our bloodline."

"Sounds complicated to me."

The girls laughed. "It is to us, too, but we just accept it. So we think when our DNA merged with Sarah's, we were brought back here. Same cabin, same family line. Make sense?"

Luke scratched his head. "If you say so. But I have a question. How are you going to explain Dora's sudden disappearance?"

Dora suggested her idea to them. "You can say I had to go home suddenly to an ill family member, so Luke took me to Muskegon to meet up with some other family members there. Then we went on to Canada from that point."

"I'm not so sure they won't question why you didn't take the train from Twin Lake," said Luke, still not sure this plan would work.

"You're probably right," said Fran. "We'll say they came to the cabin and picked her up late at night and then went on to Muskegon. The train was not running at that hour. We have been communicating with them and had not mentioned it, because we weren't sure if she was leaving."

"It could work except for one thing. Mr. Porter knows every piece of mail that comes through his office. He'll know Dora has not been getting any letters."

"Shoot, I had not thought of that." Mr. Porter was known for keeping a close watch on all of the mail.

Dora got an idea. "How about we say, I had always planned to leave on a particular date. We already knew in advance that it was only a short visit, and that I would be getting a ride with family as they passed through. We're so sorry no one had a chance to say goodbye, but they showed up a few days early, so I had to go on my way with them."

"Okay," sighed Fran. "It's not perfect, but we can work with that."

"All right, then. It's show time."

"What's show time?" asked Luke.

"Oh honey, it's just another phrase you'll have to get used to," laughed Fran. "Now let me hug you goodbye, my dear sister. Then we'll sit on the couch opposite you. I hope it works if someone is watching. We've never done it with an audience."

"Oh boy, another thing we had not thought of." It was time to say goodbye, as difficult as it was going to be. Dora smiled at Fran. "Come here Franny. Look at you. A real pioneer woman and doing just fine. And now a wife. I love you, you know that, right? You're the best sister ever."

"I love you, too, Dora. Please take care of yourself. Maybe at some point you'll try to come back. Huh?"

"Maybe," sniffed Dora.

The sisters wrapped their arms around each other, and now that parting was real, it was not difficult to get the tears flowing.

Luke sat quietly on the sofa, and Francine joined him. They held hands, almost afraid to see what was going to happen. Even though Dora's tears were seeping, there weren't enough there to drip and do what they needed to do, until Dora began to talk about the real reason she was leaving.

"Luke, you are a wonderful husband. Please always treat Francine right. And if your brother Wade ever mentions me, tell him, in private, that I will always love him. Your brother broke my heart, Luke. I've never loved anyone like I love him."

"I'm sorry, Dora. I had no idea. He never mentioned it at all, although the whole town did see some kind of attraction when you danced with him last."

"It's more than an attraction, Luke. It was a powerful love. I thought we were going to be together, and I had decided to stay here with you and Franny, but then Myra came back and pulled the rug out from under us."

The more Dora talked about Wade the more she cried. She told them how they first met at the mercantile, and the barn dance, and again at the creek. She left out the private parts, but it was clear they shared a great passion. When she went into her own world of hurt and began to sob, calling out his name, tears dripped onto the cloth. Right before Luke and Fran's eyes, Dora began to sway. For a split second her eyes went back into her head, and then her head dropped forward. In an instant, she was gone.

"Dora," cried Fran. "Oh, Luke, she's gone. My sister's gone. It worked. It truly worked." Fran sobbed into her husband's shirt, happy for Dora but missing her already. Luke's fear built with the realization that this could happen to his Franny, too.

"Fran, promise me, you'll never hold this quilt again! I'll put it away tonight."

∞

Dora felt herself spinning and falling, whirling and tossing about. It was much rougher than the first time. The next thing she knew she was standing in her grandmother's living room. With blurry eyes, she tried to focus on her surroundings. The most puzzling thing was when she detected a man sleeping on her couch. Had someone moved in while she was gone? She squinted her eyes and gasped when he sat bolt upright.

"Daniel?"

§

Thank you for reading Yesterday's Hopes, Book Two, in a 'Slip in Time.' If you enjoyed reading it and are interested in what happens to Fran and Dora, here is a sneak peek of Book Three, Yesterday's Dreams. Continue reading for the Author's Notes which immediately follows.

Yesterday's Dreams

Chapter One

"Dora? Is it possible? Is it really you?"

She heard her name, but she couldn't see well; her vision was still blurry. She blinked slowly trying to clear the image in front of her. She thought it must be Daniel, but the man before her was unshaven, and looked like he had slept in the same clothes for days. With a quick scan around the room, she noticed the quilts all laid out just like she had left them, but the coffee table was littered with beer cans, a pizza box, and some bags and wrappers from the last meal of burgers and French fries. The house smelled different. Stale and closed up, like old food and sweat. She gagged, then she heard her name again.

"Dora? Are you real?"

He was moving slowly toward her, afraid if he reached her she would disappear again, but he had to try.

Just as he reached out to touch her, she felt herself losing consciousness. She was slipping away, falling, and try as she might, there was nothing she could do about it.

Daniel caught her just in time, and the moment he felt her body in his arms, he knew it was true. She had finally come back. His Dora was home.

He choked back his sobs, picked her up, and gently carried her to her room, the very one he had been sleeping in when he wasn't passed out on the couch. He was embarrassed now that he had left the room in such a mess. Once she awoke she was sure to see that he had moved in. When he had assured himself she was in a deep sleep, he tiptoed around the room and picked up the dirty laundry he had left on the floor; socks, underwear, a stained tee shirt. He collected the used towels in the bathroom and replaced them with clean ones. Thank God he had done some laundry a few days ago, or was that last week? He placed a fresh towel on the towel bar, and quickly wiped the sink out, removing his shaved stubble. He wet down a comb and ran it through his hair, then he grabbed a clean shirt and pair of pants, and left the room. Daniel quickly dressed in the next room, and then began the chore of cleaning up the kitchen. Try as he might, he occasionally banged a pan or dropped some silverware. None of it seemed to matter, though, because she was out like a light. He couldn't wait for her to wake up. His heart was singing. Dora was home.

Author's Notes

So, you've read Book Two of 'A Slip in Time.' I hope you liked it. Now I can tell you that when I started writing I had no idea that a man named Wade even existed. Dora was meant for Ned, but it just didn't fit right. Ned is a sweet and simple man, while Dora was an experienced woman from the 21st century. When Dora and Ned went into town and she spotted an attractive man, he was supposed to be a villain, but when the characters tell you what they want, as an author, you have to follow. So Dora led me to Wade, and as I continued to write I fell in love, also. I was unsure if there was room for two love stories, but I had no choice. Wade would not be stopped, and Dora was just as guilty in pursuing him.

I loved researching the post Civil War era. I found lists of costs of goods, lists of songs, and pictures of clothing for both men and women. I knew prices were going to be way less than I expected, but I had no idea how much a dollar could buy.

Below, I have included a link to some of the sites I used to find my facts, including an article on how 'Aura Lee' became 'Love Me Tender.' If you like history like I do, you may find this very interesting.

I have just started to write Book Three, Yesterday's Dreams, so if you're reading Yesterday's Hopes shortly after publication, I'm sorry, but you'll have to wait a few months, before I can get it published. If you're coming late to the party, you can find all of my books at my Amazon Author page at:

amazon.com/author/obrienjane

Thank you so much for following me. I really do appreciate my readers. Here are more places to keep up with what's going on in my world.

You can also follow me on Facebook at:

www.facebook.com/janeobrien.author

Or my blog at:

www.authorjaneobrien.com

On Twitter I'm :

@janeobrienbooks

Links to research:

Love me Tender article:

https://www.telegraph.co.uk/culture/music/3562247/The-story-behind-the-song-Love-Me-Tender.html

Cost of Goods:

http://www.choosingvoluntarysimplicity.com/what-did-things-cost-in-1872/

Weekly Wages in 1860:

http://www.choosingvoluntarysimplicity.com/what-did-people-earn-in-1860/

Music of the 1800s:

http://www.bfv.com/cwb/

https://en.wikipedia.org/wiki/Category:1870s_songs

About the Author

Jane O'Brien discovered her love of writing at the age of ten when she wrote her first ten-chapter book in pencil on notebook paper. She passed it around to all of her friends at school and told them she wanted to be an author. And that planted the seed.

O'Brien's career life has been varied. She was a piano teacher for over 50 years, a librarian, and a professional proofreader. She is also interested in genealogy, having worked on her own family tree, as well as her husband's, for over 36 years, which helps to color most of her novels. Today, as a grandmother, Jane is finally fulfilling her lifelong dream, after successfully having her fifteenth book published, which includes two trilogies, one five-book series, and two Christmas novellas, as well as a time slip series. She lives in West Michigan and writes clean romance with a little history, mystery, and family entanglements, all set in her part of the state. The stories she weaves are about family and the intricate connections of relatives, past and present.

O'Brien loves to write about her experiences living along the Lake Michigan shoreline as a youth, and then later in the woods near inland lakes and rivers. Jane recently moved back to her hometown of Muskegon and is currently residing a few miles from her beloved Lake Michigan once again. She takes pride in being able to introduce her readers to her beautiful state.

Made in the USA
Monee, IL
27 March 2020

24003106R00269